Readers love the Forced Mates series by GRACE R. DUNCAN

Devotion

"Shifter fans are going to flock to this one of course, but there is so much more to the story."

—MM Good Book Reviews

"I really, really loved this book. It was awesome… I devoured this from start to finish."

—The Blogger Girls

"This is a sweet little shifter story (one of my favorite genres) and I enjoyed it…"

—Hearts on Fire

Patience

"This book was beautifully written and I could see the connection strengthening between them."

—Two Chicks Obsessed with Books and Eye Candy

"I really loved it… it was a fantastic read and I'll be pre-ordering every book still to come in this series."

—*Divine Magazine*

"Fans of the first book are sure to love *Patience*. The characters and story line pull you in from the beginning."

—Top 2 Bottom Reviews

By GRACE R. DUNCAN

Beautiful boy
No Sacrifice
Turning His Life Around
What About Now

FORBES MATES
Devotion
Patience
Acceptance

GOLDEN COLLAR SERIES
Choices
Coronation
Deception

PANDEMUS CHRONICLES
Celebrating You
Healing

Published by DREAMSPINNER PRESS
www.dreamspinnerpress.com

Acceptance

GRACE R. DUNCAN

Published by
DREAMSPINNER PRESS

5032 Capital Circle SW, Suite 2, PMB# 279, Tallahassee, FL 32305-7886 USA
www.dreamspinnerpress.com

ISBN: 978-1-63477-405-5
Digital ISBN: 978-1-63477-406-2
Library of Congress Control Number: 2016907030
Published July 2016
v. 1.0

Printed in the United States of America

This paper meets the requirements of
ANSI/NISO Z39.48-1992 (Permanence of Paper).

To everyone who stuck with me so far,
I hope you like Quincy as much as I do.
To Joe, for his continued love, support, and encouragement.
I truly couldn't do this without you.

Chapter 1

QUINCY KNEW they were there. It didn't take a preternatural sense of smell or hearing to pick them out. He wasn't sure if he should be offended they thought his senses were that dull, amused because they seemed that inept… or perhaps annoyed because they were so sure of themselves and their abilities that they didn't have to hide.

He wondered why they weren't suppressing their scent. He was fairly certain everyone in the jaguar world knew Pittsburgh had a pretty big number of wolves. Did that mean they were willing to fight—and possibly kill—any wolves they came across?

That thought brought a scowl to Quincy's face. Entirely aside from his new… appreciation… of the wolves, picking a fight with them would cause all *sorts* of problems, not the least of which might actually involve starting an interspecies war. And while he might still feel rather disdainful about most of the wolves out there, there were a choice few he didn't want to see anything bad happen to.

Quincy sighed and took another sip of his latte. He really was not interested in getting into a fight. Since there were only two of them, it would be pretty easy to give them the slip. He needed to do it carefully, however, because he wanted to draw them away from Pittsburgh, if at all possible.

For one thing, Miles was still working in the Presby ER. Chad and his new mate, Jamie, still lived in the Oakland apartment—though they'd been away for a while. With any luck Quincy could get the two jaguars out of town before any of his wolves got dragged into a fight because, for reasons Quincy didn't quite understand, they'd come to his rescue. And while he'd hang himself before admitting it out loud to them, he liked them and didn't want them hurt.

He downed the last of his latte and stood, gathering his laptop and stuffing it in his messenger bag, then packing the rest of his things. The idiots loitered across the street, in front of the Primanti Brothers, trying to appear inconspicuous and failing. Neither of them looked even remotely like a college student *or* medical professional, which was what made up the biggest chunk of people in Oakland.

Shaking his head, Quincy hitched his bag over his shoulder, tossed out the coffee cup, and stepped out of the Panera he'd taken over for the better part of the afternoon and evening to get work done. Going to ground didn't mean he could completely disappear. He had money, but he had a reputation to maintain, and that included finishing jobs he'd started.

As soon as the door closed behind him, Tweedle Dee and Tweedle Dumb stepped away from the shop and started across the sidewalk. Quincy sighed, pushed his glasses farther up on his nose, and turned down Forbes, grateful for the twilight. With any luck the dark would help him lose them. He kept a reasonable pace, not willing to give them the satisfaction of letting them know he was aware of them. They wanted to scare him or take him in to his dad, now that Aubrey Archer knew the private detective he'd hired—Chad—wasn't going to turn him over. And it would only feed their ego if they thought he was scared. But they looked like they didn't care about what might get in their way in the process, and Quincy had no wish to break the secrecy laws or get others hurt.

He took a quick left and did some bobbing and weaving through the alleys and side streets, leading them away from the hospital and in the opposite direction of Chad and Jamie's apartment. Despite masking his own scent and making enough turns that they shouldn't have been able to keep up with him, they seemed to be having no trouble.

His annoyance level rising, Quincy took another turn into an alley, then a left to go around the back of the building. He loved that Oakland had so many of those. It made for plenty of opportunities to stay off the street and keep them moving.

He *did* want to lead them away, but he'd rather have the chance to lay a false trail first. They were too damned close for that this time. He shouldn't have even been in Oakland in the first place, but he'd just *had* to get a glimpse of Miles.

Scowling, he moved faster, jumping fences rather than trying to run around. He cut across a few yards, scaled some chain-link this time— grateful his cat's grace translated to his human form—and took another alley.

And stopped dead when he was staring at a smooth wooden fence even *he* couldn't scale. He spun around, already sure he wasn't going to be alone, already sure it was too late to go back that way, and he was right. He saw black metal out of the corner of his eye and looked up to see if he could catch the ladder of the fire escape above him, but damned if there wasn't a *third* cat up there.

"For the love of Bastet," he muttered, then sighed. "Knew I should have stayed in the hotel today." His calendar had said today was an unlucky day—he and many of the other cats still kept that old Egyptian custom—but he hadn't heeded its warning. At least a third cat explained how they'd kept up with him so well. He cursed himself for not looking for another, then let it go. He had a bigger worry right then.

Quincy set his bag down, cracked his neck, took a deep breath, then started the shift. His claws came out, his eyesight turned to grays, and his teeth dropped almost at the same time. He stopped there, hoping he wouldn't have to shift completely, though he somehow doubted it. He turned to Tweedle Dee and Tweedle Dumb, studying their movements, the way they stalked toward him, parting to flank him at almost exactly the same time.

He narrowed his eyes, considering his options and not liking the lack of them he came up with.

"We're just here to deliver a message," Tweedle Dee said.

"I'm not interested. I don't eat Girl Scout Cookies, I donate anonymously to the Humane Society, and I already have a timeshare."

Tweedle Dee snorted. "You're funny."

"I'd say I'm here all week, but I doubt that." Quincy flicked his eyes up to the fire escape, but Tweedle Dumber hadn't so much as moved a muscle. It irritated Quincy to no end to conclude that, while he could have bested Tweedle Dee and Tweedle Dumb in a fight—either human or cat—Tweedle Dumber would be just a little too much. He really wished he hadn't left his SIG Sauer back in the hotel room.

If Quincy had one thing going for him, one thing he could usually count on over others, it was patience. He flicked his eyes from one to the other to the third—still on the fire escape—then back again. Dee and Dumb had stopped a few feet away, just out of reach. Dumber still hadn't moved.

He took slow, deep breaths through his mouth since the alley stank, keeping the best outward calm he could project. He was actually glad to be mostly human right then, because despite himself, if he'd been in cat form, his twitching tail would undoubtedly give his anxiety away. And he'd be damned if he gave them any advantage.

There was nothing specific Quincy could point to that was a signal of any sort. But one second all three of them stood frozen—including Dumber on the balcony—and the next all three had moved in.

Quincy might have been an information broker and artist. He might have preferred pencils and Wacom tablets to weapons and claws. But he was *tepey-sa*, heir to the leadership of his pride, which he wouldn't still be—whether he wanted it or not—if he wasn't worthy of it. So he could fight when he needed to.

The three of them obviously hadn't expected him to fight back. Quincy didn't know what his father had told them, but clearly he'd caught them by surprise. It allowed him to get a good kick in on Dumb, rake his claws over Dee's chest—slicing open the shirt and leaving a nice set of deep scratches—and bite down on Dumber's arm when he moved in to punch Quincy.

Unfortunately, now that they knew he could fight, he was out of surprises. They regrouped, surrounding him but approaching him a little more carefully. Quincy wasn't dumb enough to believe for one minute they were going to leave him alone.

"I'm not going back," he growled, his cat itching to take them out, pissed at being held back as much as he was.

Dee shrugged one shoulder. "No skin off my nose."

Quincy was too focused on Dee, so when Dumber moved, it was too late to react properly. He took claws to his back, then a punch to his kidney from Dumb before he could retaliate. He still attempted a swipe, though it missed, and instead of landing the kick he'd hoped for, he ended up slightly unbalanced.

He'd need to shift fully. His only hope was that these cats would take longer and give him a chance to get a few hits in on them midshift. He tried to take a breath, but the solid thud to his back knocked it out of him, and he knew if he didn't shift *now*, he might not be able to.

So he let go of the control on his cat.

Solid black fur erupted over his skin, and a few seconds later, his perspective changed as he landed on four paws. He shook his tattered clothes free and took advantage of the seconds of shock from his shift. He aimed for the neck, but Dumber recovered too quickly and dodged, so the claw swipe only grazed the skin instead of causing the damage he'd hoped.

All three backed up briefly, moving around him, obviously reevaluating. Quincy's tail twitched and ears flattened as he considered the cats still in human form in front of him. He couldn't hold back the growl in his throat completely, but he managed to subdue it a little. He didn't need to alert the entire neighborhood and bring humans into the fight.

The only warning he got next was a quick glance Dee gave to Dumber. It wasn't quite enough—or they just worked together too much and too well—because though Quincy managed to dodge the worst of their fists and feet, he couldn't avoid them entirely.

In jaguar form, however, he *could* jump better than them, so he managed to leap clear, though the only direction he could go was farther into the alley. Not that he should be going *out* of the alley in that form, or naked if he shifted back. Damn the secrecy laws, right then. Damn them to the underworld.

With a soft growl, he prowled to one side, then the other, looking for any opening he could. But it seemed they'd had enough of waiting for him. It *did* take them longer to shift than it took Quincy, just long enough for him to get a good swipe at all of them, but not enough to do any more real damage. And before he was ready for it, he faced three *huge* spotted cats.

Fucking hell. I really should have stayed in the hotel.

He briefly considered trying to jump for the fire escape, but he'd have to shift back first, and as fast as he was, he didn't think he had time.

Dee, Dumb, and Dumber apparently were tired of playing with their prey. They moved in at once, and despite his best defense, Quincy knew he wasn't getting out alive. He didn't understand why they'd kill him, had been so sure they were there to take him back, but in the end, it didn't matter.

He swiped, used his teeth and claws—front and back—dodged, did everything he could think of, but three against one—even against a *tepey-sa*, was too much. He lost track for a moment of claws and teeth and flying fur, of growls and the alley. He *could* fight, but he didn't like to, and right then, he sincerely regretted not practicing more.

He also regretted not spending more time with Miles.

A final harsh set of claws nearly slicing open his underbelly sent him crashing to the ground. He tried to stand, but one of the cats—he couldn't tell them apart in that form—stood on his hind leg, and the excruciating pain nearly drowned out the loud *crack!* of his leg breaking.

They weren't satisfied with one, though. They made sure there was *no* way he was getting up anytime soon.

As Quincy lay struggling to breathe through wetness in his lungs, they shifted back. Dee crouched over Quincy, reaching out, and petting his head. "This was just a warning. You *will* come back. You *will* take your place. And you *will* cooperate. Or next time we won't go so light."

Quincy was glad he was in cat form and unable to speak. He didn't know what he'd have said back, but whatever it was would only have earned him more broken ribs or something possibly worse. He could do nothing but lie there, fight to breathe through the pain, and watch them climb the fire escape and disappear over the rooftops.

He stared at the moon, struggling for the strength to shift, which would start his healing. He was positive they hadn't left him for dead. They knew he'd heal. It would be excruciating until he did, but he'd heal. No, they wanted him scared.

All it did was piss him off.

HE DIDN'T remember closing his eyes, but he wished he had. He might have avoided a whole mess of trouble when he opened them again.

He couldn't have been out too long. The moon hadn't gone very far; maybe an hour at most had passed. He struggled to move, and that's when he realized he was back in human form. Better if someone found him, at least as far as secrecy was concerned, but he healed better in cat form. Shifting once to human, then back to cat would have been even better, but that obviously wasn't happening.

Quincy took a quick inventory. His legs were both still broken, as was one of his arms. He was sure at least half a dozen ribs were broken as well. He groaned as he tried to move again, but nothing seemed to be obeying his orders.

A siren's wail split the night, much too close for comfort, bringing a curse from Quincy. If someone had seen him and called an ambulance… how the fuck was he supposed to handle this? He needed to get going, get *away.*

He closed his eyes and tried to summon his jaguar, but he was too injured and they were both too exhausted. *Fuck. Fuck, fuck, fuck.* With a long groan, then sharp cry, he managed to get himself onto his back, only to see the huge still-bleeding gashes across his chest and stomach. He couldn't even look at his legs. He could feel well enough how bad they were.

Bastet, give me strength. Thoth, I need your wisdom.

Neither deity seemed willing to listen. Unlucky day, indeed.

A moment later, the lights from the ambulance filled the tiny alley as it came to a stop at the end. Paramedics Quincy couldn't quite make out—his glasses, he was sure, were shattered and lost by now—jumped out of the vehicle and ran to the back. *Bastet, what do I do?*

But no wisdom came from his patron deity, and before he could come up with anything on his own, the paramedics approached him.

"Hey, what happened here?"

Oh, I don't know, I just got jumped by three jaguar shifters intent on taking me back to my father to take my place as heir to the leadership of our pride, which I didn't want to do. So they beat me up and left me like this.

Instead, Quincy croaked, "Fight."

He had to give the paramedic credit. Despite the "duh" he could see on the man's face, it was kept unvoiced. "And what—or who—did you fight?"

"Um… don't… know." It was getting harder to speak, and the pain threatened to pull him under again. "Don't… don't need help. I'll be—"

"Don't even try," the paramedic said, shaking his head.

Quincy was oddly and momentarily transfixed by the lights reflecting off the dark, shiny skin of the man's bald head. *Fuck. Not good. Bastet! Really could use some help about now….*

"Can you give me your name?"

Quincy thought fast, though he guessed it wouldn't matter if he gave his real name. The assholes weren't going to do more to him yet. They'd left their message and would leave him to heal and follow orders—or not. And if he was going to have to go to a hospital… but was that the right thing to do? Shit. Did he have any other choice? Aside from Dee, Dumb, and Dumber, he was the only cat in town. The only one he knew of who had knowledge about shifter physiology was the *one* person he shouldn't see, should *not* draw attention to.

"Quincy," he spat out, though his ribs hurt like hell and he was pretty sure he'd punctured a lung. He didn't think he had many more words in him, at least for now. He'd heal, even in human form, but it would take a while and be a bitch in the meantime.

"Do you have a hospital preference?" the guy asked as they eased the board under him.

He bit his lip to keep in the scream as they shifted him. No matter how gently or carefully they did, it felt like he was being ripped apart.

Bastet, let me be doing the right thing, he prayed one more time, then, before he could change his mind, said, "Presby. My... partner. Dr. Miles Grant."

Chapter 2

MILES FLOPPED down on the end of the couch in the tiny break room and rested his head on the back. His eyes closed on their own before he could tell them to. He didn't have long—maybe twenty, if he was lucky.

He was seriously regretting taking on so many shifts. But he'd been missing Quincy and needed something to occupy his mind, to distract him. It was ridiculous, he knew that; they'd met twice. But they were mates, destined, and their bond had already started forming. His wolf had been driving him crazy, pushing him to try to find Quincy and mate.

The problem was, whether he liked it or not, he didn't doubt for a moment Quincy spoke the truth about why they couldn't be together yet. He'd talked to Chad and Jamie a little and got the gist of the problems Quincy was having, though Chad wasn't in good enough shape to do much talking yet. He was still recovering from the change, still learning how to filter sounds and light, still learning how to be a wolf.

But Miles's wolf didn't understand, didn't give a shit about any of that. In fact, he was pushing Miles to protect Quincy, which was more than a little laughable. He'd been truthful—he wasn't afraid of a cat—but he had no knowledge whatsoever of the jaguar world. It still killed him that Diana had given him a cat. He'd been ready for his mate to be either male or female; he would have been content with either, even if his family and former pack had other ideas about that. But *no*, he had to get a different species altogether.

And a species he didn't know a damned thing about. He didn't know how far someone like Quincy's father would go to get his way. And Miles was a healer, not a fighter. He *could* fight—all shifters learned how—but that didn't mean he relished it, so he wasn't as good as most others.

He needed to see Quincy again, even for a little while. He could appease his wolf a little, make himself feel a little better, and maybe find some patience to wait more.

Quincy had sent a few messages since he'd seen his mate last—in the emergency room waiting area two months ago—mostly texts and a couple of e-mails to let Miles know he was still alive and still in hiding. They'd exchanged little bits about each other, but Quincy hadn't wanted to say a lot lest it was intercepted. It wasn't much, but at least knowing Quincy was okay helped keep Miles from going completely insane. He'd like to think he'd know if Quincy was killed, but he wasn't sure how far their thin bond went, for something like that. When he'd asked Chad how Quincy had gotten his contact information since he'd never had a chance to give it, Chad had told Miles not to wonder about it. But Miles knew at least part of what Quincy did and wasn't worried. He didn't think for a moment Quincy would use it against him.

The last two months had been pure hell. He had no idea how Tanner had managed to keep Finley at arm's length for two years. Granted, they'd been able to date, hang out together, that sort of thing, and he hadn't so much as glimpsed Quincy in two months.

So he'd spent most of it working. A few times he'd been told point-blank to go *home*, that he'd been working too much. Whether he'd liked it or not, they'd been right. He'd been so tired he'd barely been standing. But after getting a few hours' sleep—filled with some very vivid dreams of Quincy—he'd needed to do something.

Since he couldn't go back to work, he decided to do the other thing he was good at: learn. He'd gone down to the Carnegie Library in Oakland and begun reading up on all things Ancient Egypt, starting with Bastet. He had no idea how much of it was accurate to the jaguars and how much was pure myth, but he figured having a basis to start from wouldn't hurt.

Miles sighed and sat up again, eyeing the coffee machine in the corner. It was clear he wasn't going to get any sleep, so he might as well get going the only other way he could. But as he stood and turned to the counter, he got hit with a huge tangle of emotion that wasn't his. Anger seemed the primary emotion, though there was fear mixed in. And *pain*. Too much pain.

Quincy?

Miles raced out of the room, not thinking about how it would look—not thinking much at all. If Quincy was close, something was *very, very wrong*.

Just as he rounded the corner near the ambulance entrance, one of the nurses ran up to meet him. "Dr. Grant! Your pa—"

"Partner," Miles interrupted, then stopped himself when the nurse simply blinked at him. He'd never told them about a partner—because he hadn't actually had one, as far as he knew—but he'd deal with that later. "A friend called me," he said, thinking quickly.

"Oh. Okay. They're bringing him in now."

"Thanks. How bad is it?"

Just then the doors opened and the paramedics pushed Quincy in on a stretcher. He was naked except for a sheet, his normally pale skin *way* too light. He had long gashes on his chest and stomach, but the rest was covered by the sheet. It looked like the scratches—probably caused by shifter claws, if he was any judge—had already started healing, though plenty more still looked wrong with him.

Miles had to take a quick breath, then a second as Quincy's scent hit him hard—the hint of graphite and paper that overlaid a sweetness incongruent to Quincy's outer personality. Miles had to shove *hard* on his wolf. He wanted out and wanted to go after whatever or whoever hurt their mate. *Not now. We'll help our mate, but not now.*

With another breath through his mouth, he went into professional mode, falling back on his training and knowledge so he could make sure Quincy healed properly and didn't raise too many eyebrows in the process.

IT TOOK quite a bit to reach a point Miles could safely get Quincy alone. Thankfully Quincy had apparently passed out on the way to the hospital. The emotions had all been subconscious, and Miles guessed that was why they'd been so strong. He suspected an awake Quincy wouldn't let that much out. Miles would love to talk to him, but that would have to wait for now. It was much better for him to be out when they had to treat him, anyway. Painkiller—especially with a shifter metabolism—didn't do enough.

They'd had to set both legs, and he'd had to stitch the gashes on Quincy's chest and around the open gashes on his legs from the breaks. The bruising around Quincy's ribs told Miles at least six had been broken, and the X-rays—which didn't normally provide proof of broken ribs— had confirmed it, telling Miles how bad it really was.

Miles hadn't liked doing any of it. He knew Quincy's best bet would be nourishment and shifting, but he couldn't very well explain that to the nurses and assistants.

But now Quincy was in one of the treatment rooms, waiting for a bed in the main part of the hospital. Miles was going to be damned if he let Quincy check out in this condition. Quincy would probably be okay on his own, but Miles didn't think his wolf would let Quincy out of their sight yet. At least with the set legs and stitches, he could pretend Quincy had to stay for the benefit of the rest of the hospital staff, giving him a chance to rest and heal better.

The problem was, Miles *also* suspected Quincy had some internal bleeding. He hadn't said anything to the rest of the staff and had kept it out of Quincy's chart, not wanting to end up having to actually operate on Quincy. Oh, he'd *look* normal if they opened him up, but it wasn't necessary, and Miles didn't want to take any chances with Quincy in the weakened state he was in.

Miles pulled the privacy curtain now, pushed the door all the way closed, and prayed no one came in as he approached the side of Quincy's bed. Deep bruises marred his skin, making Miles's blood boil. How could someone do this to their own child? He didn't care who had actually carried it out. The order had been given—and he had no doubt who'd given it—and that was enough to make Miles want to punch something. He simply couldn't understand it, and it was certainly not endearing him to his mate's species.

He put a hand gently on Quincy's shoulder, leaned in, and called to him softly.

After only two tries, Quincy opened his eyes. He blinked up at Miles, looking adorably confused for a moment. "What—? Where am I?" He blinked once more, then said, "Aww shit." He went to move, but Miles kept a hand on him.

"Listen, we don't have a lot of time. I'm in here now, so we won't likely be disturbed for a few minutes, but I don't know how long that'll last for sure. Do you think you can shift?"

Quincy looked pensive for a moment, and Miles suspected he was checking with his cat. Quincy nodded. "Yeah, I think so. Why? And… is it safe here?"

Miles nodded. "If you can do it quickly. I think you've got some internal bleeding to go with the ribs, the gashes, and the legs. I can take you into surgery, but—"

Quincy made a face. "Yeah, no." He frowned down at his legs. "What about those?"

Miles nodded. "It's going to hurt, but I can take them off."

Quincy considered it, then shook his head. "No, I don't think my back paws will break them." He took a breath and reached for the tie at the back of his neck. Miles hurried to help him, untying and peeling the gown down, then stepped back. Quincy looked up at him. "On the bed?"

"Unless you want to put weight on those broken legs."

With a grimace Quincy nodded. "Right." He took a deep breath, closed his eyes, and in only a few seconds, Miles was looking at a *beautiful* solid black jaguar.

Miles stepped up and tilted his head. "May I touch you?"

Quincy dipped his head in something of a nod, and Miles gave a few short strokes of the fur at Quincy's neck. Miles somehow hadn't expected it to be so soft, but it was. Quincy's tail twitched, and he blinked a few times, then raised his head. Miles took it as the indication that Quincy wanted to shift, so he stepped back and nodded. A moment later he was looking at the once-more-human-shaped Quincy.

"Welcome back. How do you feel?"

"Aside from exhausted, better. I need food, though."

Miles nodded. "I don't doubt it. Listen, are they going to come after you here if I keep you?"

"Keep me?"

Miles didn't answer, just waited.

Quincy sighed and shook his head. "No. They've left their message for now."

Miles raised an eyebrow. "Message?"

"I'll tell you later. Suffice it to say, they won't bother me for a while, at least."

"Okay. Let me admit you—it's going to look really weird if I don't for a couple of days, anyway—and we'll get you meat and rest."

Quincy frowned again but nodded. "Yeah. That's probably best. Gods, I'm exhausted." He yawned.

"Lie back. Let me resettle the leg braces and see about that room."

Quincy more flopped than lay back into place, wincing as he did. "Ouch. Note to self: takes more than a couple of shifts to heal broken ribs."

Miles chuckled. "I'll remember that." He helped Quincy get resettled and readjusted the braces over both legs. It looked like the bones were a lot better, but the gashes were still open enough that the stitches didn't look out of place yet. Miles covered them with the sheet, helped Quincy with the gown, then looked back up at his mate's face. "I'm *really* glad to see you."

Seeing Quincy blush—someone normally so serious and aloof—made Miles grin. Quincy narrowed his eyes, but the effect was wasted by a slight smile. "Yeah, well... so not how I planned to see you again."

Miles grinned wider. "There are definitely better ways to meet up." He chuckled when the red on Quincy's cheeks darkened. "Let me check on your bed. Try to rest." He leaned in and kissed Quincy's forehead, smiling to himself at the stunned expression. "Back soon."

MILES COULDN'T seem to tear his eyes away from the man in the bed next to him. He had a book in his lap—more on Egyptian gods and goddesses—but he'd barely read more than a few sentences. He was still in too much awe over the fact that the man was his mate. And that said mate was here.

There *were* better ways for him to be able to see Quincy again, but if it meant he could hold on to Quincy for at least a couple of days, he'd take it. Not that he wanted Quincy to ever go through that again—he could only imagine how horrible that had been. Of course, after all he'd seen come through the emergency room over the years, he had a very good imagination.

He shook his head, closed the book, and set it aside, then leaned forward, slipping his hand into Quincy's. As he ran a thumb over the smooth skin on the back of Quincy's hand, he thought of all the things he didn't know about Quincy. It could fill volumes. He had so much he wanted to ask, so much he wanted to do, and that didn't even count actually mating and claiming.

That would have to wait, and as much as Miles didn't like that, he understood why. Until Quincy could get his father to back off, bonding would only cause bigger problems, because once bonded, mates didn't do well apart. It was why he'd been so nuts when he hadn't even managed to so much as kiss Quincy yet.

But they could talk, and once Quincy woke and had food, he planned to do just that.

As if on cue, Quincy's eyes opened, and he blinked, then yawned. Blue eyes met his for a long moment, and they just sat there, looking each other over. "We don't believe in destined mates."

Miles nodded, noting that, despite what Quincy said, he hadn't let go of Miles's hand. "You said something like that when you came to the ER."

"There are legends, stories. But I've never met a destined pair."

"I suspect it might have something to do with the fact that you're both solitary and very few in numbers," Miles said, smiling.

Quincy chuckled and nodded. "I'm sure that has something to do with it."

"Do you feel our bond?"

Quincy hesitated but nodded again. "Yeah, I do. It's like a string or… something tying us together."

Miles nodded. "Yes, very much so. We have many more destined pairs. Most are opposite-sex couples, but there are a few same-sex."

"Are Jamie and Chad destined mates?"

"Yeah, that was fun to watch." Miles chuckled again. "Every time they got close to me, Chad about went crazy."

"Oh?" Quincy raised his eyebrows.

"Um, Jamie and I used to, uh, well, we…." Jealousy spiked over their bond, surprising Miles a little.

"You fucked Jamie?"

He couldn't resist a small smile. "A few times, back before he and Chad mated. Only a few… and I never felt anything for him."

Quincy blinked at him, but the jealousy eased. "Oh. That was…." He scrunched his eyebrows. "That was weird. My cat did *not* like hearing about that."

"No, I imagine not. If I heard about any of your former, um, acquaintances, I'm sure my wolf would be rather unhappy about it."

"Weird."

Miles nodded. "I'll give you that. How are you feeling physically?"

"Hungry," Quincy said, making Miles laugh.

"I can well imagine. I have steak—I hope that's okay. The wolves tend to default to that when we're healing."

Quince nodded. "That's a safe bet. Is it cooked?"

Miles smirked. "I didn't think the natives would want to see you eating bloody steak."

Quincy laughed and sat up. "Yeah, I guess not."

Miles retrieved the thermal bag he had on the floor and pulled out the Styrofoam container he'd put inside. "It's not really hot anymore, but—"

"I'm not going to care even a little," Quincy said as Miles set the container on the table and rolled it over to the bed.

"That's good." Miles retrieved a knife and fork and handed them over next. "You can still order a meal for dinner, but I figured this would help more than the hospital food would anyway."

Quincy wrinkled his nose. "Yeah. I'll force it down." He smirked. "For you."

"Awww, thanks, sweetie." The wrinkle got worse, making Miles laugh again. "Let me go check on a few things while you eat, update your chart and such."

"Shouldn't you be down in the ER?"

Miles shook his head. "No. They kicked me out. The ER chief found out you were my partner and called in another doc, then took me off rotation for the next couple of days. Then he told me to get up here and not come back until you were discharged."

Quincy smiled. "I think I like your chief."

"Well… I've been working a lot the last couple of months, so I suppose I've earned the time off."

Quincy raised his eyebrows. "Working a lot?"

Miles shrugged one shoulder. "Couldn't have you." He leaned over and kissed Quincy's temple, then stepped back to see his mate looking pensive. "We need to talk."

Quincy nodded. "Go take care of what you need to. Let me eat. We can talk later."

"All right." Miles kissed him again and left.

JUST AS Miles was finishing up at the nurse's station, he overheard someone say, "Archer?"

He looked up to see a delivery person with a basket and frowned. "Who?"

The guy looked at the card again. "Quincy Archer."

"That's my partner."

"Oh good. Here you go," he said, handing the basket over, then taking off before Miles could say anything more.

The nurse next to him, Sara, raised an eyebrow. "Partner?"

Miles grinned. "Yeah. Quincy's my partner."

"I didn't even know you were gay," she said, shaking her head.

Miles laughed. "I'm not. I'm bi."

"Huh. Well, maybe that's why." She shrugged. "Congrats, hon. I'm glad to see you've got someone." She patted his shoulder and peered into the basket. "He have a cat?"

Miles looked down into the basket for the first time and started laughing. He took the card out to see it was signed from Chad and Jamie. He'd called them briefly to tell them he'd seen Quincy and he was in the hospital, but not much more than that.

Shaking his head, he grinned at Sara. "Yeah. Yeah, he does." With a wave he headed back to Quincy's room.

When he opened the door and stepped inside, he saw Quincy had finished eating. Miles crossed over and set the basket on the table, clearing away the container, then stepped back.

Quincy raised his eyebrows but looked back at the basket. It took about two seconds for him to start laughing. "I don't *even* have to see the card." He took it out anyway, read it quickly, then showed it to Miles.

> *Hope you get back to chasing mice around soon….*
> *Chad & Jamie.*

Quincy pulled out a furry rat and held it up, then a bag of catnip, one of those feathers on a string, and even a ball of yarn. It took Quincy a full minute to stop laughing. "Oh gods, I'm *so* getting them for this."

Miles, grinning, took the feather on the string, lifted it in front of Quincy, and shook it. Quincy snorted but batted at it anyway, making Miles laugh. As Miles pulled it away, though, Quincy batted again, chasing after it a little, nose twitching. Eyebrows raised, Miles fought the smirk.

Quincy sniffed. "I was just humoring you."

His smirk broke out into another grin. "Uh-huh."

"I was."

Miles laughed and kissed Quincy's temple. "Do you know that if we let ourselves go too long without shifting outside of the full moon, we start acting a bit like dogs… even while in human form?"

"You're kidding," Quincy said, staring. "Oh, the blackmail I'll have on Chad…."

"Not kidding at all." Miles coughed, then said, "I once chewed my own slippers right before my board exam," as all one word.

Quincy snorted, then started laughing again. "Oh, that's too much! I'm going to have to remember that. Make sure I hide my slippers."

Miles grinned, because it showed Quincy planned to be with him, at least at some point in the future. He started to speak again, but the door opened and Sara walked in.

"Time for your vitals," she said brightly.

Quincy rolled his eyes but sat still and patient as she took his blood pressure, temperature, oxygen level, and pulse. She wrote everything down on a little piece of paper, then stuffed it back in her pocket. "Can I get you anything? Are you ready to order your dinner?" She glanced over and saw the Styrofoam container. "Dr. Grant! Are you smuggling him contraband?"

Miles smirked. "I don't know what you're talking about, Sara! That was for me."

She snickered. "Right." She turned back to Quincy. "Something to drink?"

Quincy shook his head and pointed to the pitcher on the counter, still with water in it. "That's fine with me."

"All right, dear. Get some rest." She patted his foot and left.

"I wonder what she'd say if she knew just how much more healed I was," Quincy mused.

Miles laughed. "I'd probably be admitting her to Western Psych across the street."

Quincy grinned. "That wouldn't be nice, then, would it?"

Miles shook his head. "Nope. Oh!" He hurried around the bed and picked up the messenger bag on the floor. One side had a logo Miles had never seen along with a graphic of a guy with bright orange hair in a black robe with a *huge* sword resting on his shoulder. He lifted the bag and set it on the bed next to Quincy. "Apparently this got left in the ambulance. I… hope you don't mind, I checked inside. Your laptop, phone, and wallet are still in there."

"Oh good." Quincy opened the bag and pulled out a case. He took out a pair of glasses and slipped them onto his nose. "So much better."

Next he took out a slim Mac laptop, then his wallet, and blinked. "My money's still in here."

Miles shrugged. "Guess they didn't need it."

"Well. That's a surprise."

"I don't know if they'd get into the computer or phone or anything. I'm guessing you've got it locked down fairly well."

Quincy nodded. "Yeah, and the data's encrypted too. No one's going to get to my stuff."

Miles raised an eyebrow. "What *do* you do, anyway?"

"Draw things."

Miles blinked. "I'm sure you do. But what do you do that requires encrypted data?"

Quincy's lips twitched. "I'm an information broker. The kind you can't look up in the phone directory."

"Ohhhh." Miles nodded. "Well, that makes sense. I'm guessing I don't really want to know anymore."

Quincy shook his head. "No, you probably don't. Um…." Quincy tilted his head and studied Miles for a moment. "Do you think I could see your wolf?"

"Hmm…." Miles raised his eyebrows as he thought it through, but then nodded. "They won't be in for a bit. I think there's time." He kicked off his shoes, pulling his shirt off at that same time and laying it on the bed. It never even occurred to him to worry about getting naked in front of Quincy. He was used to the very sociable wolves, not the solitary jaguars. So when he turned around from taking his pants off, he realized what he smelled was arousal. It did his wolf good things to smell that, but he focused instead on giving Quincy what he'd asked for. Miles laid his pants next to his shirt and let his wolf forward.

His vision turned gray first, and then his claws extended and teeth dropped at the same time. A few seconds later, red fur that matched his human hair erupted over his skin. His bones shifted and muscles realigned, then a moment later, he landed on four paws. He lifted his front paws and braced them on the side of the bed, grinning his wolf grin at his mate.

Quincy reached out, running a hand over Miles's head. "Wow. I didn't realize your fur matched your coloring. It doesn't work that way for us. It's gorgeous."

Miles couldn't resist closing his eyes as Quincy stroked his fur. He had to be careful or he'd end up with a hard-on in wolf form. But it felt so good to have Quincy's hands on him, even in that form. To keep things *out* of the realm of sexual, he leaned forward and licked Quincy's cheek.

Quincy scowled, but there was no heat in it. "Gross. Dog slobber."

Miles snorted. And licked him again.

"Just you wait. Next time I'm in cat form, I'll give you *my* tongue."

Miles chuffed, then backed up to let himself down.

Before he could rein in his wolf and shift, Sara stepped into the room again.

Shit! Out of the corner of his eye, Miles saw Quincy throw his blanket over the clothes.

Sara stopped and stared at Miles, then looked at Quincy. "He can't be in here. No pets."

"He's a service dog. His owner stepped out to the bathroom."

Miles was going to kiss Quincy for his quick thinking.

"I didn't see anyone come in. And…." Sara raised an eyebrow, looking down at Miles. "He's not wearing a harness."

"He had to clean the harness. Got some mud on it. That's why he's out."

She blinked at him for another moment, glanced at Miles once more, then apparently accepted the excuse. Miles let out a slow breath of relief. "I came in to ask if you wanted to order something for later, even though you've eaten now. I didn't get an answer earlier."

Quincy shook his head. "I'll be fine. Besides, I can always send Miles out if I get hungry later."

She chuckled. "Right. Okay, then. Rest well… when your friend leaves." She glanced once more at Miles, then back at Quincy before she stepped out.

Miles pulled his wolf back and shifted to human form not more than a few seconds later. He took his clothes and put them on quickly. "Quick thinking." He blew out a breath.

Quincy flashed a smile. "I like to think I can do that now and again."

Miles laughed. "Right. Think I'll avoid that again until you're out of here."

"Probably a good idea," Quincy agreed, nodding.

"Now… how about that talk?" Miles asked, moving around to sit back in the chair.

Chapter 3

QUINCY BOUGHT himself a few moments by reassembling the cat toy basket. He wasn't sure he was ready for this, not sure he knew what to tell Miles. "What did you want to talk about?" Okay, dodging wasn't really like him, but he was in unfamiliar territory.

"Well, for starters… have you gotten anywhere with your father?"

Letting out a sigh, Quincy shook his head. "No. The last time I talked to him, he still wouldn't take no for an answer. I'm pretty sure he's got my apartment watched. And, well, there was Tweedle Dee, Dumb, and Dumber."

Miles burst out laughing. "Nice. I take it those were the three that attacked you?"

Quincy nodded. "Thanks. Yeah." He blew out a breath. "I honestly don't know what it's going to take to get him to listen." He scowled. "I swear to Bastet, though, if he sends someone like that again, I'm not fucking around. My fangs and claws aren't the only weapons I know how to use. In fact, this might have turned out differently if I hadn't left it behind."

Miles winced but nodded. "Yeah. Well, I wish it had turned out differently. I'm glad you know how to use other weapons, but I hope it doesn't come to that."

"I hope so too. I don't relish this shit. I just want to be left alone." He closed his eyes, annoyed at the slightly whiny tone that leaked into his voice. "I'm already tired of hiding, tired of running."

Miles's hand crept into his. "Isn't there anything I—or the wolves—can do to help?"

Quincy shook his head. "No. And right now, if you do, you risk interspecies problems."

"Ew, yeah, not good. I didn't even know we knew about you guys."

"Oh yeah. Well, I'm sure your alpha prime does. I don't know who else. But he's up there in years, isn't he?"

Miles nodded. "Yeah. Some… geez. He's over two hundred now, I think."

"Yeah, well, he'd know about us, then. And I know our *tepey-iret* knows about you."

"Tepey-iret?"

"Um... equal to your alpha prime. *Iret* is loosely translated as 'eye' and *tepey* is 'chief' or 'leader.' You know, the Eye of Ra was big with the Egyptians, so I guess they borrowed that. Where the rest of our titles and the like comes from."

"That makes sense. I've been, um, researching the gods and goddesses. Reading up on ancient Egypt."

Quincy raised his eyebrows. "Really?"

Miles blushed. "Yeah. I figured, you know, it wouldn't hurt to learn what I could. I didn't know what was myth and what wasn't, but I thought I'd read about it and ask more when I had the chance."

Quincy just stared at Miles for a long moment as he let that sink in. He'd been alone for so long—hell, even before he left for college—that it was weird to know someone wanted to do something like that for him, understand things about him.

He cleared his throat and picked at the blanket. "Um, that's... that's cool, actually. I'd be happy to talk to you about it sometime. I guess we have more important things to go over, though."

"Yeah, well, what are you going to do when you get out of here? I can probably release you tomorrow... or I could justify keeping you another day if you think it'd help."

"Um...." Quincy frowned. "I don't know, actually. Let me think about it. I'll need to call my father, try—again—to get him to stop this fucking shit." He scowled. Every time he thought about it, it pissed him off more.

"Hey, hey," Miles said, squeezing his hand.

Quincy blinked and looked up in confusion.

"I could feel your anger—beyond the scowl. I mean, I don't blame you, but...."

"Oh, I forgot about that."

Miles nodded. "For now... it's just strong emotion. I knew yesterday before they told me that something was wrong with you. I felt your anger and pain."

"That's a little... freaky." Quincy bit his lip. "And kind of cool, if confusing."

Miles laughed. "Yeah, well, when we eventually claim each other, that calms down a lot. We can still sense emotions, but we can control it a lot better."

"Ah, okay, yeah." Quincy didn't know how to address them claiming each other. He had no idea when they might be able to handle that, no clue what was different with the wolves than the jaguars—except that sometimes they didn't even claim each other. They fucked, had a cub, and that was it. He sighed. "So, uh, yeah. I need to call my father, try to figure out what the hell is going on with this. I mean... I get wanting me back, but for fuck's sake, we both know I'm not the best option for the leadership."

"Hmm." Miles frowned. "I'm afraid I don't know enough about the jaguars to say whether or not that's true. Maybe he figured he could still more or less lead through you?"

Quincy raised an eyebrow. "I never thought of it like that. I didn't really think he'd want something like that. By the time he steps down, I figured he'd be done with it."

Miles shrugged. "I really don't know enough about your world."

"It's not my world," Quincy muttered, then sighed again. "I mean, okay. I'm a jaguar, but I don't want any part of their politics, their pretense, or anything else like it. I believe in our gods. I honor our religious traditions. Outside of that, I just want to draw, sell information, and be left alone." He glanced up at Miles. "Maybe with my mate." He put the "maybe" on there, not sure himself where Miles stood in all of this. It was reasonable to assume Miles wanted him—he *had* made the claiming comment earlier—but for all that Quincy knew about the wolves, he didn't know their rules or culture.

Miles didn't disappoint. He squeezed Quincy's hand again. "I'd hope with your mate."

Quincy swallowed. It was nice to be wanted. Even if he and Miles didn't know that much about each other yet, it wasn't because it was expected of him. It just *was*—and a gift from Bastet, at that—and that made all the difference in Quincy's mind.

"Yeah, that... actually sounds nice." He smirked. "As long as I still get time to myself."

Miles grinned. "I don't know. Maybe I'll just shift and lay at your feet."

That surprised a laugh out of Quincy. "As long as you leave my slippers alone."

"I think I can handle that."

Miles got up and sat next to Quincy on the bed, brushing at Quincy's hair. "Good. I don't intend to crowd you, you know. I know the cats are solitary."

Quincy didn't know what to say to that. He *did* know the wolves *weren't* solitary, and he hoped they could find a balance… eventually. When he could worry about that stuff. "Well, maybe I'll make that call from here and figure it out, then. I suspect, though, I'm still going to have to hide for a while. This was a message: come back and take my place or worse will happen. I can't let you get caught in that. And I refuse to be forced into anything. I mean… if I thought for one minute you'd be safer if I did—"

"Don't even think it," Miles growled, and Quincy couldn't miss the hint of wolf in his voice.

Quincy raised a hand, a smile tugging at his lips at the protectiveness in Miles's voice. "Okay, okay. I don't really want to anyway."

"Good." Miles lifted his hand and kissed it. He studied Quincy for a moment, then without warning, leaned in. "Please tell me I can kiss you…. I've been wanting to for so long now."

Quincy swallowed, his throat suddenly dry, but nodded. "Yeah," he whispered.

Miles cupped Quincy's cheeks and closed the short distance, their lips brushing lightly. Quincy's eyes slid closed, and he leaned into the kiss, adding his own pressure. When he felt Miles's tongue on his lip, he opened and got the first, amazing taste of his mate. Their tongues slid, both exploring the other's mouth, the fledgling emotions they both were feeling coming across their bond. Quincy slid his hands up to Miles's shoulders and held on, deepening the kiss even more, moaning softly at the feel and taste.

His mate. Miles really was his destined mate. The pull between them intensified, and Quincy couldn't even remotely pretend it wasn't real anymore. As they kissed, that string he'd felt connecting them got stronger, thicker. Something invisible seemed to wrap around them, bringing them even closer together.

When they broke apart, Quincy stared with wide eyes into Miles's. "Wow."

Miles looked equally stunned. "Yeah, that's… about right. Wow."

"Did we… did we strengthen our bond?" Quincy decided he liked that phrase: *our bond*. He liked the link to Miles, that bit binding them together. It scared him—not that he'd admit that out loud to anyone—because the thought of something happening to the wolf he was already thoroughly attached to freaked him out. But despite that, he definitely liked and wanted it.

"I… yeah, I think so. We're not… it's not a full one yet."

Quincy shook his head slightly. "I didn't think so. But… it's… wow. It…. I think I like it."

Miles's smile was immediate and almost blinding. "I definitely do." He brushed a stray lock of Quincy's hair back. "I'm glad to have that connection to you."

Quincy took a shaky breath. "I do too. I don't…. Miles, I still don't know what's going to happen. I mean, what if… uh… what if they come back and do… more?"

Miles scowled, anger spiking across their bond. "I *will* risk an interspecies war, then. They don't fuck with my mate that way."

"Miles! That's not… there's no need to go that far!"

"Fuck that." He closed his eyes and took a breath. "You are my mate. They're already treading dangerous territory."

Quincy blinked but realized Miles wasn't wrong. "I guess so. Though… they don't know that. And I'm a little worried about putting you in the crosshairs if I tell them."

"I can see that," Miles acknowledged. "That doesn't mean I won't make their lives hell if anything happens to you—whether I've claimed you or not."

"Well… I guess I can't blame you for that. But… for now, let's just… uh… try to avoid a war?"

Miles chuckled. "Yeah, I guess. For now."

"Good. So…." Quincy mentally flailed for a safer topic. "Do you have any time to read for fun?"

QUINCY HIT the spacebar to pause the video and turned to Miles. "So… that was my very first anime."

Miles smiled. "I like it. I never had much chance to watch any, but that was mostly because I was too busy studying, then working. If I did anything for fun, it was reading a few minutes here and there where I could squeeze it in."

"I can see that. I was actually really busy in art school. They're pretty intense. Not doctor-intense, but…."

Miles nodded. "No, we're not the only ones who do a lot in college." He laughed. "So this one, is it a long series?"

Quincy considered that. "Not as long as some. This story is broken up into two different series. The first was… something like a hundred and thirty episodes, then it got canceled. They picked it up later to finish the story line. They'd stopped before the characters had managed to recover all the shards of the Shikon jewel."

"Well, uh, that's kind of dumb."

Quincy laughed. "Most of the viewers thought so too. Probably why they finished it." Quincy rested his head on Miles's shoulder. They'd spent a good hour just talking about themselves, getting to know each other. They'd talked fiction and music, and he'd discovered that, while they liked different things, they would still mesh pretty well there. His preference ran toward J-pop and K-pop, anime themes, and the like. Apparently Miles was all about dubstep, industrial, and heavy beats. While they weren't the same, there was enough crossover to keep them from killing each other. At least it hadn't been *country*.

They'd eventually gotten around to television and movies, and he'd confessed his love of all things Japan, including his love of anime. Quincy hadn't said anything, but it'd made him really happy when Miles had kicked his shoes off, settled on the bed, and suggested they watch something together after Quincy admitted to having a fairly decent collection on his laptop. Now he sat with one of Miles's arms around him, wishing, for the first time in his life, he didn't have to go back to being alone.

"There are a number of other series I like. A couple aren't done yet, though I usually prefer to wait until it's done to watch."

"I can see that. I don't have a lot of time to dedicate to a weekly thing." Miles pushed the table back, turned to Quincy, and tilted his face up. He kept the kiss slow and soft, though Quincy couldn't miss the arousal it sparked. "I like being free to do that," Miles whispered when they broke apart.

"I like it too. So, tell me, do you always trust your wolves with a mate? Knowing they're the right one for you?"

Miles pursed his lips. "Yeah. Well, it's not just that. It's Diana too, you know? Our patron goddess," he added when Quincy's confusion must have shown.

"Oh, that's right. You follow the Roman pantheon."

Miles nodded. "Yeah. You know, I suspect they're all the same gods, just… different forms for the different civilizations."

Quincy nodded. "Yeah. I'd bet you're right." He shrugged. "Not that we'll ever know. It wouldn't surprise me, though."

"No, not unless Diana/Artemis/Bastet drops down in front of us to admit it."

Quincy laughed. "And somehow I doubt we'll see that."

"Yeah, not likely." Miles grinned, wrapping his arm tighter around Quincy. "But yeah, we trust our wolves. I don't know of a single destined couple that didn't end up almost ridiculously in love and happy."

Quincy let that roll around in his head for a moment. "My cat says it's right. That you are. He wants you… even your dog." He chuckled when Miles snorted. "Besides, I somehow don't think Bastet would do that… put you with me if you're not right for me."

"I'm glad to hear it. And I'm a wolf, not a dog. Jaguars may be cats, but wolves aren't dogs." Miles scowled, but there was still a twinkle in his eyes.

Quincy grinned. "Yeah, yeah. That's why you chase mailmen and chew on slippers."

Miles rolled his eyes. "Right. Hey, are you hungry? That steak was a while ago."

"I could probably eat." Quincy frowned. "But is anything open this late?"

Miles nodded. "The cafeteria is open all but a few hours, I think." He kissed Quincy's forehead. "Let me go see what I can find for you."

"Okay. Get food for yourself too. I haven't seen you eat yet either."

Miles blushed, making Quincy grin. "Uh, yeah, okay."

"I'm betting you forget to eat a lot. Probably live on break-room coffee until your wolf threatens to burst free."

The blush got darker, and Quincy chuckled, making Miles scowl, though there was no heat in it. "Yeah, yeah. Laugh." His lips twitched. "It's true, though. I'll get food too." He climbed out of the bed and pulled his shoes on, then turned and kissed Quincy again. "I didn't think to ask if there's anything you don't like."

"I'm not one for overly sweet things." He chuckled. "No laughing....
I like fish quite a bit."

Miles nodded, obviously fighting to keep from smiling. "I won't
laugh. I'll see what they have." With one more kiss, he left.

Quincy sighed into the quiet room, *tired* in a way that had nothing
to do with his recovery. His life had taken such a ridiculously crazy
turn. Everything he was used to had been turned upside down. He'd
put together a nice, reasonably quiet life, doing what made him happy.
Even if he'd never expected a mate and he'd fought it—and he would
have, he was adult enough to admit that—he would have accepted Miles
eventually. Now he had too much of a struggle in other places to fight
against having a mate, against Miles. The rest of this, though... he needed
to get this *done* with.

He glanced at the clock. It was too late to call that night yet, but
he'd be on the phone with his father soon. This couldn't keep going. He
wanted to spend his energy learning more about Miles and working out
a life with his mate, not fighting his father and, by extension, the entire
jaguar pride.

AFTER SPENDING the night in Miles's arms—nonsexually, thanks in no
small part to their location—Quincy was even more determined to get to
the bottom of everything and get it *done* with.

He'd awakened at some point in the middle of the night when the
nurse—not Sara, who'd apparently gone home—came in to take his
vitals and clucked over finding Miles in bed with him. He'd held a finger
up to his lips, then whispered to her that Miles rarely slept as it was.
She'd shaken her head but was smiling when she left.

Quincy had spent a good deal of time after that lying awake,
thinking about destiny and mates, thinking about Bastet and the other
gods, some of which his kind had stopped paying attention to. Like
Hathor, who was, among other things, the goddess of love and quite
likely also partially responsible for mates. Many jaguars tended to focus
on Bastet, and Quincy suspected that was why they didn't believe much
in mates anymore. If they don't worship a goddess of love, why should
they believe in it?

But Quincy had never thought that quite right. While he wasn't
about to follow *every* Egyptian god—there were way too many for

that—there were quite a few he did, and Hathor was one of them. Even though he'd always thought he'd be alone, he had believed in love. And now… now he had a mate. Could he love Miles?

Quincy considered the sleeping man in his arms, sighed softly, and brushed his lips over Miles's forehead. If he trusted his gods, if he trusted his cat—and he did—he knew he'd been given Miles. Maybe the way his heart thudded when Miles looked at him was something Hathor or Bastet did. Maybe his cat prompted it. Or maybe, in the two months they'd known each other, he'd learned enough to know he loved Miles for himself. Quincy didn't really care. It was there, the want to be with Miles, the ache at the thought of leaving, and he didn't have the luxury of denying it, not with everything else trying to keep them apart. Whether that was the intention or not, it was a huge, annoying side effect, and Quincy wanted the whole situation out of the way.

To that end he also couldn't hide in the hospital anymore. He didn't want to leave Miles, but he wasn't sure he could protect Miles by himself, and he also couldn't end this from a hospital room.

He watched Miles sleep, smiling a little at how young Miles looked in that moment. The worry lines that had been around his eyes and mouth had smoothed out. The slight scowl he had every time he talked about what was going on was gone. Just fiery red hair and almost ridiculously pale smooth skin sprinkled liberally with adorable freckles. He had sharp cheekbones and lips Quincy could *not* let himself think too much about or the morning wood he was already sporting would only get worse.

But when Miles shifted in the bed and tugged Quincy a little closer, his arousal got worse anyway. Because Miles was just as hard. Quincy stifled a groan as their cocks brushed, thankfully through several layers of fabric. He might just go off like a teenager if they'd been naked against each other. It'd been a *long* time since he'd done anything sexually with another person.

He couldn't resist burying his face in Miles's neck, though, and inhaling deeply. Miles's scent drove him—and his cat—crazy. This man was theirs, and his cat was pushing him to bite and claim. *Mate.*

His cock jumped at the thought, precum beading, making a mess on the inside of his hospital gown. He didn't—couldn't—care, though. It just felt too fucking good to have Miles there, against him, in his arms. Especially since he had no idea when he would again.

He slid his hand up into Miles's hair, kissing the soft skin at the base of Miles's neck. He rubbed his face over Miles's skin, then chest, unable to resist doing so.

Miles gave a quiet chuckle. "Are you scent-marking me?"

Quincy's cheeks heated a little, but he couldn't lie to his mate. "Can't help it. My cat wants to claim you, but we can't, not yet. I can't seem to keep him from wanting to mark you as ours in some way, though."

"I didn't say I minded. I rather like the fact that you want to." He pulled back and nuzzled Quincy's nose and cheek, then kissed along his jaw. "I want to make love to you so badly right now," he whispered.

Quincy would swear to every deity in every pantheon he knew that the sound he let out was *not* a whimper. He did *not* whimper. He did, however, rock, grinding his cock into Miles's and earning himself a low moan.

Miles caught his lips in a kiss, both of them opening immediately, tongues touching, then sliding, heat exploding between them. Miles cupped Quincy's ass, pulling them even tighter together. Quincy rocked with him as he poured every bit of want for Miles he had into the kiss. Miles's hand flexed on Quincy's ass, and Quincy let loose his own quiet groan, which Miles swallowed with their kiss.

It was Miles who pulled back, though not far. "If I don't stop now," he growled, his wolf obviously close to the surface, "I won't be able to stop myself from making love to you."

Quincy panted hard, trying to remember why that was a bad idea. He closed his eyes and rested his forehead on Miles's chest, working to find some kind of calm. "Gods, I want you," he muttered, still doing his damnedest to take in oxygen, let it out, and do it again.

"Want you too, baby. But we can't. If we make love now, our animals will drive us crazy when you leave."

Eyes still closed, Quincy nodded against Miles's chest. "Yeah. I get it."

"I don't like it either," Miles murmured, kissing the top of Quincy's head.

They lay in silence for several long minutes. Somewhere along the way, Quincy managed to get control of his body and finally let out a long breath. "I'm going to take care of this. I…." He cleared his throat and took another breath. "I don't want to be apart any longer than we need to be."

Miles didn't answer for a few seconds, and Quincy started to wonder if he'd read things wrong. Then Miles whispered, "Thank Diana." He took another breath before speaking again. "I'm so glad to hear that, Quincy. Gods, so glad."

OF COURSE, it took forever for Miles to get him discharged. There were final checks of his vitals and the removal of the IV, among other things. Plus he'd had to give Miles his room key for the hotel so Miles could go get him clothes, as his were probably still lying in tatters in the alley Dee, Dumb, and Dumber had attacked him in. That had taken time, but Miles had returned in fairly short order because Quincy had, maybe stupidly, been staying right there in Oakland. He dressed in a pair of cut-off sweats, since he still had braces on his legs, and an anime T-shirt.

Miles got the discharge paperwork, then pushed him in a wheelchair to the elevator and down to the first floor. Then he found an unused room where he took the braces off Quincy's legs, and Quincy could put his jeans and shoes on. Finally he could get out. They stood outside the hospital entrance by the valet parking, leaning against the wall.

"We could do this together, Quince."

Quincy shook his head. "It's better if they don't know about you, at least not yet. I have no idea what my father might do if he knew we were mates. He doesn't believe in destined mates, but if he knows I do…."

Miles frowned but nodded. "I get it. I just… I can't help but think we'd be better off together."

"I wish that were true, Miles. I really do. I… gods, I want to be with you, okay?"

Miles's Adam's apple bobbed, but he nodded.

"I do." Quincy sighed and pulled until Miles was close. He liked that they were almost the exact same height—Miles had maybe an inch or two in height on him, but that was it.

Quincy tilted his head and brought their lips together, cupping Miles's face. Miles moaned softly and pulled him in until they were against each other. Quincy couldn't resist that—he seemed to have exactly zero willpower when it came to physical affection with Miles—and he deepened the kiss, pushing his fingers into Miles's hair.

But only a moment later, Miles broke away. "Come home with me. My apartment is barely a mile from here. We could be there in no time. We'll figure this out."

Quincy struggled to breathe and eventually managed a few deep breaths, though that was a bad idea with the exhaust around them.

He forced himself to ignore the stench and shook his head. "Not yet. I can't even promise soon, but I *will* work on this. Okay?"

"You'll contact me? Keep me informed?"

"Absolutely." Quincy closed his eyes, his heart thudding at the thought of leaving Miles. "I know it's fast, I know it's crazy, but I… I care about you a lot, Miles. I won't let this be the end."

Miles nodded, rubbing his hands up and down Quincy's back, then leaned in. "I'm pretty sure I already love you. It's okay; you don't have to say it. We don't know all that much yet."

Quincy looked up at him. "You trust your wolf, though. I trust my cat. He says you're ours. *He* thinks I should trust in our bond, in us. And if I do, if I believe you are a gift from Bastet and Hathor, then you deserve my full honesty." He took a breath and blew it out, but what he'd realized over the time lying in bed with Miles still felt true. "I love you too. We're mates. Destined. I don't think that's out of the question at all."

Miles's smile was so wide, Quincy wondered how he wasn't lighting up the entire hospital with it. He yanked hard, pulling Quincy closer again and kissing him.

When they broke apart, he cupped Quincy's face. "Be careful, please. I don't want to lose you."

Quincy nodded. "I will, Miles. I promise." He took a breath, kissed his mate one more time, then stepped back. "I'll call."

Miles nodded. "I'll wait for it. I love you."

"Love you," Quincy said, voice barely a breath as he backed away. He had to fight his cat, who was trying to get him back to their mate, but he was stronger than his beast. It took everything he had in him to turn around and *walk* to the corner. When he turned, looking back, Miles still stood there, watching him. He waved, Miles waved back, and Quincy started down the hill.

If it was a little fast, no one could blame him.

Chapter 4

MILES TOSSED his shoes into the trunk of his little Honda and shut the lid. His key went into the magnetic box he kept for it, and then he took a deep breath and let it out. He always loved the pack lands, loved the fresh mountain air, the smell of the pine, fir, and spruce that reminded him of back before life got complicated.

Almost the same scent had surrounded him from an early age. The specific types of pine, fir, and spruce were different in eastern Washington, but the scents were similar enough. He remembered running through them as a pup, rolling in leaves and grass, and playing with the other pups in his pack.

He shook his thoughts away and focused instead on his wolf. He needed to let go of complicated thought for a while. After Quincy had called to let Miles know he was okay and suggested perhaps he let his wolf out, Miles had realized his mate had a point. It'd been way too long since he'd shifted outside the full moon. And even if it didn't mean he'd chew his slippers or something, he needed to let his wolf out a bit more.

With one more deep breath, he let go of the hold on his wolf, giving him control. As always, he loved the shift, as natural as breathing to them, and in seconds he was appreciating the world from a whole different point of view.

He shook hard as he settled into his fur, then lifted his muzzle and sniffed. He caught the scent of hare, and not letting himself think about it, he took off. It gave a merry chase, and Miles was reminded again how long it'd been since he'd been out there. He'd even spent a couple of full moons locked in his apartment, rather than out on pack lands, because he'd been working so much. He poured the speed on and finally managed to catch it. His wolf relished the chase and savored the kill.

It was the one truly incongruent thing about him. His wolf could be—and was—a killer. He chased, hunted, and had no qualms about any of it. Yet the human side of him was a healer, and the violence and death *he* caused, if his human side had been more in control, would have seriously conflicted him.

When he'd finished eating, he cleaned up and took long drinks of the cool mountain water. Then he ran through the trees and underbrush, leaping logs and streams, pouring on speed and simply feeling the freedom of the wind through his fur.

He'd denied himself that freedom for way too long. It was understandable; he'd been so focused on Quincy. But he needed to remember how good it felt to run, how much he needed it to clear his head and let go of so much.

Miles found his favorite hill and settled down, looking out over the forest. The lights of Pittsburgh shone in the distance, even from that far, illuminating the sky. He had just the right angle, the mountain just high enough to see which direction the city was.

His mate was out there, somewhere. Quincy had texted him from the hotel room to say he was safe for the moment and focusing on relocation before he did anything more. He wouldn't tell Miles his destination, undoubtedly in case their communications were being intercepted. Quincy could do a lot to hide from people, but as proven by the fact that he'd been in the hospital, he couldn't do everything.

Miles tried not to let the ache get to him, but his wolf missed their mate as much as he did. They both knew there should be a sleek black jaguar next to them, tail twitching. Instead he was Mercury knew where, doing Diana knew what.

Miles was grateful he'd found Quincy. He hadn't been sure what he'd find for a mate—male or female—but he'd never expected another species. But as he'd told Quincy, he trusted the gods to know what they were doing. He cringed to think what might have happened if his younger life had never changed the way it had.

He'd known what his sexuality was from early on. He was confused—no doubt about that—because he'd understood there to be gay and straight, but he liked both, which frustrated him for a while. When he finally got a handle on it in high school, he did what he'd since read a lot of bisexuals do: hid in the closet halfway. He didn't admit to his attraction to men, kept it very firmly to himself.

But when another of the guys in their pack came out as gay and his parents hadn't freaked, he'd taken the encouragement. Still, he wasn't ready to put it all out there just yet.

Until he'd met Jacob.

Miles chuffed at the memory, realizing Jacob looked quite a bit like Quincy. Long, lean form, sinewy build, long black hair, and pale skin. He'd been fascinated by the human. Jacob had just moved there from a tiny town farther in the Coleville forest region, and he and Miles had become fast friends at school. It didn't take long for Miles to figure out Jacob was gay. He had no idea how to handle the fact that Jacob was human, but he figured he had time for that.

Except, when their senior year was winding down and Miles wanted to take Jacob to prom instead of the nice female wolf his parents had picked out… all hell had broken loose. It had never occurred to him that it would be okay for another guy to be gay, but not *their* son. Miles had never seen his parents behave like that.

The screaming had lasted days. Every time he showed his face, his father picked it up all over again. Mostly it was about "putting that gay shit aside" and "finding a nice girl" and "no son of mine." Miles usually shut it out at that point.

Eventually Miles learned to just keep to himself. He came and went when his father either wasn't home or was in bed. He'd been working part time for the pack, so he even spent some of his money eating elsewhere. When the beta's mate recognized him at the diner for the fourth day in a row, she'd tried to talk to him, but Miles wasn't ready to tell them what was going on.

Of course, Jeannie cared about her pack and knew something was wrong. So she went to the alpha, who tracked Miles down at the diner the next night. If Miles had ever wanted to be an alpha, he would have wanted to be like Karl Phillips. He'd never raised his voice, and in all the years Miles knew him, he'd used his alpha power less than a dozen times.

Karl sat opposite him at the diner, and Jeannie brought coffee. "How about we have a meal together?"

He might have asked, but Miles knew better than to cross the alpha. "Sure, Alpha," Miles said, when he'd made sure there weren't any humans on that end of the room.

With a smile Karl picked up the sugar and dumped a spoonful into his coffee and stirred it. Miles focused on his own cup, sipping slowly. Karl would speak when he was ready.

"So, I try to make it my business to know what's going on in my pack. If one of my wolves is unhappy, I want to know why, because if there's any chance I can do something about it, I'm going to."

Miles knew that about him. He'd seen Karl help more than one family find work or other help over the years. It was one of the reasons he respected the man so much.

"I don't have to ask if something's wrong. I *will* ask—for now—what it is." The unspoken addition was that he wouldn't *ask* the second time.

Miles took a deep breath and let it out. Karl hadn't kicked Wyatt out of the pack when he'd come out. The alpha wasn't going to kick him out either. The problem was, Miles wasn't sure anymore if he wanted to stay. He looked up through his lashes. "I… came out to my parents."

The only reaction Karl showed was a slight raising of his eyebrows. "You're gay?"

Miles shook his head. "I'm bisexual. But… there was a guy I wanted to take to prom." He shrugged a shoulder. "Hell, I don't even know if I could have, but I wanted to try. So when I told my parents I didn't want to go with Layla—the girl they'd picked out for me—and wanted to take Jacob instead…."

Karl actually winced. "I'm guessing Martin didn't like that."

Miles chuckled humorlessly. "No, no he didn't. Um… his favorite phrase was 'no son of mine,' though I don't know what followed because I stopped listening."

Karl nodded. "I can understand that."

Miles took another sip of his own coffee, then stared into the dark liquid as if it could offer wisdom he lacked.

"You were planning to go to EWU down in Spokane, right?"

Miles nodded. "Yeah. I was accepted to their Biology/Premed program."

"Then what?"

"I was hoping to go to Seattle for UW for the actual medical program." He frowned. "I don't know if I'll manage that now. One of the things my father said was that if I insisted on 'that gay shit,' as he called it, he wasn't paying for school. I didn't even know he could." Miles shrugged.

Karl didn't reply for a long moment, and Jeannie brought over thick cheeseburgers, a huge pile of fries, and the ketchup bottle. "Anything else right now?"

"No thanks," Karl said, smiling at her.

She winked at Miles and retreated behind the counter. Miles busied himself with ketchup and assembling the cheeseburger, then stuffing a fry in his mouth.

"Good grief, boy, I ought to come down on your dad just for your eating habits."

Miles blushed. "Uh…," he started, mouth full, then blushed harder. When he looked up, though, it was to see Karl grinning at him, and the heat in his cheeks faded.

"Do you still want to go down to Spokane? Did you pick that school for a reason other than location?"

Miles frowned, then shook his head. "No, not really. It was closer to home, to the pack. I could still come up here for full moons."

Karl nodded, taking a bite of his burger. They ate in silence for another few minutes, then Karl sat back. "I could kick Martin out of the pack for the way he treated you."

Miles's eyes widened and he stared at his alpha. "But—"

Karl held up a hand. "I could. But I don't think it'd be the best thing for you *or* the pack. Instead, I have a different thought."

Miles didn't reply, simply blinked and waited.

Karl nodded. "Do you have anything against going to Seattle a little early?"

Miles thought it through, but he'd already more or less lost his family. Unless he was willing to ignore half of himself, he'd never be able to make them happy. And, truthfully, *he'd* never be happy that way.

"No, I don't."

Karl nodded. "All right, then. The Rainier pack has a guy in the UW admissions office. I'll give Alpha Scott a call tomorrow and see what I can do. I think you'd be a lot happier with a fresh start."

Miles swallowed around the lump that formed and tried to remember how to breathe. He didn't want to leave what he knew. He'd been *happy* there in the Colville pack. But Karl was right, and Miles wouldn't be happy there any longer.

"Thank you, Alpha. I'm so—"

"Don't you dare apologize, boy." Karl scowled. "It's your father that owes apologies. I can't force him to accept you, though." He shook his head. "I can help you get a better start. Colville will get you to Seattle and get college paid for, at least your undergraduate degree. The rest'll be up to you."

Miles nodded. "Thank you. That's… more than I can expect."

Again Karl shook his head, but didn't say any more, except, "Eat. Jeannie'll skin us if we don't finish our dinner."

Miles laughed.

HE'D GONE to Seattle and put everything into his studies, graduating with honors. He'd officially joined the Rainier pack, which was a *lot* more accepting than his father had been. In fact, Seattle in general was very LGBT-friendly. Miles spent the next eight years throwing himself into his studies. He ran with the Rainier pack now and again, but although they'd been welcoming, it hadn't felt much like *home*.

When Miles graduated with his doctorate in medicine—the graduate degree courtesy of the Rainier pack, to Miles's shock—Alpha Scott got him to Denver, to the national headquarters, where he could study shifter physiology, and he'd spent two years learning all he could about the differences between humans and shifters. It wasn't until he'd finally finished that portion of his studies that he'd been at loose ends. He'd spent so much time focused on school and becoming a doctor that he hadn't let himself think about what came after.

As much as Miles loved the Pacific Northwest, though, he needed to get away, make a real fresh start. Alpha Scott had come through for him again, suggesting he talk to Alpha Noah of the Forbes pack in southwestern Pennsylvania. Miles hadn't been too sure about moving all the way across the country, but Noah had been more than happy with the thought of having a shifter doctor nearby, and when he'd outright asked Miles to go, Miles couldn't turn him down.

Forbes, the forests of southwestern PA, and the city of Pittsburgh had become home to him like no other place since Colville. He had no doubt in his mind that Diana had been guiding him. Finding his mate there, when he likely never would have come across Quincy's path otherwise, settled any possible lingering doubt that he might have been in the wrong place. This *was* home now.

Miles stood and shook himself, giving in to the ache for a brief moment. He lifted his muzzle and howled out his worry to the stars. He hadn't expected an answer, but he got not one, but two return howls. He tilted his head, trying to figure out who it was. He howled again, and again they replied. That's when he recognized them: Jamie and Chad.

He took off at a full run, dodging trees and rocks, following their voices when he howled again to find them. In a very short time, he cleared a tree line to see the two of them sitting in a small clearing. Jamie ran at him, pounced, and knocked him over. He chuffed and got out from under his friend, only to be pushed over again by Chad. He'd have laughed if he could. Chad was still very much a puppy, having only been changed a couple of months ago. He play-fought with the two of them for a while, the worry and fear fading for the moment.

Eventually he flopped down onto the grass, panting hard. The other two joined him, and to his surprise, Jamie lay on one side and Chad on the other, both curling up against him. Miles closed his eyes and let himself enjoy the closeness. He'd missed his pack. He needed to get out there more often, be with his own kind. He hoped before too long there'd be a cat along with him.

When he opened his eyes a short while later, it was to see a big wolf that, despite his current gray eyesight, he knew to be red, and his black-furred mate trot into the clearing. Miles couldn't resist a wolfy grin. Finley ran up and licked his face several times before plopping down next to him, though Tanner was a *little* more dignified… and bopped him on the nose with a paw instead.

Miles chuffed. He'd needed this, needed his friends. But he realized they'd become more than that. They were much closer to family than friends. Sure, he was part of the pack, and to a large degree, the pack *was* an extended family. But Tanner, Finley, Jamie, and Chad had become a lot more than friends or pack.

They lay together for a while, and then Finley jumped up and tugged on his ear. Miles shook him off, but got up and knocked him over in retaliation. Finley snorted, and Tanner got in on it, nipping at Finley's neck. They played for a while, Miles feeling lighter than he had in a long time.

Finally Finley shifted and squatted in front of them. "You guys want to go back to our place? Have some coffee and stuff?"

Tanner nodded in agreement and three barks answered him, so Finley shifted back. Together the five of them ran back through the woods, scaring rabbits and squirrels and splashing through the stream behind Tanner and Finley's house before they all trailed into the mud room. Finley handed out towels while Tanner grabbed sweatpants and handed them to Miles. Chad and Jamie went up to the room they were using currently, and Finley and Tanner pulled the clothes on they'd left behind in the mud room, then led the way to the big table in the dining room.

Miles loved their house. It had a rustic feel without losing any of the comforts or technology he knew they both loved. The river-rock fireplace had a huge LCD TV hanging above it. The kitchen may have been polished rosewood with copper fixtures, but those only complemented the stainless steel appliances that made cooking much easier on them.

He wondered what kind of house he and Quincy might build. He could imagine something with Japanese influence, maybe, alongside a stream. They could even build a small pond and running stream if they couldn't find one to build near. He pictured a tile roof and shoji-style doors. He smiled to himself, thinking about Quincy's face if he suggested it, and he decided right then and there that he would.

"So what brings you out tonight?" Finley asked, bringing coffee cups to the table. He and Tanner took spots on one side, and Miles took one on the other.

Before he could answer, though, Chad and Jamie joined them. "I suspect it has something to do with his mate."

Finley blinked at him and Tanner grinned. "Mate?" Finley shook his head. "When did you get a mate? And why am I only now knowing about it?" He narrowed his eyes at Jamie, who ducked his head.

"I promised I wouldn't tell yet. There's a good reason," he said, holding up a hand.

Chad kissed Jamie's cheek. "It is, actually."

Finley seemed somewhat mollified but still frowned. "Can you tell me now?"

Miles sighed but nodded. "Yeah, well…. My mate… is the jaguar you met at Chad's house."

Finley's eyes widened to huge saucers. "Your mate is a *cat*?"

Tanner, Chad, and Jamie all laughed, and Miles nodded, giving his own chagrined smile. "Yeah. You know, I was ready for a guy or girl, but noooo. Diana *has* to have a sense of humor."

Finley snorted. "That's one way of putting it."

Miles grinned. "But… I'm not unhappy with who it is. I'm not happy about what's going *on*."

"What is going on?" Tanner asked.

Miles glanced at Chad and Jamie and sighed. "I don't know everything, but…."

IT TOOK two cups of coffee and quite a while to tell everything, including the two months they were apart, the fight—Chad about blew a gasket over that—and the subsequent hospital stay. Jamie had wanted to hunt down Dee, Dumb, and Dumber right that second. Miles made a mental note to tell Quincy about it.

"I mean, we knew he was in the hospital, but we didn't know it was that bad," Chad said, shaking his head. "For the love of Diana, what is his father thinking?"

Miles shook his head. "I wish I knew. I mean… it still boggles my mind what all people can do to one another, you know? But… to your own child? I just…."

"Wait, he wasn't there, was he?" Finley asked.

"Oh no, it was just the three goons," Miles said. "But… it was under his order. That's just as bad and maybe even worse. He couldn't even bother to show up in person."

Tanner frowned. "Yeah, I don't…. I'm not sure I'm very impressed with the jaguar world, from what I know."

"Me either, but it looks like I'm going to be involved whether I like it or not," Miles said.

"Hey, uh, you'll be careful, right?" Jamie asked.

Miles smiled. "They don't even know about me. And the whole reason Quince doesn't think we should be together yet is because he's worried that if they find out… I'll be a target."

Chad wrinkled his nose. "And he'd be right. Maybe you ought to stick around here for a while. I'd go in to the city with you, but I'm not sure I'm quite ready for the noise and smells yet."

"Fuck me, I'm so wrapped up in Quincy. How are you doing?"

"He still can't seem to stop chasing skunks," Jamie said, smirking.

Chad rolled his eyes. "That damned gray vision is messing with me. They just look like big squirrels."

"Still haven't learned to trust your other senses as much yet, huh?"

Chad blushed. "Still working on that, yeah."

Miles grinned. "You'll get it. Did you get sprayed?"

"Twice. Man, that shit does *not* come out of fur either. And the worst part?" Chad looked up, and Miles stifled a grin. "It sticks to my hair in human form. Ugh!"

Miles lost the battle and not only grinned, but laughed. "Yeah. Uh, most of us learn that when we're pups."

"Guess I still kind of am a pup, huh?"

"Yeah, well, that's okay. How are you otherwise? Everything still feel okay? Should I look you over?"

Chad shook his head. "Naw. I'm fine. We have other problems to worry about, anyway."

Miles sighed. "You guys can't get involved yet."

Jamie frowned. "Why not?"

"Interspecies politics," Tanner answered for him. "If we get involved, the cats could see it as us pretty much declaring war."

"I will if anything happens to him," Miles said softly. He stared into his coffee. "It's killing me. I can't claim him. We can't even make love."

Jamie put a hand on his shoulder and squeezed. "It'll work out. I'm sure of it." He looked over at Chad, then back. "Sometimes it's just a rough road to get there."

"We've all had stuff to get through before we figured it out," Finley agreed. "It'll get better."

Miles nodded. "It will. It has to. I'm not letting him go."

Chapter 5

QUINCY SIPPED his coffee as he browsed the bookshelf in front of him while keeping one eye on the travelers passing by. He hadn't yet seen the Three Ds, as he'd come to think of them, but he didn't doubt for one minute they were there. Quincy had made no secret of the fact that he was leaving Pittsburgh.

It'd taken a lot of patience and will to do it. The day he got out of the hospital, as he was packing his suitcase to move to a different hotel, he'd received a picture of Miles via text message. He'd nearly lost his shit when he saw it, ready to run back to his mate. It took him several minutes to calm down and realize that picture could have been taken anytime. He'd pulled it off his phone, done his best to trace the number and dig into the picture's meta information, but to no avail. The number was a dead end and the picture's info had been wiped, which meant it could have been pulled from a surveillance camera in the hospital, rather than directly taken from someone's camera or phone.

It still pissed him off but was not worth throwing his carefully made plans out the window. He'd saved the picture, though, and would spend time later investigating further.

He'd forced himself to get out of Oakland and get a room out near the airport. He'd stayed another five days to work out the arrangements he needed to try to draw the Three Ds away from Pittsburgh. It had taken a frustratingly long time to move everything around and get set up. He was sure they were still there. He didn't believe for one minute they'd left him alone. They hadn't found his hotel, but that was probably because he was using a new name for it.

Now he was waiting for his flight, watching for Dee, Dumb, and Dumber to show up. He'd used his real name and identification to purchase two of the tickets. He had another one under Uther Isaacs and one more under Niles Perry, the new name he'd had in reserve but had yet to use. He wanted them to know he was leaving, but he wasn't a fool. He had no wish to find himself facing off the three of them again.

Finally he caught sight of Dee crossing the center court of the airport, making a beeline for the B terminal. Right behind him, Dumb stepped off the escalator. Quincy didn't see Dumber yet and that bothered him, but he'd have to worry about it later.

Once the other two had passed, Quincy joined them on the way into B terminal. His tickets had him leaving within twenty minutes of each other: one in Quincy's name to San Francisco, the other to Chicago. Niles's ticket went to Newark. Uther's ticket to Dulles. All four tickets and gates were through United or its subsidiaries, so all of them were together.

Dee had decided to watch the San Francisco gate, while Dumb had his eye on the Chicago gate. Quincy's Dulles gate was right next to the San Fran one, so he went over to the San Fran waiting area and took a seat, not bothering to hide. As stupid as he was sure they were, he didn't think they'd be so stupid as to start something in public.

Quincy, of course, had purchased first-class tickets, but he waited before getting in line when they'd called boarding for the San Francisco flight. When the gate agent announced the boarding would begin for Washington/Dulles in a few moments, Quincy got up and found the back of the queue for the San Francisco flight. He made eye contact with Dee as he did so, and Dee smiled, got up from his seat, pulled out a piece of paper, and got in the end of the line behind Quincy.

It was almost too easy. Just as Quincy got up to the gate agent, the Dulles flight announced boarding for first-class passengers. Quincy handed the San Fran ticket to the agent, made sure Dee and Dumb were only a few people behind him, then quickly sidestepped to look in his bag. When he saw Dee one person back from the gate agent, he smiled, crossed the waiting area, and got in line for first class to Dulles. Dee scowled as he stepped up to the ramp.

Quincy grinned, waved as Dee and Dumb were herded onto the San Fran ramp, and made his way along the Dulles ramp and onto the plane to Washington.

THE REPRIEVE wouldn't last. Quincy was sure they'd get right back off the plane. They'd never actually go to San Francisco. Still, it bought him at least a few hours. As far as Quincy knew, the next flights to Dulles were a couple of hours away—*if* they could even get tickets. If they drove, it was at least four hours, depending on traffic and how many speed laws they broke.

His flight, however, wouldn't even be long enough to nap, much less get his laptop out of his bag and work. Instead, he got fresh coffee and went over the things he'd need to do when he landed. He'd regretted the necessity of checking his suitcase, but he wasn't about to leave his SIG Sauer behind, not with the Three Ds on his ass, and he couldn't take it otherwise. Oh, he *could* get another one in DC, but it would take a lot longer than claiming a suitcase, and he didn't want to waste the time.

When he'd told Miles about his plan—briefly and more or less in code—Miles had been surprised at the thought of him flying. Quincy could understand—apparently the wolves didn't take well to it without help—but Quincy had been doing it so much and for so long, he and his cat had come to an understanding. His cat had learned they weren't going to crash, and though the pressure was uncomfortable, it wasn't too bad. He'd promised both of them not to fly more than he needed to.

The amount of time they spent in the air amused him. It always seemed like it took longer to get from the gate into the air and from the air back to the ground and gate than it did to do any actual flying.

Quincy was anxious to get the rest of his plan into motion. He needed to buy himself a little bit of time without the Three Ds too close.

So he could finally have it out with his father. This had gone on too long now.

After claiming his bag and getting the rental car—under his own name—he took a breath. He still had at *least* three hours if they drove straight for Washington. Before he could rest, he had one more stop.

The drive took him ten minutes, even though the hotel he'd chosen could be seen from the airport. The weird loop he had to take added the time. Just as he was getting out of the car to go into the lobby, his phone beeped. Hoping it was a message from Miles, he picked it up, but what greeted him instead made his blood boil.

Another picture of Miles.

Quincy took a few deep breaths. The lighting in the picture *could* mean it had just been taken. Or like the other picture, it could mean nothing and they were just trying to get to him.

He had no doubt it was Dumber. They were trying to draw him back, to get him to abandon whatever it was he was planning. But Quincy still didn't think they actually planned to *harm* his mate. At least, not yet. He'd hope his father wouldn't risk an interspecies war over this. Taking another deep breath to calm himself, he climbed out of the car, grabbed his suitcase and backpack, then hurried into the hotel.

The lobby to the Hyatt Dulles was undoubtedly pretty, but Quincy paid no attention to it. He greeted the desk attendant and gave his information, including his real name and credit card, grateful no one else was waiting. It took too long—then again, everything took too long right then—but eventually he had the key to a deluxe room.

He thanked the attendant, who he supposed was cute—he would have noticed before Miles—and turned for the elevator. A few moments later, he opened the room door and braced it with the slide-latch. He dropped the key on the desk, turned on some lights, then stepped back out, letting the door close behind him.

Two minutes later, he stepped out of the stairwell and into the parking lot, suitcase and backpack with him. And the hotel's system registering he went into the room but hadn't yet come out.

He didn't take any sort of breath until he was off Highway 28, and had taken the exit for US Route 50. He only stopped long enough for food. There seemed to be about a billion Subways and nothing else along his route—according to Google Maps—so Quincy stopped to grab a sandwich. He could shift and go hunting, but he wasn't sure he wanted to take that risk, at least not yet. He had something else to do first.

Finally he pulled off 50 onto the driveway of the Little River Inn. The stretch of road he was on had an antiques store, a fire department, an elementary school, a country store, and a pastry shop. Oh, and three churches, of course. But it butted up against the Bull Run Mountains so he could let his cat out later, they wouldn't likely even raise an eyebrow when he paid cash, and it would take the Three Ds a little while to find him.

The downfall to choosing something like a bed-and-breakfast in the middle of the country in nowhere Virginia was that the proprietor inevitably wanted to be sociable and ask a million and one questions. Quincy did his best to not look annoyed and kept his answers polite but short. Mrs. Timmons was nice enough, but his patience was already thin. Just as he was about to say something, her husband came out and patted her shoulder.

"I think he probably just wants to get into the room and settle in."

She chuckled and nodded. "Of course, of course. It's very nice to meet you, Niles. See you for breakfast."

Quincy nodded. "Of course. Thank you." He held up the key and followed the directions she'd given some five minutes before to the stairs and his room.

He flopped down on the bed and sighed. The room they'd given him had a nice-sized bed, pretty wooden antique furniture, a big round area rug, an armchair, and a private bath. If he didn't need to be so disconnected, the complete lack of technology—with the exception of an alarm clock on the bedside table—would have driven him nuts. But it would do for what he needed.

He pulled his backpack over to him, unzipped it, and took out his laptop and the three throwaway phones he'd brought along, as well as a few other things. He picked up the first of the throwaways and stared at it, willing himself to make the call.

In all the years he'd fought with his father over things, he'd never have expected something like this. He remembered a time when he and his father had gotten along well, when they'd chosen to spend time together.

He shook the thoughts off. Those days were long gone. Longer than he realized, but gone nonetheless. He stood and paced next to the bed, trying to figure out how to approach this. His anger, his worry over Miles, his downright exhaustion from hiding for so long hadn't faded. Other people had hidden for longer, he was sure, but it was past time. He was done.

He dialed the number before he could talk himself out of it, checking the time on his watch as he hit Send.

"Hello?"

"Father." That was all, and Quincy knew it would be enough.

"Thank Bastet! Where are you? When are you coming home? What—"

"Can it, Father."

Silence greeted him for a long moment. "Quincy?"

Quincy fought to hold back the pure fury flowing through him. "How *dare* you act like you're worried? Where do you get the nerve?"

"I don't like your attitude, son," his father growled.

"I don't like what you've done, Father. I think that makes us even, doesn't it? Why? Why did you do it?" Quincy pinched the bridge of his nose, trying to hold on to his patience. He kept an eye on the seconds hand on his watch, then sent a bid to Thoth for wisdom and patience in dealing with this.

"I was worried about you."

"Worried?" Quincy snorted. "Hardly." He hung up the phone and picked up the second one, dialing his father again.

"What was that for?"

"You didn't think I'd make it easy on you, did you? You're not tracking me that easily. I know how long it'll take you to get into what you need to find me." If it'd been him, he'd have already had some of the information, but his father didn't have the same access he did— undoubtedly why he'd hired Chad. So it would take him quite a bit longer, thankfully, made more difficult because none of the phones had a real name attached to them, were different services, and had been purchased in separate places. "Never mind that. How can you say you're *worried* about me when you sent not one, not two, but *three* enforcers after me? Did it even bother you a little that I ended up in a human hospital?"

"*What?*"

"Don't play dumb with me, Father. What did you think I was talking about?"

"The investigator I hired to find you."

"Unfortunately for you, he's a friend of mine." Quincy hung up and picked up the third phone. "Fine, you want to insist you didn't do it?" he said when his father picked up again. "Whatever. *Any* hope of ever seeing me again is now gone. Let me make this *very* clear. I am not now, nor will I *ever*, come back to New York to take the place you want me to. I am not, nor will I ever, choose a *hemet*. As you are apparently aware, I have a mate."

"You have—"

"Can it," Quincy said, cutting him off. "My mate is not up for discussion." He took a breath and let it out. "We're both well aware I am not the right person for the leadership. Back off. I swear to all the gods we worship, I will make your life *hell* if you don't stop this."

"Quincy, I don't know what you're talking about. I didn't call any enforcers. I didn't know you were in the hospital."

"Whatever, sorry. I don't believe you, not after the hell of the last few months. Back off or I swear, you will regret ever crossing me."

Quincy disconnected the call, then dropped all three phones onto the carpet and smashed them. The calls could still be tracked since the phones' identifying information was recorded, but without a live connection, it'd take a lot longer for his father to find the data, and with a prepaid, triangulating the location would still not necessarily get him everything. Since the nearest cell tower was at *least* three miles away, he was pretty sure he was far enough from the tower that it'd take even longer to find him. With his father's lack of access, he felt fairly confident he had at least a good twenty-four hours.

He collected the pieces of the phones and tossed all but the circuit boards into the garbage. He took the boards into the bathroom and soaked them in the sink, just to be sure, then threw them out as well. He was being overcautious, but he hadn't survived the last three months without it, despite his hospital visit.

Pacing the small room, Quincy couldn't wrap his head around his father not even taking responsibility. That wasn't like him. For all he was ruthless and could be a total asshole, he usually took responsibility for his ruthlessness. Quincy went over to the window to look out into the late afternoon. The sun was already sinking. It'd taken him longer to get there and make that call than he'd thought.

He shook his head and crossed the room again. His cat prowled just on the edge of his control, and Quincy knew he needed a run, needed to let his cat out. Maybe with instinct guiding him instead of overcomplicated thought, he could figure out what the next step should be, how to deal with the questions, worries, fears, and anger still swirling through him.

He grabbed his room key, made sure his phone was turned off, and went down the stairs.

Mr. Timmons sat on one of the chairs in the main room with a newspaper open.

"Is there a time the door is locked?" Quincy asked.

He shook his head and smiled. "Nope. Someone's always up. Might be one of the kids."

"Thank you. I need to get some air."

Mr. Timmons nodded. "Country's good for that. You could always visit the donkeys."

Quincy raised an eyebrow. "Donkeys?"

He laughed. "Yeah. We have a couple of donkeys in the back field. We call them our 'permanent guests.' They like to meet people."

Quincy couldn't suppress the chuckle. "I'll… have to do that. Thank you." Before he could get dragged into more conversation, he was through the door, around the house, and walking along the driveway.

He'd seen the forest at the edge of the property—it was one reason he'd chosen the place—and made a beeline for it.

Just inside the trees, he looked around to make sure he was alone, then quickly stripped, wrapped his clothes up carefully and stuck them under a bush, then closed his eyes and let his cat out. In seconds he was on four paws again, and he stretched, savoring the feel of the powerful muscles.

HE RAN. He ran as if Osiris himself was trying to catch him and drag him to the underworld. Or perhaps more accurately, he ran as if Seth, the embodiment of chaos, chased him.

For once, though, he didn't think. He let his cat guide him, stretching his muscles, focusing on the forest under his paws, on cool mountain air, on the scents of animals and trees and summer. He didn't know where he was going, but the beauty of his beast was that he didn't *have* to.

He ran until his muscles ached, until his stomach growled, until he couldn't run anymore. Then he ran some more. He let instinct find prey, let it guide him to the fight. But *he* savored the kill and the meat and the blood. He ate voraciously, thrilling in the satisfaction of such a basic, primal need.

But when he finished, when he'd cleaned himself and settled in a tree to rest, the other thing his cat wanted brought his humanity back to the surface. He laid his head on his paws, tail twitching, trying not to let himself think. But the image of a beautiful red wolf danced in his mind, and the human side of that wolf, smiling at him, whispering words Quincy thought he'd never hear—had thought, for so long, he didn't want to hear.

He'd been so wrong.

The pictures bothered him. Now, with the fury at his father cleared from his mind, he realized there was more to them than he'd wanted to believe, and he knew what he needed to focus on next. Regardless of whether those pictures were recent or not, they were clearly a threat. Leaving Miles hadn't worked—at least, not as he'd hoped. He'd bet the Three Ds split up, but that still left one—probably Dumber—too close to Quincy's mate for his peace of mind.

He stood and stretched, then leapt lightly from the tree. He looked up at the moon to see he'd been gone far longer than he'd hoped. He'd go back, get some sleep, and decide the rest in the morning.

WHEN QUINCY stepped through the door a short time later, intending to go straight for the stairs, he was surprised when Mr. Timmons called to him. "I thought you'd be in bed," Quincy said as he crossed the room.

Mr. Timmons smiled. "Sometimes I don't sleep. It's part of that old-man thing."

Quincy couldn't help but laugh. "So… was there something I could help you with?"

"Oh, right. This was in the door this evening. I'm not sure how it got there, but…." He held out a small manila envelope.

Quincy took it, frowning at the *Niles Perry* on the front. He glanced at the clock, but it was barely after midnight. That was awfully fast. He'd worry about that later. He flipped it over, opened it, and tipped out a picture.

Another of Miles.

It took a moment for Quincy to realize what was special about that one. Miles was in the Presby waiting room, talking to someone. Behind him, the television up on the wall was showing a news channel. And right there, clear as day, was the picture of some celebrity Quincy wasn't familiar with and the news of his death.

That had only happened this morning.

Fuck.

The blood drained from his face, and his heart started pounding. Quincy forced himself to calm down, peering closer at the photo. Could it have been fixed? Photoshopped maybe?

But the artist in him knew immediately it wasn't. It was real, and that meant those bastards really *were* watching Miles.

Quincy flipped the photo over to see a simple line:

That little phone call is going to cost you.

His face went pale. *Oh shit.*

"Um…. It appears I'll be checking out in the morning. I'm sorry. Please, keep the payment I've already given." With that Quincy bolted for the stairs and went up them two at a time. If he hadn't been worried about freaking out the human, he might have even leapt farther.

He tore into the room and snatched up his phone, waiting impatiently for it to start up. His shaking hands made dialing impossible. It took

Quincy a full count of sixty before he could calm down enough to dial. *Please be there. Please be there. Please answer.*

Except, of course, Miles's phone went straight to voice mail.

Quincy sat hard on the side of the bed. Okay, it didn't mean anything yet. He could be treating a patient—hell, he could be performing surgery. There were a billion reasons why Miles might not answer his phone. He could be in wolf form, for that matter.

Taking a deep breath, Quincy brought up his contacts and hit a different number.

That one picked up on the second ring. "Q?"

"Oh thank Bastet," he whispered. "Chad, I need a favor."

"What's going on?"

Quincy swallowed. "They're watching him. I got a picture from today, Chad. In the ER. And a warning."

"Fuck. I'm still not sure how well I can handle the city, Q."

"Chad… I wouldn't ask but—"

"No, I get it. I would if it was Jamie. All right. I'll deal with it. Where is he now?"

Quincy appreciated the shift in tone of voice. Chad was all cop—or former cop—now. "I don't know. He didn't answer his phone, but he could just be in the hospital somewhere."

"I'll find out. Jamie and I will go as soon as we get dressed."

Quincy managed a snort. "I didn't need that mental picture."

"Jeans, Q. For the love of Diana."

Quincy buried the hysterical giggle with effort. "I'll be on my way home in a few. It's going to take me about four hours, though."

"Where are you?"

"Outside DC. Just… find him. And call me when you do."

"We will."

He kept his voice steady for a little longer. "Thank you, Chad. See you soon."

Chapter 6

MILES FROWNED at the computer screen as he tried to read the blood test results from the lab. His eyes were swimming, and when he glanced at the clock in the corner of the screen, he grunted. No wonder he couldn't see. He'd been working for twelve hours straight so far.

"Dr. Grant?"

Miles looked up, grateful for the interruption. "Ah, Lainey, what do you need?"

One of the new residents sighed. "It's Mrs. Henderson again." She shook her head, her black hair flying around her face. She batted at it. "Same stuff, different day."

Miles chuckled. "She comes in at least twice a week. Run some blood tests—just to be sure—then tell her she's got nasopharyngitis, give her a 'scrip for ibuprofen, and send her home."

Lainey blinked. "You want me to tell her she's got the common cold?"

With a smirk Miles nodded. "Yes, but make sure you use the *naso*pharyngitis. I used rhinopharyngitis last week. You could also try coryza as well. I haven't used that one in a while."

She laughed. "Well, okay, then."

"She's just a lonely old lady. You'll do more for her if you just talk to her for a few minutes."

Lainey nodded. "I gotcha."

Miles's phone went off and he sighed. It'd been buzzing on and off for a while. He looked down and saw it was a text from Jamie.

911. Answer your phone, dork.

Miles blinked but looked over at Lainey. "I gotta take this. Dr. Davidson is on in a few minutes if you need something."

"Thanks," she said and hurried away.

Miles hit the button for Jamie's contact.

"About damned time."

"Impatient much?" Miles asked.

Jamie snorted. "Been trying for almost an hour. Quincy called. You've been targeted."

"Fuck."

"That's about the extent of it. Chad and I are on our way in. Stay *in* the emergency room."

"I will." Miles sighed. "What then?"

"We're thinking pack lands."

Miles frowned. "Probably best. I'll go talk to my chief… shit. It's two. I'll leave a voice mail. Where are you now?"

"Parkway East. Not far," Chad said.

"Got it. I'll be ready."

Jamie hung up, and Miles took a moment to close his eyes and let out a breath. He'd known it was a possibility. He just hoped Quincy was all right. He rubbed his face hard, then pulled up his messages and typed out a fast one to his mate. *C & J picking me up in a few. Love you.*

The reply was almost immediate. *Thank Bastet. See you soon. Love you.*

With relief at seeing Quincy's reply, he hurried to get ready to go.

"I'M GUESSING you're going to need some stuff from your place?" Chad asked as Miles met him at the door.

"Yeah. All I've got right now are scrubs."

Chad grinned. "And I'm sure you're sick of them by now."

Miles shrugged. "I wear them so much I don't even notice anymore."

Jamie was behind the wheel of the Challenger, and Miles climbed into the back seat. "Hi! Glad you're okay. You worried us there for a bit."

"Yeah, well, couldn't be helped. Hell night tonight."

"Do you need to stay?" Chad asked.

Miles shook his head. "No. There are two here and the chief has someone else coming. It's fine."

"Good. Because the city's making me nuts already."

Jamie laughed. "You should have seen his face when he opened the car door."

Miles grinned. "Yeah, I can believe it. Okay, turn right onto Lothrop, then right onto Terrace and go around. We want O'Hara."

"Got it," Jamie said, starting the car.

Miles closed his eyes and laid his head back against the seat. He tried to remember the last time he took a day off and realized it was when Quincy was still there, almost a week ago. He'd had a few hours here and there, but nothing more.

"Hey, no falling asleep yet," Chad said, poking him. "Not till we get to your apartment and on the way back to pack lands."

"Yeah, yeah. Might need coffee for that."

Jamie snorted. "More like a Red Bull."

"That shit's nasty," Miles said, wrinkling his nose.

"I can't believe coffee does anything for you by this point."

Miles didn't answer, and Jamie and Chad both laughed. "Follow Bigelow to Bayard, then almost to the end. Amberson is on the left."

"'Kay."

In only another couple of minutes, Jamie made the turn onto Amberson and followed it to the entrance.

"Parking's around back. Here," Miles said, handing over the key fob that unlocked the lot gate. He directed Jamie to a spot near the door he used, and finally they climbed out.

He was surprised when they got to his door that Chad pulled out his weapon. He held a finger up to his lips and took the key from Miles. Miles didn't argue. Chad's experience as a cop wasn't something Miles was going to get in the way of. He stepped back and let Chad work.

Miles didn't even hear the lock click. As soon as the door opened, Chad held his hand out in a wait gesture. Miles looked over at Jamie, surprised to see a gun in Jamie's hand too. Chad held his weapon up in front of him, then pushed the door open as he checked the hall. He glanced back, did the wait gesture again, then slipped into the apartment while Jamie watched the hallway both ways.

Miles guessed Chad said something over the telepathic link he had to Jamie, because with no other signal, Jamie said, "All clear."

They went in, and Miles busied himself with grabbing a bag and packing his clothes. He made sure to get his toiletries and a few other things and was about to go when he realized he should take his computer.

"Hey, you want to take this stuff out? I'll be right behind you. I forgot my computer. Take me two minutes."

Jamie took the clothing bag. "Sure. I'll get the car started."

Chad took the second bag with toiletries and the like, and Miles headed back upstairs to get his backpack.

Just as he cleared the spiral staircase, something solid and heavy caught him on the spine, knocking him forward onto his face. He hit the wood floor hard, blood spurting from his nose. He tried to roll, only to get another hit on his shoulder and a third to the side of his head. *The fuck was that?* This time he managed to roll in time to see the bat come down on his right leg. In a sort of detached way, he heard the bones crunch and thought, *Well, fuck, that's going to hurt when it heals.*

He looked up, took a deep sniff, and realized the jaguars had found him anyway. Not that he doubted it, but that confirmed it. He cursed himself for forgetting the other door. His loft had two floors, but only a spiral staircase leading to the second, so there was a normally locked back door on the second floor for moving in furniture and the like, which he'd forgotten about.

Chad's going to blame himself for this. Miles pushed the thought away and tried to get up on his good leg, but that fucking bat stopped the possibility cold. "Okay, fuck you," Miles growled, ready to call on his wolf.

Before he could manage it, the bat came down one more time. Miles tried to dodge, thinking, *Quincy's going to be so pissed.*

Then everything went black.

HE WOKE to pain and disorientation. He had no idea where he was or why *everything fucking hurt.* It took him a while to probe his mind to find the memories.

Oh right. Jaguar. Fuck.

He pried his eyes open, then slammed them closed again when the light in the room pierced his skull. He was pretty sure his head was about to explode. Or split in two. Or something. Never mind it wasn't physically possible, Miles threw science and medicine out the window for the moment and decided the pain was more accurate.

Okay. Okay. You can do this.

Miles took a breath and opened his eyes again, this time only a slit. He saw figures standing around a room he didn't readily recognize, but he couldn't make them out right away.

"Light," he croaked, annoyed at the rough sound of his voice.

There was a click, and Miles widened his visual range a little more. Without the light killing him, he could clear his vision enough to recognize Tanner, Finley, Chad, and Jamie. Chad sat in a corner chair, face buried in his hands, Jamie sitting next to him with a hand on his back. Finley had a chair up against the bed Miles was lying on, and Tanner had another chair on the other side.

"Oh good," Finley said, relief obvious. "We were beginning to worry."

Miles tried to clear his throat, but it hurt too much. He didn't remember getting hit in the throat, but then again he didn't remember anything after recognizing that it was a jaguar after him.

"Don't try to talk yet. You took some real damage to your neck and throat," Tanner said, drawing his attention. "You'll heal, but take it easy for a while."

Miles blinked at him, then gave an almost imperceptible nod. He queried the rest of his body to try to figure out how much damage he'd taken. Without X-rays, he couldn't know for sure, but he thought both legs were broken in more than one place, and possibly several ribs. His hands hurt, and a glance down told him at least a few of his fingers had been broken. And then, of course, there was his throat and head.

He'd taken a hell of a beating, apparently.

"Chad," he whispered, trying to get his friend's attention.

Chad looked up, then came over to the bed. "Hey, glad you're awake. You gonna make it, man?"

"Can't kill me that easily," Miles whispered in reply.

Chad snorted. "I wouldn't call that *easily*."

Miles started to shake his head, but when his brain banged against his skull, thought better of it. "Cat?"

"Gone," Jamie said. "We can talk more when you're better. What can we give you for that throat?"

Miles thought about it for a moment. "Warm weak tea. Honey. Lemon."

"Done. Back in a minute," Finley said, jumping up.

Miles closed his eyes and tried to stay still so it didn't hurt any more than it had to. He'd heal, but it would be slow going until he could shift. Right now his wolf wasn't even remotely interested in making an appearance. He was exhausted, trying to heal them.

"Not your fault, Chad," Miles whispered, opening his eyes again.

Chad frowned. "How'd you know what I was thinking?"

Miles didn't speak, simply raised an eyebrow. That hurt, but he let it communicate his opinion.

Jamie smirked. "Told ya. He's smart."

"Duh. Don't get to be a doctor without it." Chad shook his head. "Apparently not that smart if he said that, though."

Jamie smacked him in the back of the head.

"Ow! What the fuck was that for?"

"Being an idiot," Miles whispered. "My fault. Forgot a second door."

Chad blinked at him. "There was another door?"

"Upstairs. Locked, hidden. For moving in."

"Fuck, how did I miss that?" He frowned. "It was in the back of the closet, wasn't it?"

"Yes," Miles said, then sighed when Finley came in with a cup and a straw.

"Can't hold this yet," he said at Miles's expression. "Your hands are too damaged. Drink."

Miles obediently sipped at the warm liquid, closing his eyes as it started to soothe his throat. Once he'd had as much as he could for the moment, he gave a slight nod to Finley, who set the cup aside.

"Quince?"

"On his way. He said four hours from his call, which was…." Chad looked at his phone. "About three ago."

"'Kay." With another breath Miles closed his eyes, trying to decide what to do. He could get them to pick up painkiller for him. It wouldn't do much, but it could help. On the other hand, if he could go back to sleep and rest some more, he might just recover the energy to shift. He wasn't worried about concussions; he'd heal from anything like that. Instead, he tried to figure out if he could get a little more comfortable. He frowned down at his legs when he noticed he couldn't move them. On either side of each was a wooden stick held in place by what looked to be strips of cloth.

"Splints?"

"Yeah," Jamie said. "I didn't want you to have to rebreak them if they healed wrong."

Miles smiled. "Thanks. Would suck."

"You need to get more rest," Tanner said, standing. "With luck Quincy will be here soon, and with him close—"

"I'll heal faster, yeah. Thank you."

Jamie stepped up. "I'd, uh, hug you or pat you or something, but I have no idea where to touch."

Miles smiled again. "Not many places, and a couple I don't think Chad or Q want you to touch."

"Definitely not," Chad replied.

Miles chuckled, then groaned. "'Kay. No laughing. Got some internal shit going on. Need rest for shift."

"We're out. We'll be right out the door in the living room if you need us."

"'Kay."

All four left, and Miles closed his eyes. He didn't even hear the door close.

WHISPERING WOKE him. The sweetness of his mate's scent hit him, and he opened his eyes to see Quincy sitting on the side of the bed, staring at him with a look Miles couldn't begin to decipher. He saw terror, worry, and fury, among others, though none came across their bond. He suspected Quincy was holding them in carefully.

Tanner stepped into the room behind Quincy. "No trace from what I can tell. None of the wolves that went looking can find him."

Quincy got up and stalked toward the door. "This isn't going to stand. I'm *done* with his shit."

Tanner stepped in front of him. "Hey, wait. That's not going to help either. Miles needs you here right now."

"My mate is strong. He'll recover. But if my asshole of a father is dead, he can't hurt Miles any more."

"Tanner's right, Q," Chad said. "We'll deal with it—all of us—but it's clear it's going to take all of us, and right now Miles needs to recover before anything can happen."

"Dude, he's not going to be sitting there alone, waiting for you to come kill him," Jamie added, stepping up to him as well. "You'll walk right into a trap. That's exactly what they want."

"They're right, Quince," Miles said. It came out a whisper still, but it didn't matter.

Quincy heard. He spun around and moved back to the bed. His hands were clenched into fists, and Miles couldn't miss that the fury was currently winning the bid for control.

"Hey," Miles whispered, reaching up. He winced when he saw the bruising and swelling on his hand. "They're right," he said again, his voice a little stronger, though still horribly weak. "You'll do a lot more for me if you stay for now."

Quincy sighed and drooped. "I am so sorry, Miles," he said, shaking his head.

"Hey, hey, no. Don't you go blaming yourself either." Miles scowled, relieved to hear his voice, though still scratchy, coming out a little better.

"Either?" Quincy asked.

Miles nodded, tilting his head toward Chad, who was back in the corner chair. "He blames himself too. But this isn't on either of you. It's on whoever ordered it."

"I should've—"

Miles shook his head. "No. All that's going to do is waste time. Going over what *might* have happened if we'd done something differently is an exercise in futility. They may well have gotten to me one way or the other. We have to let that part of it go."

Quincy took a breath, closing his eyes. He went through a few more inhales and exhales, then finally opened his eyes again and nodded. Miles was glad to see the fury seemed to have died down some.

"You're right," he murmured. "You're right. So…. How are you feeling?"

"Like I was hit by a three-hundred-pound jaguar at full speed."

Quincy's lips twitched. "I don't think he weighed three hundred pounds."

"Then two hundred and fifty." Miles rolled his eyes. "Too damned much muscle."

"So, do you think you can shift now?"

Miles turned inward, prodding his wolf. "Yeah, I think so. Not sure I can do it more than twice, but even that'll help a lot."

Quincy nodded. "Um… do you want me to try to help you get your clothes off?"

Miles pursed his lips, then shook his head, wincing when his brain rattled again. "No. That'd hurt like a bitch. Just the splints, because my wolf legs won't like those at all."

Quincy carefully unwrapped the makeshift splints and set them aside. Miles gritted his teeth as his still mostly broken legs were moved. Finally Quincy stepped back, and Miles closed his eyes, giving over control to his wolf.

Normally the shift felt as natural as breathing. Normally, though the bones reformed and muscles realigned and it seemed like it should, it didn't hurt. However, because he was reforming *broken* bones this time, it hurt like hell as they knitted themselves back together for the most part. They'd still be weak for a while, until he could eat and shift more, but for now, at least, they were much more on their way to being how they're supposed to be.

When his vision was gray, his body was covered in fur, and his hands had turned into paws, Miles flopped down onto the bed, utterly exhausted. He'd overestimated the amount of energy he had, or underestimated the amount it would take for a healing shift. He wasn't going to be able to shift back right away.

Quincy helped get his scrubs off, tossing them aside. "I'm so burning those," he muttered.

Miles gave a tired chuff. He couldn't really blame Quincy for wanting to. He sighed, resting his head on his paws and looking up at his mate.

"I'm guessing you can't shift back yet, can you?"

Miles lifted his head and shook it.

"Would food help?"

Miles thought about it briefly, then nodded the best he could. His head still hurt like hell, but it was getting better.

"I'll get him something. I'm sure we've got some steaks in the fridge," Finley said, hurrying out.

Quincy looked around. "Could we be alone for a few moments?"

Chad, Jamie, and Tanner simply left.

Quincy turned back to Miles. "I thought maybe I'd shift and lay with you."

Miles looked up, warmth spreading through his chest at the idea, and thumped his tail a few times.

With a chuckle Quincy stood back and tugged his shirt over his head. "I'll take that as a yes." He kicked his shoes off, then shucked his jeans and underwear at the same time. Miles had only seen Quincy naked when he was injured, and at the time, Miles had been in full doctor mode. Now, even though he was exhausted, he could appreciate Quincy's lean, sexy grace.

Quincy grinned at him, then closed his eyes. A moment later Miles watched in fascination as the teeth dropped, claws grew, fur sprouted, and then Quincy dropped down as the rest of his body changed shape. He stretched and yawned, then stood and jumped up onto the bed next to Miles.

Miles shuffled around until he lay alongside Quincy, resting his head on Quincy's paw. Quincy licked his face, and Miles was briefly thrown off by the texture of Quincy's tongue. It felt good, though, having his mate close, caring for him.

"Oh. My. Gods. That is *adorable*."

Miles looked up to see Finley grinning at them, holding a plate of raw steaks. Quincy gave a quiet growl, but Finley didn't look the least intimidated. Quincy's nose twitched, and he went back to bathing Miles.

"That *is* kinda cute," Chad said as he followed Finley into the room.

Finley grinned at him. "You and Jamie were like that when you first shifted."

Quincy snorted.

Chad narrowed his eyes. "Don't get any funny ideas, kitty cat."

Quincy's tail twitched, and then he went back to ignoring them.

Chad laughed as he and Finley brought not one but two plates of raw steaks over.

Finley turned to Quincy. "Do you want some too?"

Quincy shook his head.

"If you change your mind, it's there." Finley leaned in. "You're a gorgeous cat. May I feel your fur?"

Quincy dipped his head, and Finley ran his fingers over Quincy's head.

Miles surprised himself with the wave of jealousy that hit at someone else touching his mate. Quincy's head whipped around, and he managed to look surprised, even in jaguar form. Miles drooped even more than his exhaustion had made him, putting his paws over his head and whining.

"What's that all about?" Chad asked.

Miles peeked out to see Finley shaking his head. "I don't know."

Quincy licked Miles's face and, when Miles moved his paws, rubbed his face all over Miles's. Scent-marking him. Showing who he was mated to. Miles sighed and nuzzled Quincy back for another moment, then looked up at Finley.

Finley was smirking. "He was jealous I was touching his mate."

"Oh." Chad nodded, chuckling. "I remember that well."

Finley grinned. "Oh yeah. Anyway, Quincy, your fur is soft. I mean, I know most domestic cat fur is soft, but for some reason, I didn't expect yours to be." He stepped back. "All right, then. Thank you, Quincy. You guys eat and rest."

Finley and Chad left, and Miles focused on getting sustenance, trying to ignore the embarrassment still going through him at his ridiculous jealousy. He downed two steaks before he remembered to even breathe. When he finished the first plate, he nudged the other toward Quincy, but Quincy just pushed it back at him. Miles sighed but could tell Quincy was going to be stubborn, so he simply finished the second plate as well. By the time he had, he was feeling a lot better.

And content and sleepy. Especially when he realized… Quincy was purring.

It was a rough sort of purr, not what he'd heard from pet cats, but there was no doubt what it was and that Quincy was trying to soothe him—very likely the jealousy *and* the pain. Miles licked Quincy's face a little, then resettled against Quincy and put his head once more on one black paw. He fell asleep to Quincy bathing him.

WHEN MILES woke, light filled the room and the vast majority of his pain was gone. He'd forgotten just how much having a mate near can help. Even though he and Quincy hadn't bonded much or claimed each other yet, the link they *did* have helped.

He sat up, yawned, then carefully climbed down off the bed, not wanting to disturb the still-sleeping Quincy. He tested his limbs, then shook and happily realized nothing was still broken. He was still sore in all sorts of places, but that wasn't going to go away for a little while. Unless he could shift a few more times.

He didn't really want to get out of wolf form yet, but he had other urgent matters to deal with. With a sigh he nudged his wolf back and brought his human form forward. Just as he settled into his human skin, he looked up to see the human version of Quincy lying on the bed watching him.

Quincy's lips twitched. "You know, for a dog, you're kinda hot."

Miles snorted and lay down next to Quincy, pulling his very naked mate into his arms. "Well, for a cat, you're kinda hot too."

Quincy laughed. "Thanks." He ran his hands up over Miles's arms, tracing his fingers over Miles's neck. Miles guessed bruises still covered his skin, since it usually took a few shifts for something like that to go away completely. "I *will* end this. They made a *big* mistake coming after you."

Miles nodded. "Yes, they did, for a few reasons. Let's just take the moment we've got here, hmm?"

Quincy didn't reply except to lean in and brush his lips over Miles's. Miles tilted his head, tightening his arms and deepening the kiss. Quincy rewarded him with a soft moan and by leaning into him more.

"Well, good to know you're feeling better," Chad said.

Miles scowled at him as he yanked the edge of the comforter, covering Quincy's ass. "Better enough to be annoyed by an interruption like that."

Chad grinned unrepentantly. "Fin made breakfast. French toast, sausage, the whole thing. He sent me to see if you're hungry, but I can tell it isn't food you're interested in."

Miles rolled his eyes and looked over at Quincy, who sighed.

"Too late for that. Besides, he needs to heal more, and food will help that."

"We'll be down in a few," Miles said.

"Damn. I was hoping to listen in." Chad closed the door just as the pillow Quincy threw hit it.

Miles laughed. "How does Jamie put up with him?"

Quincy shook his head. "I have no idea. But I guess they work. Destined, right?"

Miles nodded. "Yeah, they are. I guess we should go for food."

With a sigh Quincy kissed him softly, then climbed out of bed. "Guess so."

Miles stretched and crossed over to his scrubs, making a face. "Ew. I am so not wearing them again."

"Here," Quincy said, opening a suitcase. "These should fit until we can get your stuff. I think it's still in Chad's car."

Miles took the gray sweatpants and blue T-shirt, pulled them on, and grinned when they fit him pretty much perfectly. "Guess we'll have to be careful with whose clothes are whose," he said, chuckling.

"I doubt we'll care." Quincy smiled as he pulled out his own pair of sweats and another T-shirt and put them on quickly. After they stepped through the door, Miles took Quincy's hand, brought it up to his mouth, and kissed it. Quincy returned the kiss to Miles's hand, and they went out to the dining room. Miles still had to walk slowly, the bruising and soreness worse than he'd initially thought, but he was grateful for his shifter abilities and his mate. Without them he'd be dead.

"Welcome back to the land of the living," Jamie said, chuckling. He set plates out at the table, and Miles took a seat. Quincy retrieved coffee, then helped set the food out. When they had everything, he picked a few sausage links, then took a piece of offered french toast from Chad.

Miles looked around and frowned. "So… is anyone going to tell me what happened after I got knocked out?"

Chapter 7

QUINCY WASN'T entirely sure he wanted to hear this. The sight of Miles so bruised and broken had boiled his blood. He'd wanted to turn around right that second and drive to New York to shoot his father.

As much as he didn't want to admit it, he was glad they'd talked him out of it. Jamie had been right, as had Chad. Miles needed him here—even more than Quincy had originally thought—and running off half-cocked was hardly the way to go about things.

So despite not wanting to hear, Quincy needed to. As an information broker, he knew just how important every little piece of it was. He needed to rein in his fury and refocus.

Chad sighed. "So, Jamie and I had taken Miles's bags, but as we were leaving, Miles told us to go ahead, he wanted to grab his computer, and that he'd be out in a minute." He shook his head. "I'd checked the apartment first and hadn't seen anyone. Even the closets, but apparently—"

"There's a second door in my loft. For getting furniture and such in and out," Miles said at Quincy's raised eyebrow.

Quincy nodded.

"So, we think the guy picked the locks and got in that way. The door wasn't broken—I would have seen that when I checked the closet—so that's the best I can come up with for it, and his scent was everywhere. It was muted—I guess he was trying to mask it?" Chad asked.

"Yeah," Quincy said. "We... we used to *not* mask our scents. Ages ago, before we started hiding from the wolves, we always did what was, essentially, a partial shift. The glands we use to scent-mark, which create our particular smell, we left in place. Once we started fighting with the wolves, we had to learn how to shift those glands as well."

"Ah, I can see that," Miles said, and nodded.

"I'm surprised he left that much behind," Quincy said, frowning.

"Well, the thing is, I'm not entirely sure most wolves would have found it," Jamie said thoughtfully.

Quincy raised his eyebrows. "Oh?"

Jamie nodded. "Chad's senses are still new. He hasn't learned how to filter things and mute them in human form yet."

"Oh." Quincy considered that. "So Dumber—I'm guessing it's him—was banking on the fact that you'd all be in human form and, thus, not smell anything."

"He really is dumb," Jamie said, shaking his head.

"I think he just underestimates us," Tanner offered. "I think he believes we're truly just dumb dogs."

Quincy snorted. "Let him keep thinking that. It'll be his fuckup."

Chad pointed at Quincy with his fork. "He certainly didn't expect two more 'dogs' to show up and fight him."

"You were in wolf form?"

Chad coughed. "Yeah. So, I went out to the car and put the bag in the trunk, but something was bugging me. I've always tried to follow my instincts, and decided to go back in to walk Miles out. Well, when I got in there…. Dumber wasn't expecting someone else. I really don't think he was expecting me to go wolf." Chad cleared his throat. "I'm still dealing with control issues like that. Extreme emotion gives him control. And I was *pissed*, so the wolf came out."

"He called to me through our telepathic link, and I came running. I'm *sure* Dumber wasn't expecting two wolves." Jamie chuckled. "He took one look at me, then back at Chad, and ran like the hounds of hell were after him."

"Well, I wouldn't say we were from *hell*…." Chad smirked.

Miles laughed and Quincy chuckled.

"So what I'm not getting," Finley said with a frown, "is why the bat?"

Quincy sighed. "I think they were trying to make it look like a break in by a human."

"That explains why he tried to strangle you," Chad said quietly, glancing at Miles.

Quincy whipped his head around to stare. "Strangle him?"

Chad nodded. "That's what he was doing when I found them. He jumped up right away, but took advantage of my shift to… uh… hurt Miles a little more."

Quincy swallowed a few times, suddenly very much *not* hungry. "I need to know. I want every detail I can get."

Chad frowned. "Are you sure?"

"Yes." Quincy nodded firmly. Miles put a hand on Quincy's leg, and Quincy grasped it.

"All right." Chad sighed. "He kicked Miles in the ribs, then stepped on both hands as he came at me."

"Well, that explains that," Miles muttered.

Quincy took a few deep breaths, praying to Bastet for calm. It took a full minute before he could speak. "Well. He won't get away with it." He ate another piece of sausage because he needed fuel.

"So... now what?" Chad asked.

Quincy frowned. "Okay, well... I need to call my father. I doubt he'll take responsibility, but I have to try. Then... I think it might be best if we lay low here for a bit." He glanced up at Finley, then Tanner.

"Fine with us," Finley said. "We've got the room."

"I'll pay for our food and such."

"You don't have to—" Tanner closed his mouth and chuckled, and Quincy glanced at Miles to see him scowling too. "Fine! Fine. You can buy groceries."

"Thank you." Quincy sighed. "There's something in all of this that I'm missing, but I don't know what. Some piece that isn't fitting. I need some time to think through it."

"Well, here is as good a place as any for that." Finley smiled.

"Thank you," Quincy said again and focused back on his food.

HE HAD one more throwaway phone from his last set of purchases. The problem was, they'd found him. Way too fast last time. And the last thing he needed was to bring those bastards to the wolves.

He decided instead to call through the computer. He could send it through about a billion proxies, and once he disconnected, tracing it would be damned near impossible. If he took his time and was careful, he could avoid them finding him—and the wolves.

Quincy set up in the dining room, working slowly and double— and triple-checking every proxy, every extra server he routed through, every extra step he added to his phone call. He'd keep it brief, because he was pretty sure he already knew what his father was going to say. Even so, he wanted to take as few chances as possible.

He'd considered actually driving somewhere else to make the call, but no matter where he went, if he did it that way, whoever was feeding information to the Three Ds would trace it and their time would be much more limited. No, after careful consideration, he knew this was the right way to do it. He'd learned the hard way that they had more resources than he'd thought. He couldn't make any assumptions.

With a deep breath, Quincy glanced at the others around the table, then started the call.

His father picked up on the first ring. "Hello?"

"Father."

"Quincy, are you going to listen to me this time?"

"Are you going to take responsibility for the fact that my mate almost died at the hands of your goons?"

His answer, at first, was silence. "Someone tried to kill your mate?"

Quincy sighed. "Why do you act like you don't know this when it was under your orders?"

He wasn't surprised by the low growl that came through the phone. "I will not keep arguing with you. I did *not* order any kind of violence against you *or* your mate. I may be ruthless, Quincy Dean Archer, but I take responsibility for my actions. If I order something be done because I feel it needs to be, then I will take that responsibility."

Quincy winced at the use of his full name, but his father's words didn't change his resolve. "I can't believe this of you, Father. I really can't. How can you justify possibly starting an interspecies war over this?"

"Interspec—*what*?"

Quincy blinked and frowned. "Tell me you did it. Take the fucking responsibility that I know is yours, or I'll be forced to go to my mate's alpha."

"Alph—he's a *dog*?"

It hurt, there were no two ways about it—his outright refusal to deal with this. "Good-bye, Father. I suggest you watch your back." Quincy hit the disconnect, quickly closing out the proxies. He'd been on for barely more than a minute, so he doubted they'd be able to trace, but he wasn't taking chances.

When he'd finished, he took a breath, struggling with his emotions, but he couldn't seem to get enough oxygen. A red haze seemed to cover everything. *Damn him!* Quincy stood up abruptly and looked at his mate. Miles reached up and took off Quincy's glasses, then mouthed, *Go*.

Quincy remembered himself enough to open the french doors to the back deck, then started running. By the time he cleared the railing at the end, he'd shifted, his clothes flying off in tatters. He landed lightly on his feet on the lower level, then ran.

HOURS LATER, Quincy lay on the banks of a wide stream, exhausted. He'd run, just like he had in Washington, but the clarity he sought eluded him. No amount of giving his cat control had helped this time.

Nothing made sense. His father had never shied away from laying claim to his actions. In all the years he'd known the man, he'd never seen Aubrey Archer shun responsibility before. For as much of an asshole as he could be, he'd taken duty and his own warped sense of honor seriously.

Quincy didn't understand the surprise at Miles's species either, unless those reporting didn't *know* Miles was a wolf or simply didn't tell his father. It still felt off to him, and that, as much as anything, frustrated him. He didn't like puzzles, not like that.

He smelled them before he heard them. Quincy was proud of them despite himself. He didn't bother getting up, simply stayed put, sure they'd come to him. They surprised him, though. He'd only smelled the first two. But when *five* wolves cleared the tree line, approached him, then lay down with him, he really was impressed.

He couldn't tell them apart very easily by sight. The solid black wolf he guessed was Finley. He knew his own mate—would recognize Miles's scent instantly anywhere. The white-looking wolf had to be Jamie. But he wasn't positive which was Tanner and which was Chad and wasn't familiar enough with their scents either.

Until Chad chased a lightning bug across the grass.

Quincy snorted and, if he'd been human, would have laughed.

Jamie lay down and put his paws over his eyes, the action clearly saying, *I don't know him!*

Finley chuffed and tackled Jamie, and then the two of them started rolling around and play-fighting. Tanner shook his head and stretched out on the other side of Quincy from Miles.

It was an odd sensation to be surrounded like that. As a cat, he rarely spent time around others. He'd certainly never have considered spending time with the pride like he was with the wolves. He had to admit, it felt good. He knew he couldn't do it all the time. He'd need his solitude. But he found he was liking the feeling of belonging to the group.

He laid his head on his paws, watching Jamie and Finley play even as Chad still chased the lightning bugs around. He looked over at Miles, then tilted his head toward Jamie and Finley. Miles gave him a wolf-grin and nodded. He looked at Tanner and got the same reply.

Quincy got to his feet and crouched, slinking along the grass silently. He paused, waiting for just the right moment, tail twitching and watching as they rolled and nipped at each other. Reminding himself to keep his claws sheathed, he leaped, landing just past Finley's snout and pushing Jamie over. They rolled together for a few feet. Finley barked and chased after them, jumping onto Quincy's back. Quincy wiggled out from under him and batted at Finley's flank. Jamie chuffed, jumping up and nipping at Quincy's tail. Quincy turned around, batting at Jamie this time, when Finley jumped onto his back.

Quincy flopped down in surrender. To his surprise, Jamie dropped next to him and Finley by their heads. Chad came back from his bug-chasing, and a moment later, all six of them were in what Quincy could only call… a dog pile.

He closed his eyes, letting himself enjoy it. He'd always known he hadn't belonged to the jaguars the same way everyone else did. He'd always had a different attitude, a different feeling about what was right and comfortable.

He guessed he figured out where he really belonged. He wasn't about to admit it to all of them—at least for a while, anyway. Miles, yes, but not the others. He *did* have an image to maintain, after all.

But Quincy knew he was home. He just had to keep that home safe.

QUINCY PACED Tanner and Finley's living room, his frustration mounting. "Father and I have been at odds for years, that's no secret. I am a huge disappointment, blah blah blah." He sighed, turned around, and met Miles's gaze before continuing his pacing. "I don't and never have agreed with the way he runs the pride. Sure, we survived, but…." He shook his head and kept pacing. "Maybe that's just me not agreeing with the way most of the jaguars are. Anyway, I never wanted his business. I never wanted the pride, and I made no secret of that. But even with that… he's never been… like this before."

"What if…," Chad said, drawing Quincy's attention. "What if it's *not* your father?"

Quincy frowned, stopping dead. He scowled. That had never occurred to him, the idea it could be someone besides his father. "Who else could it be?"

Chad shrugged. "Hell if I know. But your father seems awfully adamant that it's not him. Is there someone else who would benefit from you coming back?"

The head shake came automatically, but then he stopped and gave it real thought. He still came up blank. "I don't think so. I mean… our laws say that if my father is killed or steps down, I am next to take over as tepey."

"Unless they plan to kill you both."

Quincy whipped his head around to stare at Jamie. "Kill us both?"

Jamie nodded. "Yeah. What if they want both of you out of the way, but they need to make it look right? So, they get you back there and get both of you together, then… I dunno, an accident of some sort, house fire. Who knows? There's plenty that can kill us—and you."

"I still don't know who it could be." Quincy frowned, chewing on his lip. "I mean… sure, there's a line of succession. Cats like to think they're nobility." Quincy rolled his eyes. "But I can't see anyone else in the line willing to do that. I have an uncle and a cousin, both of whom are fairly decent for cats—and on the other side of the world. They travel and both have said they didn't want it either."

"Is your father the only one with power in the pride?"

Quincy nodded. "He has ultimate say. The only one who overrides him is our tepey-iret, but he doesn't get involved unless it's an interpride issue."

"What about a council? Like… we have our elders. They don't have power or anything, but as advisors, they sometimes think they do," Finley offered.

Again, though, Quincy shook his head. "No. I mean, we do, but like yours, it has no power." He sighed and flopped down onto the couch next to Miles. He rubbed his eyes, then looked over at Tanner. "I'm afraid we're going to have to talk to your father. He should know I'm here, anyway, I guess."

"I called him, but yes, he'd like to meet you. Especially since you're Miles's mate."

Quincy sighed. "Okay. See, the thing is, if—and I'm not saying I believe it—if my father *isn't* behind this, then he still should be trying to find out who is. And you'll notice he never once said anything about that."

"Well, to be fair, he might know he's being tapped," Chad pointed out.

With a groan Quincy dropped his head back. "Fuck. I'll have to deal with that part later. First, your father." He glanced at Miles, who looked ready to pass out. "After my mate gets more rest, since we do have time."

Miles waved, but Quincy snorted, stood, and proceeded to pick Miles up. "Whoa! Hey, I can walk!"

"Stow it, Grant. You're as weak as a newborn cub."

"You know I love you, Quincy, but fuck you," Miles said, scowling. He scowled harder when laughter followed them down the hall.

Quincy smirked, nudged the door open with his toe, carried Miles to the bed, then laid him down. "I'll stay with you. But you need rest."

Miles sighed. "Fuck." He frowned. "I don't have to like it."

Quincy grinned. "No, you don't. Just have to do it."

To Quincy's satisfaction, before he even got the covers situated over them, Miles was already starting to drift. He kissed a temple, then settled in with Miles in his arms.

A THREE-HOUR nap, another plate of steaks, and two shifts later, Miles was looking a lot more normal, and Quincy felt like he could breathe a little better. By that time, it was getting kind of late, so they decided to put off the visit to Alpha Noah's until the next day.

Which was fine by Quincy. As much as he wanted to move forward, he also wanted a little time with his mate. Tanner and Finley disappeared up to their bedroom, and Chad and Jamie had wolfed out and headed into the woods, so Quincy took the opportunity for the quiet with Miles.

"So…," Miles said, when the others were gone. "I wanted to ask you… what happens now? I mean, between us. Are you going to leave again?"

Quincy thought about it but shook his head. "No. I think at this point it's best if we stay together. It didn't work to keep them from you by leaving, so…."

Miles nodded. "Good. Because I want to suggest something."

"Oh?" Quincy raised his eyebrows.

Miles reached up and brushed at Quincy's hair. "Yeah. I'd like to start bonding with you."

Quincy swallowed. "If we bond… we can't be apart?"

Miles nodded. "Well, to a point. I mean, we can go do our own thing for a little while. But nothing long-term. Not until we claim each other, and as much as this pains me to say… I don't think we should claim each other yet."

"No?" Quincy blinked.

"No." He hesitated, frowning. "Not until this is all over. If… if something happens to one of us after we've claimed each other, well… at best? Pure hell. You'll wish Osiris had taken you to the underworld. At worst… you *will* find yourself facing him and your feather of *maat*."

Quincy stared at him, ignoring for the moment that Miles understood so much about his religion. "And if we bond but don't claim?"

"It'll hurt for a while, but nothing nearly as bad. But in the meantime, our animals will handle things a bit better."

"Being together, you mean? Our emotions and such?"

Miles nodded. "Yeah. It's… it'll be a little weird. You know how you got hit with my jealousy earlier?"

"Yes."

"Well, right now, because the bond was begun but not strengthened, all we feel is *really* strong emotion. Once we start bonding, we'll feel much more. And we can soothe each other if it's needed."

Quincy blinked. "Huh. That's… really cool."

Miles smiled. "I think so."

"So… when did you want to do this?"

Miles grimaced. "I'd love to say now, but I'm a little afraid I'd fall asleep."

That surprised a laugh out of Quincy. "That wouldn't do much for my ego if you fell asleep during sex."

Miles shook his head. "No. But those shifts earlier took a lot out of me, even with the food. I just… I wanted to bring it up. I thought we should talk about it. It's not just about having sex—making love."

"No, the bonding makes things more complicated, at least for now." Quincy leaned forward and kissed Miles on the forehead. "How about I put on some anime?"

Miles smiled. "I'd like that. How about that one you were telling me about? With the guy that looks like you and the kid with the orange hair. Um…. The… *shinigami*?"

Quincy laughed. "Yeah, he does look like me." He couldn't hide his grin, thrilled Miles asked. "All right. Let me get my computer."

Chapter 8

MILES FOUND himself wishing he'd bonded with Quincy that morning instead of going with the plan he'd put together. Quincy was going nuts in the seat next to him, and he wished he could send calm through their bond. But it wasn't that strong and he couldn't really project yet, so he could do nothing but hold his mate's hand.

No one else would know Quincy was so wound up. Miles swore to himself he'd never play poker with Quincy because his poker face was downright ridiculous. But there were minor tells, and Miles had spent every available minute studying him to know what they were. Granted, that wasn't a *lot* of time, but it was enough to learn when Quincy was hiding something.

He squeezed Quincy's hand now. "We'll get this all worked out."

Quincy sighed. "He's going to argue with your alpha, and I have no idea how to stop this from escalating."

Miles frowned. "Well, Alpha Noah won't jump to a war or anything. He'll try everything else he can think of first."

"That's what Tanner said." Quincy looked out the window briefly, then back to Miles. "If he continues to be stubborn, Alpha Noah will have to talk to your alpha prime, though."

"I know," Miles said, nodding. "But there are other options first. Let's just talk it out with Noah and go from there."

Quincy sighed again and nodded. "Yeah, that's best. Just… I'm still so *pissed* at him."

Miles lifted Quincy's hand and kissed it. "And you have every right to be. He would find a way to get a message to you that he was looking into it if it really wasn't him. That he hasn't is still bullshit. There may be more than your father at work here, but he's not entirely innocent either. I think we should let Chad and Jamie help like they've offered."

"Well, as long as it doesn't go straight to an interspecies conflict, I think you're right. We'll see what they can do to help."

"Good. Looks like we're here," Miles said, pointing when Tanner turned down the driveway.

"Oh good," Quincy said, and Miles wasn't sure it was possible for Quincy to sound more nervous if he tried.

They climbed out of the third row of Tanner's Outlander, and Miles took Quincy's hand again as they walked up to the porch. Tanner called out to his dad as they went inside.

After somewhat chaotic introductions and greetings with Tanner's mom, Carol, she made an offer of coffee; then Alpha Noah came out from his study. "Hey, son."

Miles, along with the rest of the wolves, tilted their head in respect. Miles was a little surprised to see Quincy do it, but he guessed it had something to do with the shaky ground the jaguars and wolves were already on with each other.

"Alpha," Miles greeted him.

Noah nodded, then turned to Quincy. "Welcome to the Forbes pack, Quincy. It's nice to meet you." He offered his hand.

Quincy glanced at Miles, then turned a smile to Noah. "Thank you, sir."

"Alpha. Or Noah, please. Let's have a seat and you can tell me what you know."

It took all six of them to remember everything. Quincy told most of it, beginning with his initial disappearance. Miles added in bits and pieces of the last two-plus months since they'd met and been apart. He had to defer to Chad and Jamie over the fight in his apartment, and Tanner talked about what the wolves who'd gone looking around Miles's apartment had found. Finally they managed to put it all together.

"Well. That is something of a mess," Noah said, sitting back. He stayed silent for a while, looking thoughtful. "I guess the first step is to see if your father maintains his innocence with me. After that, we'll have to figure out where to go from there."

Quincy nodded and sighed. "There's one more thing, though." He glanced at Miles, who nodded and squeezed his hand.

"Better for him to know everything."

"Right." Quincy wrinkled his nose. "So, it was right after my first call to my father that they went after Miles. There's a good chance they'll come after you if you call from your phone."

Noah's smile sent a chill down Miles's spine, and Quincy shuddered next to him.

"If they do manage to hurt me, that man—" Noah pointed to Tanner. "—will become alpha. And any hope your pride had of avoiding war is gone. He *will* make sure it happens."

Tanner was nodding the whole time. "I will. Quincy, I care about you and Miles. But I won't let something like that stand. I couldn't even if I wanted to. And I won't want to."

"I wouldn't want you to either. You'd have as much inside information on them as I could get you," Quincy promised.

Miles kissed Quincy's temple. "Let's hope it doesn't get there." He turned back to Noah. "Perhaps you could make a comment on the phone call to that effect? So that whoever is listening in will know just how dangerous it is to try?"

Noah nodded. "Good idea. It can be veiled—or not." He smirked. "But either way, it'll be clear."

Carol insisted on getting fresh coffee for everyone before they tackled the phone call. Once she'd handed out cups, Noah moved them to the table in his study and pulled over the speakerphone from his desk to the bigger table. Quincy wrote the number on a piece of paper for him, then sat back.

Miles pulled Quincy close and put an arm around him. Quincy raised an eyebrow, but Miles just smirked and tightened it, knowing Quincy would need the support. With a sigh they turned back to Noah, who was introducing himself.

"Good afternoon, Alpha Noah." Quincy's father paused. "I'm assuming since you are aware of my nature that you are the alpha of my son's mate."

"Indeed. And disturbed to hear about the attack on my wolf."

"I do hope you're not insinuating I was involved."

Miles tried not to snort, but he didn't think he succeeded entirely. He coughed to cover it up, but Chad and Jamie both smirked at him. He flipped them off, making them grin.

"Of course not, Tepey Aubrey. I'm not insinuating anything." Noah paused, sending an amused look toward Quincy. "I'm saying outright that a jaguar in *your* territory attacked my wolf. That makes it your responsibility."

Finley slapped a hand over his mouth, and Tanner and Chad were both laughing silently. Miles was having real trouble keeping a straight face. Even Quincy was smirking, because he knew his father knew Noah was right.

"Do you have proof it was a jaguar?"

"*Several* of my wolves identified his scent. Do we really need to beat around the bush? What are you going to do about it?"

Silence sat on the line for a moment. "Give me some time to look into it. It would be best if we didn't take this any higher for the moment."

"I can agree to that. For now. But something *better* happen. And know this. If *anything* else happens to *any* members of my pack—wolf, human, or jaguar—I will *not* hesitate to take this to my prime. Is that clear?"

"Crystal, Alpha Noah. You will hear from me soon." And with that Quincy's father hung up.

Noah hit the button to turn off the phone and sat back. "Well, was that what you expected, Quincy?"

Quincy nodded. "More or less. He still refused to admit he ordered it." He sighed and shrugged.

Miles kissed his temple, wishing again he could send comfort over their bond.

"I don't know. Maybe he didn't."

"You know...," Chad said, pursing his lips. "Maybe you ought to try to see him in person—in public somewhere—and gauge for yourself if he's telling the truth."

Miles tilted his head and considered his mate. "You'd probably learn a lot more."

Quincy frowned. "That's... not a bad idea. But I'm not sure I want to leave Miles alone again. No offense to you," he said, holding a hand out to Chad.

Chad waved it off. "I wasn't thinking you'd go alone anyway. I'm thinking the four of us should go."

Quincy blinked at him, then looked at Miles, then back to Chad. "Four?"

Jamie nodded. "He's not going without me, especially since his wolf still isn't the most stable."

"And I'm not letting you go without me," Miles said quietly.

Quincy sighed. Miles had learned the expression on Quincy's face—that he was giving in, obviously realizing he was outnumbered.

"Fine. But…. He's in New York and we should probably drive. Keep as low a profile going up there as we can."

Chad nodded. "We'll take the Challenger. They won't necessarily know it and, well, let's just say my car's good for a lot."

Quincy chuckled. "Okay. I won't argue that. When do you want to go?"

"Let's give it a few days. Make some plans and see if you can get a message to your father to meet us somewhere," Chad suggested.

"Good idea."

"Good. Let me know what happens. If he calls, I'll tell you right away," Noah said, standing.

"Thank you, Alpha," Quincy said, holding his hand out.

Noah shook it. "Nothing to thank me for. It's my job. Welcome to the pack, son."

ALL SIX of them piled back into the Outlander. "Still want to go out?" Tanner asked, looking in the rearview mirror.

"Fuck yes," Quincy said, rather succinctly.

Miles laughed. "Yes, definitely."

"All right, then." Tanner took the turn out of the driveway toward Greensburg.

Miles sat quietly for a long moment, studying Quincy. Lines of strain showed around his eyes, not that Miles would point them out. It was clear, though, that everything was starting to get to Quincy.

"How are you?"

Quincy shook his head. "I don't really know. I don't know what to think anymore." He sighed. "It's a good plan. But I just want this all over now."

"I know," Miles said, pulling him closer. "I know. We'll get there. We just need a little more patience. Surely a cat has some of that. So they can take over the world?"

Quincy snorted. "I'm not planning world domination."

Miles feigned surprise. "You mean I'm not mated to a mastermind bent on taking over the world? Damn. And here I thought Diana had it right…."

Quincy laughed and Miles grinned, glad he could get that. "Sorry, she messed up there."

"Aw, damn. So, instead I have a gorgeous man who's an otaku with a penchant for... tweaking... people's data, and turns into a beautiful, sleek black jaguar." Miles tilted his head. "Don't think I'm missing out on anything."

By the time he was done, Quincy's cheeks were bright red. He muttered something that sounded suspiciously like "not gorgeous or beautiful."

Miles grabbed Quincy's chin and tugged until Quincy was looking at him. "Definitely gorgeous," Miles corrected him, then brought his mouth down on Quincy's.

Quincy opened to him immediately, and Miles got lost in the feel and taste of his mate. He, in fact, completely lost track of how long they kissed, where they were, and who else was there. He'd had so little of Quincy and couldn't seem to stop. Quincy didn't seem to mind. He wrapped his arms around Miles, tilting his head and deepening the kiss.

"Yo! Stop making out in the back seat like teenagers!" Tanner shouted.

Miles flipped him off and kept kissing Quincy out of spite.

"Hey, fine, stay there if you want, but we're here," Tanner said. "I'll eat all the steak myself."

Quincy snorted and Miles pulled back, grinning. "He probably could."

That brought another laugh from Quincy, who shook his head. "Somehow, I don't doubt it."

THE JAPANESE hibachi steakhouse was one Miles had been to a couple of times since he'd moved to the Pittsburgh area. He had a feeling Quincy would like it, and he wasn't disappointed. The six of them took up half of one of the grill tables, laughing and taunting each other about how much they could each eat as they took menus.

Quincy immediately ordered a big bottle of sake. "Not that it does much, but that's not going to stop me."

"I hear you on that," Miles said, then looked up at the waitress. "I'll have the same, and tea."

She smiled and nodded, then continued down the line.

After taking Finley's and Tanner's drink orders and moving on, the two leaned in together over their menu, Finley looking worried.

Miles turned to Quincy. "When the waitress comes back, make sure she puts this on one bill and gives it to us."

"Of course," Quincy said, blinking.

Miles shook his head. "I think they think they're paying for their own." He nodded toward Tanner and Finley.

Quincy stared at him another moment. "That's ridiculous. Miles, between the two of us, if we quit working *now*, we'd have a hard time worrying about money if we were even halfway careful with it."

"And as I have no intention of quitting—"

"And neither do I."

"Then—" Miles paused and raised an eyebrow. "Do I want to know how you know my bank balance?"

Quincy smirked. "No."

Miles snorted. "Not that it matters. We're mated. What's mine is yours."

Quincy beamed at that. "That's good—not because I want it. I certainly don't need it. But because I know a little bit about finance. I can take good care of it for you and help you grow it."

Miles raised an eyebrow. "Is it legal?"

Quincy sniffed. "Of course it is. Finding out about what you had? No. But the rest is quite legal." He turned his attention back to his menu.

Miles laughed and kissed Quincy's cheek. "Remind me to actually authorize you to get to my money."

Quincy sighed. "If you insist."

"I do." Miles considered Quincy. "I want to help the pack too." He leaned in, glancing at Jamie and Chad, then murmuring into Quincy's ear. "I paid for Jamie's schooling. He doesn't know it and I don't want him to. But there are still kids in the pack who can't afford it."

"Well, *we* can certainly afford it, and *we* will help," Quincy replied, keeping his eyes on the menu.

Miles grinned. "Thank you, baby," he murmured, kissing his mate again.

Quincy sniffed. "I don't know what you're talking about. I'm thinking we should get the *nigiri* and *sashimi* appetizers. They look like a good mix of sushi types."

With a chuckle Miles read the descriptions, letting the money talk go. "Sounds good. Now…," Miles said louder, to the table at large, "I think I want the steak and scallops. Finley, I bet you'd like that. Or the shrimp."

He met Finley's eyes for a moment, then Tanner's.

Tanner nodded, then glanced over at Finley. Miles guessed they were communicating telepathically.

Finley smiled. "I think maybe the shrimp, yes."

"Me? I think I'd like that steak and chicken," Tanner said, turning back to the menu.

CHAD AND Jamie had actually argued over the bill for a bit, but finally gave in when Quincy and Miles agreed they could buy the movie tickets. They were obviously not nearly as much as dinner was—with the sushi appetizers, the sake most of them had ordered, and the plum wine Finley had wanted to try—but it at least made up for it a little. Miles and Quincy both understood the feeling—neither wanted charity—but they were well aware that while Chad and Jamie weren't *poor*, Quincy and Miles still had a lot more than they did.

Miles had originally thought a date with all six of them would be a bit much, but it turned out to be fun. He'd wanted to take just Quincy out, since they hadn't actually had a chance to go on a date yet—not that they had to; they were destined, after all. But Miles *wanted* to, wanted to be able to romance his mate a little. But Quincy hadn't been comfortable with them going out alone. It was Tanner who suggested they all go together, and in the end, Miles had been glad for it.

Chad started a popcorn war with Finley, then Miles and Jamie not long after they sat down in the theater. Tanner and Quincy both tried to pretend they didn't know the rest of them, but all it took was a piece of popcorn landing in Quincy's hair and apparently he couldn't resist. A moment later Tanner was in on it.

Tanner managed to stop it before they got kicked out of the theater. He made Chad and Finley go get more popcorn for starting it. Their response was to bring back chocolate... for everyone but Tanner. He raised an eyebrow while staring at Finley—again, likely communicating telepathically. Finley didn't look quite as amused after that and shared his candy with Tanner.

Luckily the previews started then, and they could turn their attention to the movie.

AFTER THE movie, as they piled into the SUV, there was brief discussion about going for ice cream, but Miles was getting antsy. He had other plans that night and didn't want to delay a whole lot more. He suggested they go running, and since the rest of the group—sans Quincy—was aware of the rest of the plans, he got no argument.

Instead, Tanner drove to the pack clearing and parked. Everyone piled out of the car and immediately started undressing. Quincy looked a little uncomfortable, and it took a moment for Miles to realize what it was. As a cat, Quincy didn't usually shift—and, thus, get naked—around other people.

He tilted his head, leading Quincy around to the side of the car. "We can wait until they're done."

Quincy looked a little embarrassed but nodded. "I just, uh, usually I'm—"

"By yourself, I know." He smiled. "It's not like I'm overly thrilled with the idea of them seeing you naked, anyway. I'd prefer to keep you to myself. Besides, it's not like we can't catch up to them." Miles looked up over the roof. "Hey, you guys go on. We'll catch up in just a minute."

"Don't be too long," Chad called. "Wouldn't want the kitty to tire himself out trying to catch up."

Quincy kept it mature. He flipped Chad off.

Chad laughed as he stripped off the last of his clothes and threw them in the car.

A moment later the other four had shifted, and Miles and Quincy were alone. Miles made quick work of his clothes, tossing them onto the seat as he went. Then finally they were both naked.

Miles paused to look Quincy over. "You *are* gorgeous, you know that? Sleek and lean, and yet still powerful, just like your cat."

"Stop," Quincy mumbled.

"I wouldn't have thought you'd be insecure about that."

Quincy cleared his throat. "It's…." He looked up. "I didn't have a lot of exposure to others growing up. My father hired private tutors. And how I looked, building my self-esteem, wasn't anything he worried about. He was all about grooming me to be tepey and just *assumed* I'd get the self-confidence I needed somewhere along the way." He shrugged a shoulder. "All while not really wanting anything to do with me outside of training me to take over for him eventually."

"That's a seriously shit thing to do to your kid." Miles shook his head. "I got lucky up until my senior year. My parents *did* do their best to help me learn self-confidence and have good self-esteem. For the record,

I don't say things like that for any reason other than because I mean them. No, the bond doesn't make me think you're gorgeous. You've figured that out, haven't you?"

Quincy nodded. "Yes."

"Then you know I mean it. I love you, Quince, very much. But I don't think you're hot because I love you. I'm attracted to you, want to get my dick inside you, because you're hot."

The crude words did what he'd hoped. Quincy smirked. "Thinking you're going to top, are you?"

Miles grinned. "I know I am."

Quincy's smirk turned into a grin. "If you can catch me." And on that note, he started shifting.

Miles was only a few seconds behind him, but it was enough for Quincy to get a head start. He didn't mind. His wolf liked the chase, loved the challenge. He also loved running through the woods in wolf form, loved the feel of the wind in his fur. And knowing what was at the other end made it even better.

Quincy didn't make it easy, which Miles appreciated. It took a good while before he finally caught up, but once Quincy's trail got stronger, it didn't take long to find him. That's when Miles realized his mate had an unfair advantage. He stopped, sat down, and chuffed.

Quincy was up in the tree.

He lay sprawled over a couple of the branches, his tail swinging back and forth, taunting Miles.

Miles watched in amusement, trying to decide what he wanted to do. Before he could make his decision, the other four wolves found them. Chad sat at the base of the tree, head cocked, looking for all the world like a confused puppy. Tanner simply snorted and stretched out off to the side. Jamie and Finley barked at Quincy, and if Miles could have translated, it probably would have been something like, *Awww, is the kitty hiding in the tree from the big, bad wolves?*

Miles saw it coming before anyone else did. He backed up and lay down next to Tanner just as Quincy batted at the first pine cone hanging next to him. He knocked it loose and it dropped, hitting Chad in the head.

Chad yipped, jumped back, then growled up at Quincy. Finley fell over, snorting and chuffing, rolling around as he did so. Jamie made a sort of snorting noise that Miles thought meant he was trying to keep from laughing at Chad.

It didn't work. Chad turned his attention to Jamie and growled instead.

Quincy got Jamie back for Chad, though. The second pine cone hit Jamie's nose. The third caught Finley on the belly.

By this time even Tanner was having trouble holding in his mirth. Miles had amusement and pride battling inside him. He couldn't decide if getting the best of the wolves was funnier… or if Quincy was just that awesome because he did.

As fun as it was, though, Miles had something better he wanted to do yet. He shifted and grinned up at Quincy. "You know this means I win, right? I caught you. Just because I'm not up there doesn't mean I didn't catch you."

Quincy sighed, twitched his tail a few more times, then leapt lightly to the ground. He sat, licked his paw, and ran it over his face, looking like he hadn't just been called out.

Miles grinned and shifted back, padded over, and sat next to his mate.

The other wolves came up and, one by one, bopped Quincy before taking off. Quincy managed to look very put-upon even while still in cat form, growling quietly until they left. Miles chuffed at him, then stood and tugged Quincy's ear. Quincy looked slightly confused but stood as well.

Miles led Quincy through the woods again, past his favorite stream—the one they'd found Quincy next to the other day—then along another path. Finally, they came out at a small clearing, surrounded by thick forest. Above them, the waning crescent moon provided just enough light. Miles sniffed until he found what he was looking for, then shifted and pulled out the blanket and small bag.

When he turned around, Quincy had shifted back as well. "What's this?"

"I asked Jamie and Chad to bring this out earlier. I thought you might appreciate a little privacy, rather than have the others so close." Miles spread out the blanket, then held his hand out. "Bond with me, Quincy."

Quincy closed the distance and took his hand. He reached up with the other and cupped Miles's cheek. "I'd like that. A lot."

With a smile Miles pulled Quincy closer. He ran his hand up along Quincy's arm, then cupped a cheek in a mirror of Quincy's movement. He soaked in the incredible vision in front of him. His *mate*. It still amazed him that he'd found this man, the one destined for him. He probably would never have chosen a jaguar—even if he knew they existed—but now that he'd gotten to know Quincy, finally was able to spend time together, he couldn't imagine anyone else.

He caught Quincy's lips with his own, taking his time building the kiss. He brushed his mouth over Quincy's, nipping and nibbling, then finally running his tongue over Quincy's lip.

Quincy opened to him, his hands going up into Miles's hair as he tilted his head.

Miles moaned softly, losing himself to the taste and feel of Quincy. He didn't think he'd ever get tired of that, of having Quincy in his arms, against him, of the scent of sweetness surrounding him. He broke the kiss only to dip down and kiss a trail along Quincy's neck. He realized when he opened his eyes that his vision had gone gray and his teeth had dropped.

It gratified him to see Quincy's eyes had bled black and his teeth were out as well. Then Quincy rocked against him, brushing their hard cocks together, and Miles damned near forgot everything in that moment and bit Quincy.

He reined it in carefully and pulled back, then kissed his way slowly along Quincy's chest as he knelt. He paused to brush his lips over the light treasure trail on Quincy's belly, then skipped his cock and kept moving to one hip, then back across to the other.

Quincy threaded his fingers into Miles's hair and dropped to his knees, nearly crashing into Miles and kissing him again. Miles let his hands go where they would, not paying too much attention to what he touched or teased, only thinking he needed more. More of Quincy, more touch, just *more*.

He managed to guide Quincy onto his back. "Let me taste you," he murmured, and after groaning, Quincy nodded.

So Miles did. Every dip and muscle, every line and inch of skin he could find. Everything except Quincy's cock. He found every sensitive spot he could, every place that brought the tiniest of sounds, the barest of gasps, and he exploited them, teased them until Quincy's sounds turned almost begging. Then he moved on.

He settled between Quincy's legs, but still avoided the one thing he knew Quincy wanted him to taste more than anything. Instead, he dipped down and kissed and licked his way over both balls, then along Quincy's taint. With a glance up at Quincy's black eyes, he dove farther and ran his tongue over the tight muscle guarding his mate's hole.

"Oh *fuck*, Miles!" Quincy was none too quiet, and Miles was glad he'd brought them out to the forest. He'd been sure Quincy wouldn't want to share this with the others, and there'd be no way to *keep* it from a house full of wolves.

Miles savored the sound briefly, then went back to teasing Quincy mercilessly. He spread Quincy's cheeks and licked slowly, making circles, then dipping the tip of his tongue in slightly, before circling again. Another dip, then more teasing until Quincy rocked, grabbing Miles's head and tugged on his hair.

With a chuckle Miles pushed his tongue in farther, thrilling when he got another loud moan. He poured everything he had into pleasuring Quincy and got a little lost in it. So he was surprised when Quincy pulled on his hair again.

He sat back, and Quincy said, "My turn."

Miles couldn't very well argue too much with that. He lay back, and Quincy started with his lips, kissing him again, then followed a similar trail over Miles's body that Miles had taken over Quincy's. There were spots Miles had never known were sensitive, places he'd have sworn wouldn't react. And yet Quincy managed to get him to moan with all of them.

When Quincy swallowed Miles's cock, it took all Miles had not to pour months of missing Quincy down his throat. Miles gritted his teeth—nearly punching a hole in his lip with his canine—and gripped the blanket to hold himself back. He was *so* not coming in Quincy's mouth.

"Quince… fuck, stop! Not…."

Quincy pulled off and looked up at him.

It took Miles several deep breaths, a prayer or three to Diana for calm, and some mental recitation of scientific terms before he felt like he could handle more.

Miles tilted his head. "Turn around," he murmured.

Quincy did as Miles asked and knelt over Miles's face. Miles grabbed the bag he'd had with the blanket, pulled out the lube, and popped it open. As he took Quincy's cock into his mouth, he coated his finger, then slid one into Quincy's ass.

The concentration it took to pleasure Quincy *and* prepare him was enough to help Miles not go completely nuts. By the time he felt like Quincy was sufficiently stretched, however, even that wasn't helping much. That got worse when Quincy snatched up the lube and coated Miles's cock in the slick. He closed his eyes and gritted his teeth to hold back again.

Finally Quincy let go and turned around. Without a word he stretched out next to Miles, then lay back. "Want to see you," he whispered, and warmth spread through Miles that they were on the same wavelength.

He got into place and lined up, then leaned forward and kissed Quincy softly. "I love you," he whispered before pushing.

"Love you," Quincy said, though it was a little stilted because Miles managed to get the tip of his cock in at the same time. "Oh fuck, that feels good."

Miles grinned. "I hope so, or we're in for a *long*, boring mating."

Quincy laughed. "Well, I could always top."

"True," Miles agreed, leaning forward. He kissed Quincy again, then focused on working his length into Quincy, inch by slow inch. When he'd seated himself completely, he sat up a little to give himself better leverage, then started thrusting. Quincy rested his hands on Miles's arms, lifting his legs a little, and Miles thought he was going to go crazy with the change in angle. He did his damnedest to hold on, but knew—with all the buildup, all the time apart, all the waiting—he wasn't going to last very long this first time.

It seemed Quincy wasn't far behind him. He arched his back and, almost as if he couldn't stop himself, gripped his own dick and started stroking it.

"That's it, baby. So fucking hot," Miles whispered. He pumped his hips a little faster, thrust a little harder, pleasure filling him in a way it hadn't in a long time. The tight heat surrounding his cock nearly did him in before he was ready.

Quincy moaned, his hand moving even faster with the encouragement. His eyes—still black with his cat close to the surface—locked onto Miles's. "Too… can't…."

Seeing what he was doing for Quincy had Miles's balls drawing up. "I know, baby, me too." He leaned forward again and kissed Quincy once more. "Come with me, Quince. Let's strengthen the bond."

"Yes," Quincy nearly hissed. He tightened his muscles, and that was all Miles could take.

He threw his head back and shouted Quincy's name. The base of his cock swelled, the knot forming, tying him to his mate. Quincy groaned, his back arching hard and Miles's name spilling from his lips as he shot white heat all over his hand and chest, even splashing Miles.

He'd heard about what to expect when the bond strengthened, but hearing about it and experiencing it were two different things. The link between them seemed to solidify, thicken. Then it was like something wrapped around them, pulling them even closer to each other.

As he came, pumping his pleasure into Quincy, the echoes of a climax not his own hit him. Quincy's eyes widened, and awe and love followed on the heels of the pleasure.

It took Miles a moment to be able to think clearly. As he did, he realized little shocks of pleasure were still hitting him. He'd understood the physiology of mating, of what happened when a wolf knotted, but *feeling* it was so much more.

"That feels… weird," Quincy muttered, and Miles laughed.

"I can imagine." He tilted his head. "You guys don't knot, do you?"

Quincy shook his head. "No. At least, I don't think so. Our wild cousins don't, so I doubt we do."

"Good to know. So if we do anything in public, *you* top, then."

Quincy laughed. "Noted." His smile didn't fade as he looked up at Miles. "Is that love…?"

"Mine, yes. Love, awe. Amazement. I can't get over that we're bonding."

"It's… incredible," Quincy agreed. He brushed his thumbs over Miles's cheek.

"It'll be a little… unstable, I guess, is the best way to put it, until we claim each other. We can't really control how much or how little emotion transmits across the bond. We can send emotion—calm, love, that sort of thing. But when we're emotional, we can't hide it from each other."

"That's a little scary and yet… we can't lie, then, can we?"

Miles shook his head. "No, we can't. I think that's a good thing."

"It is," Quincy said, nodding. "Um… are we going to be stuck like this for long?"

Miles shrugged. "I actually don't know exactly. Sometimes it's short, sometimes much longer. My understanding is it shouldn't last more than thirty minutes. If it does, something's wrong. Of course… I'm the only shifter doctor I know of in this part of the state. So if there *is* something wrong, it's up to me to figure it out."

"That's… comforting. I guess we'll be glad we don't have to wait for someone to show up? Or go to them?"

Miles threw his head back and laughed. "There's an optimistic way of looking at it." He dipped his head and kissed Quincy softly.

"Thank you, by the way," Quincy said when they broke apart, and Miles raised his eyebrows. "For arranging this. I'm not sure I want Chad and Jamie knowing about this, but I'd guess they probably all do, and… well… that's *way* better than them hearing it."

"You're welcome," Miles said, smiling. "I'm glad you appreciate it. I… I didn't want to share you with them either."

"Don't want to share you either." Quincy sighed. "All the more reason to get this mess taken care of. I'm thinking we make our plans for that tomorrow."

"Sounds good. Tonight, though… tonight I want to hold you for the rest of the night."

Quincy smiled. "Can we do it in a bed, though?"

Chapter 9

IT TOOK a little more doing than Quincy would have liked to make all the plans. Now that he had a course of action, he wanted to get moving on it and, hopefully, get *done*. He wanted to work on plans of a different sort—like figuring out where he and Miles would live together and when they could make that happen. He wanted to focus on building a life with his mate, rather than fighting with Thoth-knows who over Bastet-knows what.

Instead, he had to think through each aspect of the plan, each step, to make sure he wasn't missing something, wasn't forgetting anything. He had not just himself to worry about now, but three wolves he'd come to care a lot about—not that he'd admit that out loud to either Chad *or* Jamie. He had no doubt that when it came down to it, Chad and Jamie and even Miles could take care of themselves—in most situations. But whoever was behind all of this had already proven they didn't give a damn about fair. If it was still Dee, Dumb, and Dumber as their hired muscle, Quincy had no doubt any and all three of them would fight as dirty and unfairly as they could if it meant they'd win.

At the same time, if his father really *wasn't* the one ordering all of this, he was going to have to be able to lure Dee, Dumb, and Dumber somewhere and question them. Because if his father didn't know, then they were the only ones he could possibly get the information from. Quincy wasn't sure if he was looking forward to that or not. He was quite sure they'd put up a fight, and he wanted the slightest excuse to get back at them for both his injuries and nearly killing his mate.

After careful consideration, he picked a hotel, and they decided the best route to take to the city. There were two major interstates they could take once they got to Harrisburg, but the Turnpike was quite a bit more populated, and at least until Quincy had an answer about his father, he wanted to possibly keep the Three Ds from being able to get to them. So they stuck to the Pennsylvania Turnpike and, despite none of them being fans of New Jersey, took the New Jersey Turnpike north through the state.

The Challenger had more backseat space than Quincy had expected. He was grateful, though. He hadn't been looking forward to being squished for the six-odd hours it would take to get to New York. Not that he minded being against Miles, but there were limits.

Chad noticed the Three Ds first. He pointed out the Camaro that seemed intent on keeping up with them. Quincy had no doubt who it was, especially when they pulled off at the same rest stops and left with them. He and Chad both agreed their plan to stick to lots of people had been a good one.

Apparently Chad was not a fan of driving in Manhattan. Though actually quite amused by the expletives Chad shouted at the other drivers, Quincy couldn't help but be impressed at how well he handled the car and avoided idiots. Despite the fact that they only had approximately two-dozen blocks of Manhattan to get through, Chad looked about ready to shoot someone by the time they pulled up outside the Plaza Hotel on Grand Army Plaza near Central Park.

One of the things that had taken so long to get them ready for the trip was that Quincy needed to create a new identity. Since they were aware of not only Quincy Archer, but also Uther Isaacs and Niles Perry, he needed something else. Acquiring the physical identification had taken the longest, though creating his credentials online also took time. He'd only picked up the Pennsylvania driver's license under the name Dean Grant the day before.

Once Chad stopped the car and they all climbed out, Quincy focused on getting his backpack to go check them in. Miles turned to go with him, while Jamie and Chad apparently argued with the valet that they didn't *need* valet parking, to please just point them to a garage. After making sure Jamie knew to leave their bags with the bellman, Quincy left them to it, and he and Miles stepped into the Plaza lobby.

He'd been there so many times, the marble floors, huge chandeliers, rich wood, and gold accents barely even registered anymore. It took him a moment to realize Miles wasn't right beside him. He turned around and smiled at his mate's reaction. He stopped then and tried to see it through the eyes of someone who'd never been there before, and realized there was definitely reason to stop and admire a little.

The crystal chandeliers alone inspired a bit of awe. The classical furnishings, sweeping staircase, and even something as simple as the gilt railings were enough to want to take a moment. Miles cleared his throat, and when he caught up, red tinged his cheeks.

Quincy leaned in and kissed one cheek softly. "I grew up here—well, not here as in the hotel, but here as in New York. My family's home is in Connecticut. I forget what it's like to see some of these things for the first time. You should have seen me. I embarrassed the hell out of my father." He laughed, and Miles raised his eyebrows. Quincy nodded. "Yeah. I stood right there—" He pointed at the biggest chandelier that hung over the gold design inlaid in the marble. "—and gaped at everything. I thought he was going to have a fit."

Miles shook his head. "It's just that…. I mean… it's not exactly *typical* of most hotels."

"No, it's not. There's a reason the Plaza is such a big deal, you know?"

"Yeah." Miles took Quincy's hand, and they moved over to the registration desk.

It took Quincy a moment to remember what name he'd put the room under. "Dean Grant," he finally said when he remembered. Miles raised an eyebrow and smirked. Quincy ignored him, though he had picked the name on purpose. "And this is my husband, Miles Grant."

"Very good, sir," the desk clerk said without even batting an eye. Quincy figured that had something to do with the fact that they were booked in one of the larger suites and under the Archer Enterprises account. Considering all they were going through, he had no qualms charging this little venture to the company—and, thus, his father. Quincy had put out enough money while on the run. The company could more than afford it. "And how many keys would you like?"

"Four, please. There are two more in our suite."

In only a few moments, Quincy got the keys, signed them in, and handed one of the keycards over to Miles. "We'll find the other two, go up, and figure things out when we're settled."

Chad had finally found the garage apparently, and Jamie waited for them by the door. A couple of minutes later, Chad joined them. "I'm not exactly a fan of New York yet," Chad said, shaking his head.

Quincy laughed. "There's a reason I like Pittsburgh. New York's too big. Here." He handed keys over, then led them to the elevator. He noticed Jamie fidget a few times and wondered about it until he leaned in and whispered to Chad.

"I *really* don't belong here."

It just went to show how uncomfortable Jamie was, if he spoke out loud—even in a whisper—instead of communicating telepathically to his mate. Quincy turned around and sniffed, then answered before Chad could speak. "You absolutely do. Do you know why?"

Jamie blinked at him, cheeks red. "Uh… why?"

"Because anyone belongs at the Plaza who wants to be at the Plaza. People come from all over to see this place. You're a registered guest just like anyone else. It doesn't matter one bit who's paying for it. I'd bet half my biggest bank account a large number of people who stay here don't pay for it themselves either."

Jamie stared at him for another moment. "Kind of hard to argue with that."

Chad snickered. "I'm going to have to remember that."

Jamie elbowed him, scowling.

Chad winced. "Sorry, baby." He kissed Jamie's temple.

"Uh-huh." Jamie shook his head but took a breath and looked a bit better. "Thanks, Q."

Quincy waved it off as they stepped out of the elevator. "Let's just get settled. Six hours on the road drives me nuts."

He couldn't resist watching them walk around the suite, looking at everything. He'd stayed there a few times himself, so he'd already seen the classical furnishings and decor.

Once the bellhop had delivered their luggage, left, and they'd sorted it out, Quincy went straight for the wet bar. He started with the Chivas, then moved on to the Grey Goose. Miles watched in amusement, and Quincy sniffed, ignoring the expression on his mate's face, then finished the Grey Goose and tossed the empty bottle in the garbage. "Six hours cooped up with three dogs."

Miles threw his head back and laughed. "I can see that prompting a wet bar raid." He chuckled and pulled Quincy close. "Sorry we're so onerous."

Quincy rolled his eyes. "Okay. *Two* dogs and a wolf."

"I heard that!" Chad called from his and Jamie's bedroom.

Quincy laughed, feeling a lot better all of a sudden. He had friends with him, friends who were more than capable of watching his back, helping him, and who wanted to be there because they liked him, not because they had to be. He was still getting used to the idea that he wasn't alone.

He took a deep breath, grabbed a bottle of Grand Marnier, and called, "How about we work on the next step?"

AFTER USING his proxies again to call his father's office through the Internet to make sure his father was in, Quincy and Chad decided to have one of the wolves deliver a message directly, in public. Still concerned about the possibility of being intercepted—there was always the chance someone in his father's office was watching him, even if there were only a couple other cats working for him—Quincy decided to keep it simple.

> *In town. Let's meet.—Q*

He paced the hotel room, nervous as all hell, until he heard from Jamie. As soon as his cell rang, Quincy snatched it up. "Hello?"

"Got the reply. He didn't seem surprised to find a couple of wolves in his office."

"My father's poker face makes mine look amateurish."

"Wow. And I wouldn't play poker with you for all the ham bones in the world. Okay," Jamie said, chuckling when Quincy laughed. "Anyway, he wrote a reply right away. We'll be there soon."

"Don't get in the elevator alone. Or the stairs."

"No worries. There's a crowd waiting."

"Good. See you soon."

It took less time than Quincy expected for them to be at the door. Either that or he'd made more laps around the living room than he realized.

"Either he needs a good dose of catnip or you need to fuck him into the mattress, dude," Chad said as they stepped in.

Quincy rolled his eyes, too anxious to even rise to the bait.

Chad raised his eyebrows, likely at the lack of response, but handed over the piece of paper. Apparently, his father was being just as cautious.

> *Will arrange something. Don't forget your duty to*
> *your ancestors.*

"What's your duty to your ancestors?" Chad asked, looking over Quincy's shoulder.

"Tomorrow is the Beautiful Festival of the Valley," Quincy muttered. "It used to be held over twelve days, but that's been brought down to one."

"Uh... what is it?"

Quincy shook his head. "Sorry. We're supposed to spend the day at the cemetery, sharing a meal with the spirits of our dead relatives. Usually it's a day-long affair. They have catering bring in a buffet, and each of the families comes from all over the region. There are prayers, of course, and it's also a chance to see cats you don't get to see other times. I can't actually go tomorrow, not the way I should. But I'm guessing my father will find a way to get me a message there." He sighed. "Something more is going on. He suspects something, or he'd be more direct. Shit."

Miles came up and wrapped his arms around Quincy. "Isn't this good, though? That it's probably not him?"

Quincy frowned. "Yeah. But then... I've been accusing him for months. What—"

"Hey," Jamie interrupted. "Hey, he hasn't exactly gone out of his way to find out for you or let you know he was looking, has he?"

"Well, no."

"No, he hasn't," Chad said. "And are you telling me he couldn't have traveled to Pittsburgh himself to see you? Talk to you? Find out what was going on?"

Quincy sighed. "No."

"No," Miles said, nodding. "Maybe this isn't him—or all him—but he's hardly blameless."

Quincy swallowed, turned around, and buried his face in Miles's neck. "Thank you," he whispered, then stepped back. "You're right. All of you." He frowned. "Okay, then. Obviously we've got to get to the cemetery tomorrow."

"Is it far?" Chad asked.

"No." Quincy shook his head. "But we need to figure out where to park, what to do, and how to otherwise stay out of sight."

"Let's bring up the map on Google and go from there, hmm?"

"Right," Quincy said, grabbing his laptop and setting up at the table.

"Could we get some coffee for this? I have a feeling we'll be working on it for a while," Jamie asked.

Quincy pointed to the table sitting under the mounted LCD TV. "It's on the iPad. Order whatever. It goes to the room."

"Thanks," Jamie said, crossing the room.

"Hey! Get a burger. I'm starving," Chad called.

"You're always starving," Jamie said with a snicker.

Quincy grinned and opened his browser. "Just don't empty the hotel kitchen. I want food too. See what they have in fish. Now, let's see...."

As Quincy expected, the normal access road into the cemetery was clogged with vehicles. Natural forest bordered the private cemetery the pride owned on three sides. Quincy would be able to approach and watch from a distance, and with the population of cats there that day, he was pretty confident no one would pick up an extra cat's scent. No matter how faint the cats' scents normally were, he knew they wouldn't disguise their scent for something like this. But with so many, Quincy didn't worry about himself.

Wolves, however, were a different problem. He'd had Jamie and Chad put on extra cologne so their wolf scent wouldn't be automatically recognizable. They were also sticking to the downwind side of the cemetery. They'd keep an eye out for Dumber, since they hadn't seen Dee and Dumb and wouldn't recognize them, and just be ready should they be needed for anything—like a weapon or a fast set of wheels. The Challenger was parked in the shadows at the edge of the forest.

Miles, however, was *not* wearing extra cologne. Quincy had wanted him to stay back at the hotel, but Miles had flatly refused. In truth, Quincy was glad Miles had insisted. He had no idea what it was going to be like to watch this from a distance. So his mate was at his side.

And pretty much *covered* in his scent. He'd marked Miles everywhere he could possibly manage it. Apparently he'd managed so well, Chad declared he *stank* of cat. Quincy had grinned... and rubbed his face along Miles's shoulder again. Chad had snorted, made a comment about jealous mates, and proceeded to grab and kiss Jamie to within an inch of his life.

Quincy and Miles crouched on a small hill overlooking Quincy's family crypt. On one end of the cemetery, a tent had been set up with a buffet and tables. Several families had already collected plates and blankets and sat by their own crypts.

It took Quincy a moment to find his father. As tepey, of course, he'd be expected to greet the others, talk to each of the families, and in general show he was there for the pride. He moved through the cemetery slowly, stopping at each crypt to offer words before moving on. Quincy tried not to be angry, but he couldn't seem to help it.

He should be down there.

He should have a plate of salmon and steak. He should be sitting on the blanket in front of the crypt, talking about the grandparents he'd only known for a short while before they died. He should be sending up his prayers to Bastet and Osiris and Thoth that his grandparents and the rest of his ancestors had safely passed the test of maat and found their place. He should be introducing Miles to them in their way, telling Miles about the memories he did have.

Instead, he was on a hill, lying in the grass in cat form, next to Miles in wolf form—who also would not be welcome down there, not even if the current mess wasn't going on. Quincy tried not to let the anger turn into hurt. He'd never missed a Festival of the Valley. Every year he'd made his trip to the cemetery.

He took a deep breath and let it out.

The elders sat at their table under the tent, looking as righteous and ridiculous as always. Every last one of them wore absurdly expensive suits and jewelry, flaunting the wealth they had as if it was some symbol of their true worth. There were families in the pride who could have used that money—families Quincy could at least say his father helped.

Quincy shook his head and took in the rest of the gathering. He spotted his mother with her family. He'd long since gotten over her walking away. He *did* understand. They were a solitary species. He and his mother still spoke, but as tepey-sa, he was to be raised by his father and groomed to take over. Since there was *no way* she and his father were going to get along, it meant she stepped away. It wasn't that they never talked or saw each other. They still did during events and the like. But they were little more than polite to each other.

He leaned a little harder into the warm furry body next to him, then let his tail curl over Miles's. Miles licked his face, and Quincy felt the calm Miles was sending over their bond. He returned the licks, then forced his attention back to the cemetery.

His father had finally taken his place at their crypt. Quincy's gaze was glued to his father with the fascination of watching a train wreck. He could have repeated, word for word, verbatim, each prayer his father gave and, in fact, found himself thinking each prayer along with his father. Each successive prayer, each bite of fish, made breathing harder. Quincy fought it all, the effort aided by the warmth and love next to him.

They weren't going to be there too long. Quincy had shown up toward the end, well aware of how dangerous it was. So by the time his father collected his empty plate and picked up the blanket, the sun had started to sink. Quincy lost track of it all as the emotional knot inside him expanded.

It wasn't until a nose worked its way under his chin that he realized he'd been growling softly. He took a breath, turned his head to his mate, and buried his own nose in the scruff of Miles's neck. He inhaled deeply, then turned back just in time to see his father look around, then tuck a piece of paper into the flower pot in front of the sphinx outside their crypt.

When night fell a short time later, the gathering dispersed fairly quickly. Many of his fellow jaguars felt they were tempting Seth to cause problems if they hung around too long. Quincy thought they were nuts—for all he believed in the gods, he didn't believe they were that involved in the cats' individual lives.

Their departure to the tepey's residence to continue the social aspect of the festival actually helped Quincy. When all that were left were the human caterers packing up, Quincy and Miles made their silent way to the tomb. Quincy sat briefly, bowing his head and asking Bastet's forgiveness for not being able to honor his relatives properly. With a heavy sigh, he shifted and plucked the paper out of the pot.

Le Bernardin. 8 pm tomorrow. Bring the wolf.

He'd written dog first and crossed it out before writing wolf. Quincy didn't have the emotional capacity to even get pissed about the name. He showed the note to Miles, then crumpled the paper. He glanced around and, when he saw a neighboring crypt that had a candle burning, crossed over and dropped the note into the flame. When he was confident it was ash, he shifted, and together he and Miles made their way back to the Challenger.

He wanted to just be *angry*. He could handle anger. But there was so much more swirling around inside him. Frustration at the situation, the way his life had spun *so* out of control. Confusion over who could want him back so badly, who could want his mate dead. By far the biggest piece was something he didn't even want to name. But his heart ached and a lump filled his throat so much that he was having trouble simply breathing again.

Miles did the talking with Chad and Jamie on the way back to the hotel—telling them about the note and listening to their report. Quincy let the talk flow over and around him. He'd get the rest later. He just couldn't deal with it right then.

He let Miles hold him on the way back to the city, then be the one to get them back up to the room. It was a testament to how fucked up he was that he didn't even make a peep when Miles stripped him and got him into bed. Part of that might have been because Miles climbed in right after him, pulled him in, and curled around him. But Quincy could admit part of it was just how bad he'd let the night get to him.

For once in his life, he didn't care what someone else thought. Instead, he burrowed into Miles's arms and let himself be comforted.

Chapter 10

MILES LEANED a little closer to get a better look at the map Chad had laid out on the table.

"Okay, so, Le Bernardin is here," Chad said, tapping his finger on the entrance of the building on 51st. "There's a Starbucks in the building just on the other side. Or there's Café Duke right across the street. I'm actually thinking that might be better. More direct." He tapped each option.

"I'll trust your judgment on that," Quincy said. "You know what you're doing here."

Chad flashed a smile, then went back to the map. "I think as long as we don't, like, go into an alley or anything, we should be out of reach of the Three Ds, both going there and coming back. Unless you want to take a cab."

Miles wrinkled his nose, and Quincy laughed. "Miles has it right. If you think the streets of New York stink, you'll *love* the cabs."

"I was here once for a conference. I seriously held my nose the whole way from the airport," Miles said, shaking his head.

Chad blinked, then nodded. "Uh, okay, then. I'll take your word for it. We walk. Now," he said, turning to Jamie, who handed him what looked like a tiny flesh-colored button. Chad held it up. "Bluetooth. It works along with this." He took a black wire from Jamie and held it up too. It made one big loop, then came together to hang down. "Microphone and transmitter," Chad said. "They work together. Single charge should get us more than twelve hours, and despite being a four-course meal, I doubt you'll be in there that long."

Quincy snorted. "I couldn't put up with my father that long."

"Right. So these will connect to this." Chad tossed a cell phone at Quincy. "Motorola Moto G. Eighteen-hour continuous talk time. Prepaid through Verizon. I'm not worried about anyone tracing it, but I didn't want to actually use your phone either. They know you're here. They know where to find you if they want you."

"That's comforting," Miles muttered, tightening his hold on Quincy a little.

"But true," Quincy said, sighing.

Chad paused and looked up at them. "There are four of us. All of us know how to fight. We can protect you, especially now that I have a better idea of what we're up against. I'm guessing you've never used a weapon besides your claws, right?" he asked, looking at Miles.

"Yeah. I prefer to heal, not hurt."

"I get that, but that might not be an option." Chad frowned.

Miles held up a hand and met Chad's gaze. "I know. And if it's a choice between Quincy or you guys—or me—and them, then, well, I'll do what I have to."

Chad turned to Quincy. "Do you have a weapon—other than your claws—with you?"

Quincy nodded and got up, then hurried down the hall. A moment later he returned holding a handgun. "SIG Sauer P250," Quincy said, checking the safety, then handing it to Chad.

Chad checked it over, including the magazine, then handed it back. "I carry a Beretta. Jamie prefers a Glock. He hasn't spent a lot of time with one, but he's a pretty damned decent shot when he trusts his instincts."

Jamie blushed.

"Anyway, the three of us will be armed, so Miles, with any luck, you can keep to your healing. I'm *really* hoping it won't be necessary." He took a breath. "Jamie and I will wait in the cafe across the street, then. We'll get the call set up before you're seated. All four of us will be listening. I'm going to record everything on this." He held up an identical phone to the one he'd tossed Quincy.

"Do you really think all this is necessary?" Quincy asked, frowning.

"My instincts say something bigger than family issues is going on here. And if I trust them, then we're going to want all the details we can get. Aside from not avoiding skunks, I've been pretty damned good at trusting my instincts."

Quincy burst out laughing. "Skunks?"

Miles snickered. "Still?"

Jamie nodded, grinning. "He keeps chasing them in wolf form."

"Damn things just look like big squirrels to my wolf."

Quincy grinned. "Still a big pup, huh?"

Chad shrugged. "I'll learn. I'm still adjusting to trusting my other senses more."

Quincy nodded. "That takes time. Especially if you've been human for a long time. You're used to trusting your sight."

"Exactly. See?" Chad said, elbowing Jamie. "He gets it."

Jamie grinned and kissed Chad's cheek. "I do too, but I'm your mate. If I didn't give you shit...."

"I'd wonder what was wrong with you," Chad finished for him, chuckling. He cleared his throat. "Okay, so, yes. I think it would be wise to record it. It may be nothing, but there's a chance things could get emotional and you might miss a detail one of us might pick up on."

Quincy sighed but nodded. Frustration hit Miles over their bond, and he kissed Quincy's temple. "That's true. And if you tell anyone, anywhere, ever, that I got emotional—"

Chad held up a hand. "Your secret's safe with me."

Quincy narrowed his eyes a moment, then nodded. "Fine." He took a deep breath and let it out. "I'm not sure if I want this to be my father or if I want him to not be involved. Because if he's not—"

"Things could get really ugly," Chad said, nodding. "Yeah. It would be nice if this time my instincts weren't right."

"But that's not likely," Quincy said, shaking his head.

Miles kissed him, doing his best to soothe him as much as he could, sending calm over their bond. Quincy sat a little tighter against Miles, and Miles smiled when he felt the gratitude coming back.

"Is there anything else we need to worry about?" Miles asked, still looking at the map.

Chad shook his head. "I don't think so. As dumb as the Three Ds are, I doubt they'll try anything in the middle of Manhattan—again as long as we avoid alleys."

"All right." Quincy sighed and checked the time. "Okay, we've got a little while, then. Let's make sure everything's charged and ready."

When Miles and Quincy got into the bedroom to get ready, Quincy flopped down on the bed, rubbing his face again. "I am so sick of this. I never wanted to get into this cloak-and-dagger stuff. I mean, yeah, I'm pretty damned sneaky when I get the information I need or fix things I need to fix. But... that's not the same, you know? I never wanted to fight with my father like this. I just wanted to be left *alone*."

"Well, not *too* alone, I hope," Miles said, sitting next to him.

Quincy moved his hands and looked up. He pulled the tie out of Miles's hair and played a little with the long, thick red locks. "Before all this, I would have fought you. I don't think I'd have accepted you nearly as quickly. But now… there's just too much shit. I don't have the energy to fight you *and* the rest. I'm glad I didn't."

Miles kissed his forehead, closing his eyes briefly to savor the sweet scent his mate had. "I'm glad you didn't too. I'd understand, though, how it would have gone before. Hell, I'm pretty sure *I* might have fought it more. You know I'm bi, right?"

Quincy nodded. "You said something about it in passing a while back."

"So I was all set to accept a male *or* female mate. To find out not only are we not the only shifters in the world, but my mate is a *cat*?" He chuckled.

Quincy snickered. "Yeah, no doubt."

"So, I think we'd both have had a harder time, but all this other stuff just showed us how important we are, how ridiculous it is to fight what's between us." Miles tilted his head, brushing some of Quincy's hair back. "Thankfully we've recognized that and we're together." He glanced at the clock and grinned. "You know, I think there's *just* enough time for something."

Quincy raised his eyebrows as Miles slid off the bed and moved in front of him.

Miles popped the button on Quincy's jeans, then tugged the zipper. He pulled Quincy's cock out, licking his lips. "Yeah, just enough time for an afternoon snack," he said, then swallowed Quincy in one move.

IT SEEMED the blowjob had done what Miles had intended: Quincy looked a lot more relaxed after. He'd tried to return the favor, but Miles had refused. On the way to the shower, he had finally confessed, despite being a bit embarrassed by how fast it had happened, that he'd already come while blowing Quincy.

That stopped Quincy in his tracks, and he stared wide-eyed at Miles, who grinned at the new arousal. However, Miles was well aware they were getting short on time, so he managed to get them focused on cleaning, then getting dressed.

He'd had to make an emergency run to a clothing store earlier in the day when he realized he didn't have a suit coat with him, since the restaurant required one. Miles refused to wear a tie, though. He'd always felt like he was strangling in one. He'd worn them a few times, when he really needed to, and he really would have if Quincy insisted. But Quincy had just chuckled, kissed Miles, then pulled out his own—a deep navy with tiny Japanese characters on it—and finally was dressed himself.

Chad whistled as they stepped into the living room. "Well, don't you two look fancy. I'm feeling underdressed. What about you, baby?"

Jamie snorted. "We're not going to a prix fixe dinner either."

Chad stared at him. "A pre what?"

"Prix fixe. That's what they call those. Fixed price for each person." He shrugged.

"Huh." Chad blinked. "I've never been to one. And how do you know about them?"

Jamie wrinkled his nose. "My parents used to be big into stuff like that."

Chad winced and Miles frowned. He remembered all too well hearing about the shit Jamie had gone through with his parents over his orientation, culminating in him getting kicked out.

Chad pulled Jamie in and kissed him softly. "Sorry, baby."

"You're not missing much," Quincy said, and Miles would have kissed his mate, but he didn't want to draw attention to what Quincy was doing—comforting Jamie. Because he was well aware Quincy wouldn't *want* attention drawn to that. "Don't get me wrong. I love the food at Le Bernardin, but honestly there's plenty of good food at much less expensive places."

As they walked the eight or so blocks to the restaurant, all four of them had to work to ignore the stench of New York. "I promise, a cab would have smelled even worse," Quincy assured them. "Really."

"Should have gotten the Challenger out," Chad muttered.

"You'd probably have to park eight blocks away anyway," Jamie said, shaking his head.

Quincy laughed. "Maybe not, but it wouldn't necessarily be right there, that's for sure."

Despite the banter, Miles couldn't resist looking at every person he passed, peering at doorways and stairwells. He couldn't shake the feeling that the Three Ds were close. He'd only ever seen Dumber, but he had a feeling he'd recognize the other two as well. But by the time they turned onto 51st Street, he hadn't seen them. Either they were hiding *really* well or biding their time.

"I wonder," Quincy murmured as they walked the last block. "Since I'm here in New York, I wonder if they might be thinking I've come back and are leaving me alone because of it?"

Chad pursed his lips but shook his head. "Even though they know you're here, if you were *back*, wouldn't you have actually shown up at the Festival yesterday?"

"Good point," Miles said. "I'd think that would be enough of a tipoff."

Quincy wrinkled his nose. "Dammit, you're right." He scowled, and the now ever-present frustration coming across their link got even worse.

Miles kissed Quincy again, squeezing his hand. "We'll get this worked out, baby," he murmured.

Quincy took a deep breath and nodded. The frustration lightened a little, and Miles felt a little better at having helped him.

At Le Bernardin they split up, Quincy and Miles turning into the restaurant and Chad and Jamie crossing the street. It took a few moments for them to get the call set up, but eventually all four of them were on the line.

"Testing," Quincy said.

"*Got it,*" Chad replied. "*Miles?*"

"I'm here."

"*Good,*" Jamie replied. "*Let's see what we can find out.*"

"*Right,*" Chad said. "*Don't forget to use that scary poker face you've got, Q. He shouldn't know we're listening.*"

"I got it. I know," Quincy said, snorting.

"*Right. Good luck.*"

Quincy took a deep breath. "Thanks." He turned to Miles. "Don't let him get to you," he muttered.

Miles smiled and kissed his temple. "He won't. I've got a half-decent poker face, myself."

Apparently Aubrey Archer was already waiting for them. The maître d' led them to a corner table—probably one of the most private in the restaurant. A semicircular bench sat to one side, with two place settings in front of it, and on the other, Aubrey Archer sat, sipping at a dark brown liquid and doing something on his phone.

Money could do so much, Miles thought.

Up close, Miles could see small telltale signs that the man was stressed. He was lean and toned, the cut and fit of his suit reflecting that. Quincy had told him that his father had always insisted on making sure he looked the part of a strong leader, both physically and mentally, which, whether Miles liked him or not, made sense. The jaguars didn't show age until they were quite a bit older than Quincy's father was— much like the wolves—but the stress lines around Aubrey's eyes and lips and the hint of dark circles under the dark eyes spoke of sleepless nights.

"Father," Quincy said when they stepped up.

His father looked up and stood. "Quincy," he said, holding his hand out.

Quincy shook it, and Miles hid his surprise at the gesture. Quincy had told him more than a few times that they were *not* a demonstrative family. "Father, this is my mate. Miles Grant."

Aubrey looked him up and down before extending his hand. Miles shook it and held the hand as tight as Aubrey did. He would *not* show weakness to this man. He wasn't interested in earning Aubrey's respect. After the way he'd treated his son—whether he ordered it or not, there was too much he should have done and didn't—Miles couldn't give a shit what Aubrey thought of him. At the same time, he also wasn't going to let this man think he was a pushover either.

Finally Aubrey let go and they took their seats. "So, tell me what you do, Miles."

Miles smiled. "I'm a doctor. ER doctor, for the moment."

Aubrey raised his eyebrows, and Miles simply waited, knowing the man very likely already knew exactly who Miles was and what he did. It was obviously a test of some sort. "Any particular reason you do that instead of private practice?"

Miles smiled, understanding the minor dig—that he might make a lot more in a private specialty, rather than as an emergency room doctor. "I care more about actually helping people than money. I make plenty of it without being greedy. Besides, any of our kind who are injured come into that ER if possible, so I can guide their care so as not to raise suspicion."

Aubrey studied him for a long moment, then nodded. "It's good you're there for that." Miles wasn't sure what to make of that reply, but Aubrey was already turning to Quincy. "And how have you been?"

Quincy was saved from answering by the server. They both ordered scotch, then focused on the menu.

Miles frowned at it, not even sure where to begin. It claimed "four courses," but he couldn't really figure out *what* four. He leaned in to whisper in Quincy's ear. "Uh…. What… err…."

Quincy smiled. "Do you trust me?"

"Of course," Miles said without hesitation.

Aubrey's eyebrows went up, but they both ignored him.

"Then let me order for you."

"Happily," Miles said, sitting back.

Quincy flashed him another smile, then turned to the waiter. "My partner will have the wild salmon tartare, the warm Peekytoe Maryland crab, and the white tuna-Kobe beef. I will have yellowfin tuna carpaccio, the scallops with brown butter dashi, and the poached skate with braised daikon, charred scallion jam, and the confit-kimchi broth."

In his ear Chad said, *"Damn. I'm glad I'm eating a burger. That sounds disgusting."* Quincy coughed and Miles cleared his throat, both of them obviously fighting snorts.

Miles turned to Quincy. "Um… so what am I eating?"

"Salmon, crab, tuna, and beef."

"Okay, then," Miles said, chuckling. "That sounds good."

They waited in silence for Aubrey to finish ordering, then turn back to the table. Quincy took a sip of his scotch, and his anxiety spiked over their bond.

Miles squeezed Quincy's hand as he studied his father's expression, then said, "Tell me, right now, to my face, that you didn't order any of that."

They all knew he wasn't referring to the caviar or lobster. His father looked back at him and said simply, "I didn't."

Miles kept his gaze firmly on Aubrey, but he couldn't see anything in the man's eyes to say he was lying. Nothing about his smell indicated it either, though Miles was sure a tepey would have learned how to lie convincingly.

Quincy deflated a little, apparently believing his father. "Then… what? Who? *Why?*"

"I'm still working on that, but I have a few theories. I'm fairly certain we can speak freely, but let's not go out of our way to be specific. And I would like to get to know your… mate."

Quincy sighed. "You could at least pretend to be nice to him, Father."

Miles squeezed his hand under the table. "I'm pretty sure we're both leery of the other, and I think that's fair."

Aubrey nodded. "We can agree on that much." He turned to Quincy. "But why a d—wolf?"

Quincy scowled, and Miles tried, again, to soothe him. Chad growled in his ear, but the "*Oof!*" that cut off the growl made him want to smile. He could totally picture Jamie elbowing Chad.

He focused back on the people at the table with him as Quincy said, "He's destined, Father."

Aubrey raised an eyebrow. "There's no—"

"Don't. Just don't," Quincy said, raising his hand. "As much as I want to know what you know, I will leave."

The muscles in Aubrey's jaw jumped for a moment, but then he nodded. "I didn't know you believed in them."

"I didn't used to," Quincy said. "It's hard to ignore when it's happening, though."

One of Aubrey's eyebrows went up. "Oh?"

Quincy nodded, glanced around, and lowered his voice. "You feel it. There's a… pull."

Aubrey dropped his gaze to the glass. "I don't know about that. But… I guess if you believe it…." He shrugged a shoulder, and it looked like Quincy wanted to reach across the table and punch him.

Miles tried to send calm again, rubbing his thumb over Quincy's hand, and Quincy seemed to settle a little. "I certainly do. I knew your son was my mate the second I saw him. I understand that, as few of you as there are, it would be difficult to believe. I imagine if they're unusual for us, they'd be almost impossibly rare for you, especially as solitary as you are."

Aubrey considered him for a long moment, then nodded. "There are stories, of course. Most of them we've come to believe are nothing but legend." He gave a small smile. He cleared his throat, but at that moment, the first course of the dinner arrived.

They ate in silence for a while. The food tasted wonderful, though Miles still wasn't entirely sure what he was eating. Aubrey was actually pleasant—asking about the hospital, Miles's background, where he was from—and sounding rather nonjudgmental at the same time. Quincy looked downright stunned.

Miles didn't quite know what to make of it, but figured he'd just go along with it. In the end he was there for Quincy.

He finished what turned out to be the salmon and, when Aubrey went to the bathroom, turned to Quincy. "Would you think me horribly crass if I said I still preferred the Japanese steakhouse?"

"*I know I'd prefer that and I'm not even eating it,*" Chad said.

Quincy snorted but shook his head. "Not at all. This kind of thing isn't for everyone."

"*I take it he's not there?*" Jamie asked.

"Bathroom," Quincy said.

"*Good. I know there's quite a bit of the meal to go, but see if you can't nudge him back to the issue at hand,*" Chad said.

"Yeah. We need to get this moving," Quincy grumbled. "I don't know what his game is, but it's driving me fucking nuts."

Aubrey chose that moment to return. As he took his seat, he looked steadily at Quincy. "So… what have you been doing?"

Quincy frowned. "Hiding. I thought you knew that."

"Well, yes. That's not what I meant."

"Working as much as I can since I've been on the run," he said, scowling.

"Have you done any drawing lately?"

Quincy blinked at him, mouth dropping open.

"*Come to think of it, I haven't seen him draw anything either, in all the time he's been with us,*" Chad said.

"Uh, no. I haven't really been able to," Quincy murmured. "I… I didn't even know you knew I drew."

Aubrey snickered. "I did pay for art school, remember?"

Quincy rolled his eyes. "Yeah, but I didn't think you paid attention to what I did there."

"I know more than you realize" was the only reply.

Miles cleared his throat. "So, tell us, what are these theories?"

Aubrey raised an eyebrow but didn't reply right away. "I suppose there's more to the wolves than we've let ourselves believe," he said, surprising Miles—and Quincy, if the shock coming over their bond was anything to go by. Aubrey sighed. "I don't know anything for sure. Right now it's all conjecture. I have no proof. But…." He glanced around, then leaned in a little more, picking up a piece of bread. "There are three separate people I'm not sure of. There's another line set to inherit if neither Quincy nor I are in power."

"I thought my uncle would," Quincy said, blinking.

"He's already stated he'd refuse it, so they all know it's not going to him. The Lewis family, on the other hand, would take over if I was… no longer able to lead and you weren't there."

"But… why would they tell me to come back?" Quincy asked, scowling. "Why not just get rid of me?"

Aubrey shrugged. "I don't know yet. Frank's crafty. I doubt he'd trust actually getting *rid* of you—or me—to the thugs. I suspect he'd want to make sure it got done himself. He's only one, though."

Quincy tilted his head. "Who else?"

Aubrey glanced at Miles. "This is not meant as anything toward you or your pack." Miles nodded once, and Aubrey continued. "The wolf pack here knows we exist. I think that's a fairly recent thing."

Miles frowned. "Why would they have been told? Who told them?"

Aubrey shrugged. "I don't know. Could have been Frank. Could have been someone else. Again, this is conjecture."

"But…." Quincy scowled again. "But if it was the wolves, why would they send cats after me—us?"

"Actually," Miles said, frowning. "I think I get that. If they hire someone—and if they're successful at hiding the money trail—it'll look like infighting in the cats. If they get rid of both you and your father, it creates a power vacuum."

"Which is prime opportunity to send us more or less into chaos," Quincy finished, sighing. "Well, this is one big clusterfuck," he muttered.

"Language, boy," Aubrey growled.

Quincy rolled his eyes but nodded.

Aubrey held up a hand. "That's not all."

Quincy blinked. "Fu—what else?"

"You know this, but I'm not sure if you do," Aubrey said, pointing first at Quincy, then to Miles. "We have a council of elders in the pride— all prides do. The council is advisory only. They have no direct power. However, there are suspicions that a couple of the council members aren't… happy with the way I run things."

Quincy snorted. "They're never happy."

Aubrey nodded. "Of course not. I know that, but this goes beyond their typical disapproval."

"*Holy shit,*" Chad muttered. "*So it could be three different groups? Fuck.*"

Miles coughed an "uh-huh."

Quincy shook his head. "Well, fu—crap. Let me get this straight. I could be the target of not only Frank Lewis—"

"And Wyatt."

"Great. And his son, Wyatt. But also the council of elders—"

"Not all of them. I'm sure it's only a couple of them, but…."

"But still. *Or* it could be the local wolf pack, looking to stir up trouble," Quincy finished.

Aubrey tilted his head, then nodded. "That's about it."

Quincy buried his face in his hands, and the frustration, confusion, and anger transmitting over their bond got even worse.

"*Yeah, that'll be easy to pick through,*" Chad muttered.

Jamie coughed.

Miles sighed and looked up at Aubrey. "Do you have any suspicions as to who you think is more likely?"

Aubrey took a sip of his scotch, and they paused their conversation as the next course was delivered. As soon as the server left, sure they didn't need anything, Aubrey answered. "I am leaning toward the elders or the wolves. Not because I have a problem with them," he said when Quincy scowled and opened his mouth. "But because Frank has never made it a secret that he doesn't like how I lead. If he is behind this, he's being kind of stupid about still mouthing off."

Quincy's scowl faded. "That makes sense."

"*Doesn't narrow it much, though,*" Chad muttered.

"Still, let's say for the sake of argument it *is* the wolves," Miles said. "I have a hard time believing the alpha is involved. This kind of thing has a death penalty attached to it in our world."

Aubrey inclined his head. "As it does for us. Interspecies fights are not tolerated for us either. But if that's the case…."

He didn't need to finish. If it was the local wolf pack and *not* the alpha, that meant the pack had its own internal pile of shit going on. Miles sighed.

"Precisely. That said," Aubrey said as he picked up his fork. "It doesn't leave Frank off the hook and doesn't mean the local alpha *isn't* involved. I think your best bet might be to try to find Payne, Sully, and Witt."

"Who?" Miles asked, blinking.

"I think that's the Three Ds," Quincy said.

"Three Ds?" Aubrey asked, raising an eyebrow.

"I didn't stop to ask their names before we fought. Instead, I've taken to calling them Tweedle Dee, Tweedle Dumb, and Tweedle Dumber, shortened to Dee, Dumb, and Dumber."

Aubrey threw his head back and laughed. "Nice," he said, smiling at Quincy.

Quincy blinked, and confusion took over for a moment again over their bond. Miles squeezed his hand, and Quincy cleared his throat. "Thanks. Um… how do you know who they are?"

"I—discreetly—asked around for who I should hire for the sort of work they've been doing. Pretended to want to hire them to 'encourage' a pride member to cooperate with something." Aubrey shrugged a shoulder. "Those were the names that came up. The person I talked to said they were the best, and something tells me whoever this is can afford that."

"Very likely," Quincy agreed. "Well, I'll still call them the Three Ds."

Aubrey chuckled. "Anyway. I'd suggest trying to find them. Make use of that ex-cop you're friends with. I'm sure he could help you with it. The one I tried to hire."

Quincy smirked. "And told you to buzz off?"

"*Hey, I was more professional than that!*"

Miles had to fight the smile.

Aubrey nodded. "The same, though he was, at least, professional."

"*See?*" Chad asked. Miles suspected the grunt that followed was courtesy of Jamie—again.

"Anyway. Make use of him. Find them. I'm betting they're your best bet. Though… if you're going to… question them… get out of the city. There are too many eyes and ears here."

Quincy nodded and Chad snorted. "*No kidding. Does he think we were born yesterday?*"

"*No,*" Jamie said. "*The day before.*"

"So," Quincy said, ignoring them. "Any idea where to find them?"

Aubrey shook his head. "No, I'm afraid not. But… I might have an idea how to draw them out."

"I'm not going to like this, am I?" Miles asked.

Aubrey looked up at him. "No more than I will, but it may be necessary."

Chapter 11

QUINCY DIDN'T know what to feel more of: frustration, confusion, aggravation, or anger. An entire hurricane swirled inside him, and he had no idea how to handle it. He'd always thought of himself as a fairly calm individual. Certainly not *emotional*. Maybe not emotionless, but this riot was driving him crazy.

He barely noticed the trip back to the hotel. Like the night before, Miles talked to Chad and Jamie, discussing the prospects, but Quincy was still trying to make sense of the dinner. The possibilities for who might be responsible wasn't really all that surprising.

No, it was the way his father had behaved. He'd been… *nice*. He'd smiled. He'd even congratulated them as the dinner ended and said that, when it was over, he hoped they could all have a less stressful dinner together.

Quincy had been, in a word, floored.

He hadn't even asked once when Quincy planned to come back. Quincy wasn't sure what to make of that—whether his father had given up now that Quincy was mated or whether he was biding his time or what—but it certainly didn't help his mental state.

So he spent the whole walk back—all eight blocks—running the questions over and over in his head. It wasn't until they stepped into the elevator alone that Quincy forced himself to focus.

"Where are Chad and Jamie?"

"They decided to go check out Times Square. Said something about being in New York twice now and having never seen it. Jamie made sure I knew they wouldn't be back for a while."

"Oh." Quincy blinked, then his eyes widened. "Oh."

"Yeah," Miles said, nodding. "It's up to you, of course, but I thought time alone might help."

Quincy swallowed and nodded. When they stepped out of the elevator, Quincy wasted no time getting to the room. He practically dragged Miles into the bedroom and kicked the door shut.

"Strip and get on the bed. I'm topping tonight."

Miles grinned. "I thought you'd never ask."

Quincy had no idea where this sort of pushiness was coming from. He'd never been one for being very dominant in bed. Sure, he liked to top as much as the next guy, but he was usually pretty happy with the typical give-and-take during sex.

But something had him pushing this time, and since Miles seemed perfectly happy to go along with it, Quincy wasn't going to argue. Before Miles could actually do what Quincy had told him to do, he shoved Miles's jacket off him, yanked at the shirt next, ignoring the popped buttons and ripping sound, and tossed them aside. He removed his own jacket, tie, and shirt as he kicked his shoes off. Once Miles had gotten rid of his shoes and socks, Quincy crawled onto the bed over him.

Quincy stopped to catch Miles's lips in a long, thorough kiss. He needed his mate's taste, needed that connection as well. Then he bent and bit and nipped lightly along Miles's neck and chest. Pausing to actually open Miles's pants, he sat back long enough to yank them and the boxer-briefs off. Quincy tossed them over the side of the bed, then went back to tasting Miles's skin.

Miles moaned, his hands coming down to Quincy's shoulders. Quincy sat up, though, and took both hands, pinning them over his head. He met Miles's black eyes, thrilling in the teeth poking out under his lip, showing even more than the hard cock how turned on Miles was. Eyes and teeth that matched his own.

"Leave them there," he muttered.

"Yes, sir," Miles said, lips twitching. He sobered when Quincy looked up. He must have seen something in the expression on Quincy's face, because he nodded. "Okay, baby."

Quincy took the moment to dig the lube out of the bedside table and tossed it on the bed next to Miles, then went back to tasting. He exploited every spot he knew would drive Miles crazy, teased every bit of skin he could reach. He wanted—wanted to be buried in Miles right that second, but also to stretch it out, make it last. Their first time had gone so fast, as had the one other time he'd had Miles inside him, and while he understood the reasoning behind it, he wanted more.

So he forced himself to slow down and instead licked long lines over Miles's skin. He sucked up little bruises and chuckled to himself.

"Something funny, baby?"

Quincy grinned up at him. "You look like a jaguar with all those spots."

Miles looked down at himself and laughed. "I guess I do. Too bad they won't last."

"It is. That's okay," Quincy said, rubbing his face over Miles's skin. "That'll last, though, at least awhile."

"Always having to mark me. I'm not going anywhere, baby."

Quincy took a breath. "I know. My cat hasn't figured that out yet. Won't until I claim you."

Miles nodded. "I understand that."

Quincy went back to what he'd been doing, losing himself in the taste and feel of his mate. He touched everything, needing to feel everything. He paused long enough to take his own pants and underwear off, then nudged Miles to roll over. He leaned over Miles, letting his hard, dripping cock slide along Miles's ass, rocking and teasing for a long moment.

He bent to Miles's ear. "Going to fuck you hard."

"*Ohfuckyes*," Miles moaned.

In direct contradiction to his words, Quincy kissed his way slowly along Miles's spine, leaving brushes over each individual vertebra, then rib, then every muscle he could find. Every new spot brought another moan or grunt—music to Quincy's ears. He kissed his way over each of Miles's ass cheeks, then spread them and ran his tongue over the tight muscle there as well.

He had to focus to retract his teeth so he could do what he wanted to next without hurting Miles. When he succeeded, he didn't even hesitate to push his tongue through the ring.

"Fuck, Quince!" Miles shouted.

Quincy pulled back briefly. "Yes, I will. But not yet. I haven't tormented you enough yet."

Miles groaned and dropped his head onto the pillow.

Quincy grinned and went back to his task, pushing his tongue once more into Miles's hole. He worked it in as far as he could, then *slowly* back out, thrilling in the near-whimper he got in reaction. So he did it again, earning the same sound.

Miles rocked his hips, but Quincy pushed them back down to the bed. "Uh-uh. Don't move."

Miles let out another groan but stilled.

Quincy snatched up the bottle, his cock too hard for more teasing. He coated his finger in lube, then pushed it into Miles slowly. "Fuck, you're tight, baby," he groaned.

"Haven't…." Miles paused to grunt when Quincy twisted his finger. "Haven't bottomed in years."

Quincy forced himself to calm down a little. His cock was so hard, precum dripped constantly. But he wasn't going to do anything to hurt Miles, no matter how much he wanted to plunge his dick into the tight body below him.

He took his time—even ignoring Miles's prodding—and stretched the muscle carefully, going all the way up to three fingers. When he finally felt like he'd prepped Miles well enough, *then* he covered his cock with slick and tugged on Miles's hips until he was kneeling.

Taking another breath and sending a prayer to Bastet for patience, he nudged Miles's ass with the tip of his cock. It took some work just to get it in, Miles relaxing his muscle and Quincy slowly but steadily pushing. Finally, however, the tip popped in and they both moaned.

Still, he refused to rush. He pushed in another inch, then pulled back out again, then another and back out until only the tip was still in. Miles groaned and tried to rock back, but Quincy held his hips still and, for good measure, slapped his ass. Miles stilled, but Quincy could tell he needed more.

He let himself go a little faster, finally seating himself completely. There, he paused, bending over Miles's back and wrapping his arms around his mate. He couldn't seem to speak, didn't know what he could say to get his feelings across. Instead, he simply kissed a line across Miles's shoulder, hoping he would understand, at least a little. Miles had *known* what he'd needed in a way even Quincy hadn't. To control this, when so much in his life was out of control, was helping to center him in a way he didn't think anything else would. Not his art, not even shifting.

He gave himself another moment to savor the feel of being buried inside his mate, then pulled out slowly. Stopping just shy of pulling out completely, he paused, then thrust hard back in. Miles moaned but held still, hands clenched tight around the edge of the pillow.

"Fuck, Miles, so good," Quincy moaned as he pulled out again. He set a slow pace at first, still wanting to make this last awhile. He had no idea what would happen next, no clue when they might be able to be together again, and he was going to make the most of this.

Miles, however, was clearly getting frustrated.

Quincy gave in, speeding up, putting more behind each thrust. He moved until he could get a different angle, thrilled when he got the shout he was going for. He gripped Miles's hips, his own body pushing him now to get to the end. His balls were drawing up, and he wasn't going to make it last much longer. "Stroke yourself, baby," he murmured as he sped up a little more.

Miles's hand flew to his dick, and he started stroking himself almost furiously. "Oh gods, Quince… so… *fuck* close."

Quincy groaned in reply, his hips almost having a mind of their own as he nearly pounded into Miles's ass. His cat reared up in him, pushing him to bite, to claim. It took all his skill, all his control, to hold it back. Miles's neck was *right* there, hair having fallen to the side, making it so difficult.

In that precise moment, though, Miles threw his head back and shouted. "Quince! Going to… *oh fuck!*"

His muscles flexed, and Quincy's orgasm hit at the same time Miles shouted again, spraying the cover under him in his spunk. Quincy's thrusts turned erratic as the pleasure crashed into him. It stole his breath as it yanked the cum from his balls to fill his mate's ass.

At the same time, that tug he'd felt when he'd first been with Miles came again. The link between them thickened even more, and on the tail of that, the feeling of being wrapped up and drawn together came once again. As soon as that registered, the echo of Miles's pleasure, then love and happiness that wasn't his, followed.

He closed his eyes, arms tight around Miles as he savored the connection. A connection he never thought he'd want with another person. A connection he was sure that now he didn't want to be without.

Quincy eased out, and they fell over together onto the bed.

Miles turned to him, yanked him in, and kissed him thoroughly. "I love you, Quincy, so fucking much."

He returned the kiss, then brushed is fingers over Miles's cheek, then through the long red hair. "I love you, Miles. I'm… I'm so glad we met."

"Me too, baby." Miles kissed his forehead, then tightened his arms. "Me too."

Quincy had no idea what was going to happen next, but he wasn't going to let it worry him for the moment. Instead, he tugged the blanket over them, buried his nose in his mate's scent, and simply enjoyed being in his mate's arms.

"OKAY. I'VE listened and relistened to the conversation. I don't know him as well as you do, obviously," Chad said, pacing the living room of the suite. "But nothing in his voice made me think he expects you to actually get hurt."

"I don't think he does," Quincy said, shaking his head.

"We're still not going into this half-cocked," Miles said, scowling.

Chad raised a hand. "Of course not. Aubrey is right about some things, though. For one thing, I don't think this is really about you coming back anymore. *Maybe* it is, but I wouldn't bet my bank account on it."

"Then… what?"

Chad glanced at Jamie, then looked at Quincy again. "I don't know exactly. I just… this *feels* bigger to me."

Quincy frowned but sighed. "I'll trust your instincts on it. I think maybe I'm just too close to it."

Chad nodded. "That's definitely likely. I think, first, we need to call Tanner. They should know the local pack is aware of the cats."

"That's probably a good idea. I don't know that they should call the prime yet. If what you heard in Rome has any truth to it…." Miles shook his head.

Jamie scowled. "Then the prime can't be trusted."

"Wait, what?" Quincy squinched his eyes at Jamie.

Chad sighed. "When we went to Rome back in June, Mario and Luigi—"

"Anthony and Raphael," Jamie corrected him. At Quincy's puzzled look, he laughed. "They trolled us, saying they were Mario and Luigi, then told us their real names."

"Ah. So, uh, what did they say?"

Chad frowned. "The rumor over there is that our prime is xenophobic. Has more or less flipped out about anything *not* wolf. And not American wolf, at that."

Quincy blinked. "That's a hell of a thing to accuse your prime of."

Chad nodded. "Yeah. Noah hasn't done anything with it yet, of course, but it means we have to watch what we say to the prime. He was bluffing your father when he told him he'd go to the prime. Of course, if more happened, he'd have to, but…."

"But with that hanging out there, yeah." Quincy sighed. "So where does that leave us?"

"I think Noah needs to see if he can find out how many packs know about the cats," Jamie mused. Chad raised an eyebrow and Jamie nodded. "I mean, if this is as big as we think it is…."

Chad nodded slowly. "And more information is never a bad thing."

"I'm sure Noah can be discreet," Quincy said. "So we'll call Tanner."

"Then, like it or not, I think the best way to go from here is to find the Three Ds. Unfortunately I think your father's plan is best. Have him make noise about you refusing—again—to come back, possibly even staging the phone call he suggested, then let them come to you."

"I really don't like this," Miles grumbled.

Quincy kissed him. "You'll be there to patch me up if they get to me. But… I don't think they will."

Chad shook his head. "I'm going to do everything I can to make sure they don't. I didn't spend the last two months just chasing skunks." He flashed a grin, making Quincy chuckle. "I *have* been working with my sensitive senses. With the training I already have, I'm no slouch. Neither is my mate. He can kick just as much ass."

Miles took a deep breath and let it out slowly. "All right. So… he calls his dad?"

Chad nodded. "Yeah, but we don't make it too obvious. You still use a prepaid or something like it. They know you're here in New York; they'll find you from there. I think, though, we ought to be out on pride lands when you do it."

"Are you kidding me? They'll be right there!" Miles blinked at Chad, mouth hanging open in shock.

"That's the point," Chad said. "First, we don't want to be in the city. My status as a former cop isn't going to mean jack squat if the NYPD finds us toting guns that aren't registered to us or roughing someone up—whether they deserve it or not. On top of that, if they find the Three Ds with, say, a bullet hole that heals?"

Miles sighed. "You're right."

"Of course I am." Chad grinned and Miles snorted.

"Okay, that makes sense," Quincy said, to get things back on track. "So…."

"You find a place for us to lure them. There has to be someplace we can make them miserable that's out of the way. We'll call Tanner in the meantime. Then we'll work on the timing of the rest of this."

Quincy took a deep breath and pulled the map of New York over to himself. He frowned down at it, thinking about the different places he'd gone as a cub. He'd found a bunch of spots that no one else seemed to go, but he had no idea if those were still left alone now. He also couldn't exactly waltz up to his father's house, not if he wasn't "coming back." So it had to be *elsewhere* on the pride lands.

He dropped his face in his hands and rubbed it hard. "I need more coffee before I can figure this out," he muttered and went over to the iPad to order food. "Anyone want food?"

"Do I exist?" Chad asked.

Quincy snorted and turned back to the menu.

IT TOOK the rest of the evening to work out the plans. The call to Tanner had gone as Quincy had expected. Tanner hadn't been happy to hear about the New York wolf pack any more than they had been. He'd conferenced his father into the call, and together they'd discussed what the four of them had learned. Noah had agreed to do discreet inquiries and promised to let them know as soon as he could.

By that time, they were all exhausted. Quincy was comfortable with the plan, though. It wasn't perfect—nothing like this could be—but it was the best option they had. Miles was still more than a little unhappy with the prospect of putting Quincy in the line of fire, but there wasn't much Quincy could do about it.

He understood too. If their roles were reversed, he'd be just as unhappy as Miles was. So he couldn't blame Miles for feeling the way he did.

Despite the exhaustion, none of them slept very well, but with about three pots of coffee shared among them and some solid protein, Quincy felt like he could face what they needed to do. His nerves were just about shot, and he hoped he could carry out the plan like they needed him to.

"Relax," Miles murmured once they'd settled into the back of the Challenger. "I know you're nervous, but you'll kick ass."

Quincy snorted. "I'm not worried about me."

"Hey, I *can* fight, baby."

"That's… I didn't mean…. I know you can. It's not that. I just…." He shrugged and stared at his fingernails. "I never thought I'd want a mate. Now I don't want to imagine life without you."

"Oh, baby," Miles whispered, hugging him closer. "You're not going to. I have a good feeling about this."

"Me too," Chad said from the driver's seat. "We still have some major shit ahead of us, but I feel good about this part, at least."

Quincy sighed. "I hope so." He let the conversation go, watching out the window as they drove along the river. He realized, though, his anxiety had faded a little.

The drive itself only took a little over an hour. They'd timed it so they left before rush hour, but even so, there was traffic. Still, they made it to the forest the pride used for their runs in good time.

Quincy directed Chad to the parking lot they were going to use, and Chad backed in, then turned off the car. "Okay, so."

"The cabin we have is that way about a mile," Quincy said, pointing to the north. "If you go west, you can circle around and, I think, be far enough away to keep them from smelling you."

Chad nodded. "Good. Let's check the phones."

They'd refilled the minutes on the phones they'd used during the dinner with Quincy's father so they could use them again to stay in touch. Within a few moments, everyone was once again connected, and they climbed out of the car.

"Ohhh," Chad said, as the wind caught his hair. "Feel that wind."

Jamie grinned. "If we stay downwind from the cabin, we can be even closer because of that."

"Good. Less time to stall," Quincy said. "Okay, then. Here we go."

The cabin only had two rooms—one main room and one bathroom that had a stall-type shower, tiny sink and toilet, and not much else. The main room had a table and four chairs on one side, a narrow bed against another wall, and a galley-style kitchen opposite the huge stone fireplace. Two doors led into and out of the cabin, opposite each other—a front and back door. He'd chosen the cabin because it was close enough to civilization to have power—and a cell signal—but still be far enough away that any noise shouldn't carry.

Quincy and Miles set to work making it look like they'd been staying for a while. The suitcase they'd brought sat by the bed. Miles lit a fire in the fireplace—since it *would* get cold as soon as the sun went down—and Quincy found the old percolator coffeepot and cups and made the coffee they'd brought along.

"*What was the cabin for? I meant to ask earlier. I somehow don't see the cats doing much roughing it,*" Chad asked through the phone.

Quincy chuckled. "No. It was here so we had some place to leave clothes to shift and run. It also had supplies if we found ourselves in cat form and needed them."

Miles raised his eyebrows. "Ah, that's kind of cool. We ought to build something like this on the pack lands. We usually end up having to lock our clothes in the car and hope no one finds the key."

"*Oh my gods, yes,*" Jamie chimed in. "*Be a lot safer to hide a single house key than a car key right by the car it goes to.*"

Miles chuckled. "Okay, Quince. You ready?"

Quincy sighed. "As I'll ever be." He pulled out the prepaid cell phone and laid it on the table.

"*Remember to put it on speaker so we can hear it,*" Chad said.

"I will. Bossy puppy," Quincy muttered.

"*I heard that.*"

"You were supposed to." Quincy shook his head when Jamie laughed. "Here goes." He hit the speakerphone button, then the number for his father he'd programmed in earlier—so he didn't fuck up the number or something because of nerves.

He kept it short and to the point. They'd gotten a message to his father at the office the day before via Miles, who'd shown up with the excuse of "telling his partner's father off." They'd half expected *that* to bring the Three Ds down on them, but it hadn't, and Quincy guessed his father's office itself wasn't bugged, just the phone lines.

When his father picked up, Quincy gave a curt, "Father."

"Quincy. Have you come to your senses?"

Quincy sighed. "No. Or, rather, not in the way you want me to." He didn't have to fake being annoyed. The fact that he had to do this at all still annoyed him and he used that now. "Can't you get it through your head? I don't want anything to *do* with the pride. Or being tepey. Or anything like it!"

"Quincy, you need to get back here to New York, *now*. I'm tired of playing these games."

It took all Quincy had to keep from saying, "Me too." Instead, he said, "Then don't. Leave me alone." He kept his eyes glued to his watch. He had about ten more seconds to be sure they'd have enough to trace him. "I'm not coming back. Not now, not ever. Good-bye, Father."

He hit the disconnect button and turned off the phone, then sat back and sighed. "And now… we wait."

Chapter 12

THERE WAS a reason Quincy had pursued his art. Entirely aside from it being what he loved, it didn't require the kind of patience this sort of thing did. It could, conceivably, take hours for the Three Ds to find them.

"Should have brought cards or something," he muttered as he made another trip back and forth in front of the fireplace.

"*No kidding,*" Jamie said. "*Is this what surveillance is usually like?*"

"*Yup. There's a reason they drink a lot of coffee and eat a lot of donuts.*" Chad chuckled at the three snorts.

"*Can I blow you or something to pass the time?*"

"We're still here!" Miles said, shaking his head. "I do *not* need to hear that."

"And I don't want to. Just… no," Quincy said, shaking his head as well.

"*Well, next time be done before we get back from Times Square.*" Chad snorted.

Quincy closed his eyes. "I'm going to kill your mate, Jamie."

"*Get in line,*" Jamie said.

"*Sorry.*" Chad didn't sound the least bit sorry, but Quincy was too nuts to call him on it. The grunt that came through the phone was satisfying, though.

"Where did you guys end up?" Miles asked.

"*We can see the back door from here. Is it unlocked in case we need it?*" Chad asked.

Quincy went over to check, then flipped the bolt. "It is now."

"*Good. The call finished about half an hour ago. How long does it take to trace something like that, Q?*"

"Hmm." Quincy pursed his lips as he thought. "It really depends on how good their info guy is. It would take me about an hour to two to find the right cell tower and get a rough radius. After that, it's process of elimination on where it could be. The last time they found me in about three hours. But I was in BFE Virginia."

"And this time you're in home territory. So, likely less."

"If they can narrow the cell tower down, yes."

Miles sighed. "So... at least another half hour, though probably even longer."

"Yup," Chad agreed.

Quincy sighed too. "More coffee, I think."

"So not fair," Chad grumbled.

"Should have stopped at the convenience store. Or Dunkin' Donuts," Quincy replied, grinning.

His only reply was a *"pbbbt"* through the phone.

IF QUINCY hadn't been so hypersensitive to everything around him, he wouldn't have known they were there. As it was, even cats couldn't be *completely* silent when in human form, and the sound of shoes on the wooden porch—even though it was barely there—was enough.

"They're here," Quincy said.

"Roger. On our way."

Quincy forced himself to sit at the table and pick up his coffee cup. He met Miles's gaze, and Miles nodded at him.

"You got this," he whispered.

Quincy blew out a breath and nodded back. It took all the control he had, all the discipline he'd ever learned, to keep the SIG in its holster at the back of his jeans instead of pulling it out. He'd have felt a hell of a lot better facing them with it in his hand, but if he did, he'd blow things.

It annoyed him to no end that he jumped when they kicked the door in. In part because he spilled some of his coffee. He turned to them, scowling. "Oh, for Bastet's sake. Did you *have* to break the door?"

The one in front—Dee—blinked at him in confusion for several seconds, then covered it with a grin. "Hey guys, look, we get the stupid dog too." He laughed, and Dumb and Dumber laughed with him.

"We're here."

Quincy's scowl deepened. "Did you really think it would be that easy? You really *are* Dumb and Dumber."

That stopped the laughter. All three scowled. "Who are you calling dumb?"

Quincy just rolled his eyes. "Never mind. The names obviously fit. Did you *really* think I didn't know you were out there? Or looking for me?" He shook his head.

Dee hid his surprise quickly, but the other two weren't so successful. "Doesn't matter if you did. We've done this once before, haven't we?" He gave a nasty sort of smile, which Quincy returned, making Dee scowl.

"Yeah, we did," Chad said from behind them.

Dee spun around. "Another fucking dog?"

Dumber grunted. "Shit."

Chad flashed him a grin.

"Um. Two more," Jamie said, stepping up onto the porch. "I see why you use those names," he said, nodding to Quincy.

"Yeah, not all that bright." Quincy shook his head. "Well, get inside. Might as well get this over with." Quincy stood, pulling the SIG from its holster at the same time as Chad and Jamie pulled out their weapons. Miles had the other Glock Chad had brought, though he wouldn't be using it. He had it purely for intimidation purposes.

Dee shook his head. "You think that little thing is going to stop us?"

"Maybe not," Chad answered for him. "But there are *four*. And I'm pretty sure, as fast as you are, you can't beat a bullet. This isn't *The Matrix* and your name isn't Neo."

Dee scowled, and Dumb and Dumber looked confused again.

Quincy sighed, lifted his weapon, and pointed it straight at Dee. "Really? Let's get this over with."

Dee shook his head and started across the room toward Quincy. Dumb and Dumber stepped in behind him, but kept their eyes on Chad and Jamie. Quincy would have been worried if he didn't know just how well Chad could handle the weapon in his hand.

Quincy kept his gaze on Dee, and that was the only reason he knew what was coming. Dee took the last few steps between them at a near run and made a swipe at him with a partially shifted hand. Quincy dodged the hit and spun when a shot rang out in the room.

Dee crashed into the table, then fell. "Fuck!"

Quincy looked down to see a hole in the knee of Dee's jeans. He looked up and Chad shrugged.

"What? It heals in humans. I figured it'd heal easily enough in him."

"True." Quincy turned to Dee and held the gun on him. "As you can see, my friend isn't afraid to use the weapon in his hand. Neither am I. If you want to test that, all you have to do is move or try to shift."

Dee blinked at him but didn't reply. He did, however, stay put on the floor.

Dumb and Dumber both stared in shock. "You shot him," Dumb blurted.

"Duh? Did you think these were for show?" Chad asked, waving the gun and blinking at him.

Dumb didn't answer but he didn't move either.

"All right," Quincy said, getting down to business. "Rope. In the suitcase, Miles." He never took his gaze off Dee, trusting Chad and Jamie had Dumb and Dumber taken care of.

"Got it."

A moment later Miles came back with three bunches of rope. He tossed one to Chad and one to Jamie, then went to work on Dee. "Hold on to those while I take care of him." Miles nodded at Dee.

Quincy raised an eyebrow. "Those knots are impressive. Where'd you learn those?"

"Wolf scouts," Miles said, deadpan.

Quincy blinked at him. "Wolf scouts?" He glanced at Jamie. "Is that like… Boy Scouts for wolves?"

Jamie chuckled. "I think he's pulling your leg."

Quincy turned back to scowl at his mate.

Miles just grinned at him. "I spent a lot of time in Seattle during college. I did a few interesting jobs over the summers."

"We'll have to talk about those later."

The grin widened. "Maybe I can show you."

"Uh, do you mind not flirting? That's kind of gross," Dee grumbled.

Quincy pushed the gun against Dee's forehead. "You're hardly in a position to bargain. And let me remind you: don't even *consider* trying to shift or move. I have zero qualms about filling your brain with lead." That wasn't entirely accurate. Quincy had no intention whatsoever of killing. He would if it came down to the Three Ds or him and the wolves, but for one thing, it would be hard to get information out of a corpse.

Miles finished tying Dee's arms behind his back, then his feet together. He moved over to Jamie and took care of Dumber, then a few moments later had also tied Dumb up pretty well. With Chad and Jamie's help, they got them up against the walls—in different spots, with Chad keeping watch over Dumb, Jamie over Dumber, and Quincy standing in front of Dee.

"Miles, give me a hand here," Quincy said, squatting. He dug through Dee's pockets and pulled out a cell phone. Miles helped turn Dee so Quincy could get to the wallet in his back pocket and pluck it out. He flipped it open to see a New York driver's license with the name Payne Stewart on it. He raised his eyebrow. "You use your real name?"

Dee simply narrowed his eyes.

Quincy shrugged a shoulder. "Doesn't matter. I'll find it. And if somehow I don't? He—" He pointed at Jamie. "—found *me*. If he can find me, he'll find you."

Dee scowled but kept his mouth shut.

Quincy tossed the phone and wallet to Miles. "Chad and Jamie, get theirs too." He tilted his head at Dee. "There are two ways this can go. You can tell me what I want to know and I will let you and your fellow idiots go. Or you can fight me and go through a whole hell of a lot of pain. That man?" He nodded toward Miles. "Is a doctor. Anything I do, he can patch you up so you'll heal and then I can do it all over again."

Dee swallowed, but that was the only outward response.

"That's okay." Quincy smiled. "I was hoping you'd refuse." He sighed. "Let's start with something simple. Who hired you?"

Dee actually rolled his eyes. "Really? You're going to be that typical?"

"Are you going to answer my question?" Quincy asked.

Dee spit in his face.

Quincy pointed the gun at Dee's right knee—the one that hadn't been shot yet—and squeezed the trigger.

"Fuck!" Dee shouted.

Quincy brought the gun up and aimed it at Dee's forehead. "That will heal. This won't. I have nine bullets left. I promise, you won't like where I'll put them. There are *plenty* of nonlethal spots on your body."

Dee simply blinked at him.

"Now. Let's try again. Who hired you?"

"Fuck you."

Quincy shot Dee's right shoulder, then pointed the gun back on Dee's forehead.

Dee held in the shout this time, but he obviously strained with it.

"Eight bullets."

At that second, Jamie whispered into the mic, "*Four o'clock.*"

Quincy didn't even hesitate. He swung his right arm around and squeezed the trigger.

"Shit! Shit! You killed him!" Dumb shouted.

Quincy glanced over his shoulder to see Dumber fallen over, eyes open but staring sightlessly ahead. His hands were partially shifted—and thus, no longer tied—and he'd obviously thrown himself forward as if he was going to try shifting the rest of the way. Instead, a neat little bullet hole sat in the middle of his forehead.

"Seven bullets," Quincy said as he pointed the SIG back at Dee's forehead.

"Nice aim," Chad said.

Jamie leaned over. "Huh. It didn't come out the back."

"That's good. Less to clean up," Miles said.

"They don't always come out," Chad said.

"I read about that when we studied ballistics, but I never really thought that was accurate. Huh. Guess that's what I get for watching so much crime crap on TV."

"They're fuckin' crazy, P!" Dumb said, expression still complete shock.

Dee didn't take his eyes off Quincy's face.

Quincy held the gun steadily on Dee's forehead. "I've been called less accurate things." Quincy held on to the humor as much as he could. He had no stomach for this, but it was the only way he was going to get to the bottom of the whole nightmare. He had a feeling Miles, Jamie, and even Chad were using humor for the same reason. With the oversensitive senses Chad was dealing with and the fact that Jamie hadn't been in this sort of situation before... well, despite all that, it'd be a miracle if it *didn't* affect them. Quincy wasn't sure if it was because of or in spite of that, that made him want them with him.

"All right. Now. One more time, this time with feeling. Who hired you?"

Dee stared at him for a long moment, then, lip curled, said, "Go to hell."

Quincy sighed, pointed the gun at Dee's left thigh—close enough to his groin to scare him, but not close enough to do damage to it—and took another shot. "Six bullets."

Dee grunted this time, his face turning red with the strain of not reacting.

"P, maybe we ought to just tell him. We don't get paid enough for this!"

Dee's eyes darted in Dumb's direction, then back to Quincy.

"You tell me what I want to know, you can go. You and Dumb over there. You don't want to tell me, well, I've got six bullets left. That's five nonlethal and one for your brain. Then I can start on him." Quincy tossed his head toward Dumb.

"Ewwww!" came a few seconds later from Chad. "This one pissed himself! Ugh."

Quincy blinked at Dumb. "Really? You pissed yourself?" He turned back to Dee. "He's not good for much, is he? Except a bit of muscle?"

Dee blinked and Quincy smirked.

"God, it stinks now," Chad grumbled, covering his nose with his free hand. "I ought to shoot you just for that." He scowled at Dumb.

"Might not want to say more. Next he'll shit himself, and that'll be way worse," Jamie pointed out.

"True," Chad said. He glared at Dumb, then looked back at Dee. "For the love of Diana, just answer the fucking questions before we all puke from the smell."

Quincy raised his eyebrows. "Well? It can't smell any better for you. Unless you're used to the smell of his piss…. In which case, I *don't* want to know. Ew." He shuddered. "Look—"

"Fuck. Off."

"Bastet, give me patience." Quincy shook his head and shot Dee's other leg. "Five bullets."

"Abraham Thomas and Charles Ross!" Dumb blurted.

Dee sighed and dropped his head down. "Fuckin' asshole," he muttered.

"You know what?" Dumb shouted. "Fuck you! If you wanna fuckin' die for this, be my fuckin' guest! But fuck you. Fuck you and your fuckin' death wish, you fuckin' fuck! I'm not ready to meet Osiris."

"Well, that certainly illustrates the diversity of the word," Chad muttered.

"What do they want with me?" Quincy asked.

"I don't know. Really!" Dumb said when Quincy raised an eyebrow. "They didn't tell us that shit. They'd just tell us what to do—go rough you up, kill him." He tilted his head toward Miles. "That sort of thing. I don't know who they are or what they want. Just that they want you. We were s'pposed to bring you in or kill you tonight."

Dee just sighed again, shook his head, then finally spoke. "They think you'll be their puppet. They want to start a war."

The silence in the room deafened Quincy. He stared at Dee. "A… war?" he whispered.

Dee nodded. "He's right," he said, tossing his head toward Dumb. "I don't get paid enough for this shit. Fuckers want a war, that's on them. I'm done. They know your father isn't going to let them get into a war. I don't know what the fuck they think they'll gain from it." He shrugged a shoulder. "None of my business. They thought we were stupid, talked right over us."

Quincy kept his opinion of Dee's intelligence to himself. "And they thought I'd just blithely go along with it?"

Dee snorted. "Yeah, and they think *they're* the smart ones."

"Who all knows about it?"

Dee shrugged again. "I don't know. The two he mentioned. Someone else they call a lot—I don't think it's a cat, but I'm not sure. That's all I know. You want more, I'd start with Thomas. He seems to be more in the lead than the other one. There might be one more cat, but if there is, he's silent."

Quincy narrowed his eyes as he considered that. It aligned with one of his father's theories. "How do I know you're telling the truth?" Kind of a stupid question, which he realized as soon as it came out. And the information had the ring of truth to it.

Dee snorted. "You'll find it." He nodded toward Miles. "Their numbers are in my phone. Trace 'em. I know you know how."

Quincy nodded and stood. "Miles, take the bullets out while I look some of this up. If it checks out, we'll let them go."

"Oh thank Bastet!" Dumb said on a sob.

Chad rolled his eyes. "Really? Hey, can I spray him down with Lysol or something?"

Quincy shrugged. "Be my guest."

Miles collected his medical kit from the suitcase and knelt next to Dee. "You gonna fight me?"

Dee raised an eyebrow. "I'm not as crazy as your mate is. I'd like to heal, thanks."

Miles smirked. "Good. I can't give you painkillers. And if you shift now, you'll lodge the bullets in your muscles."

"Yeah, yeah, I know. Just do it."

Quincy turned away and grabbed his computer from his bag. He glanced at Jamie. "Want to help me?"

Jamie raised his eyebrows and blinked. "Me?"

Quincy nodded. "Yeah. Two of us will get it faster. You start here. I'll get into the phones." He held his computer out toward Jamie.

"All right." Jamie took it and sat next to him.

Quincy worked quickly, the sound in the room almost nonexistent, save the ping of the bullets hitting the pan Miles used, the clack of the keys as Jamie typed, and Dee's grunts as Miles worked.

Until they heard retching.

"Oh for the love of Diana." Chad hauled Dumb to his feet and carried him into the bathroom. "Puke in there. Fuck's sake. How do you survive this line of work?"

Dumb retched again.

Quincy shook his head and turned back to the phones.

In what could only be a few more minutes, Jamie tapped Quincy's shoulder. "I've got it. I assume you knew who those two men were."

"Yeah." Quincy nodded.

"Addresses, phone numbers, etcetera here," Jamie said, pointing. "Bank accounts here. Including…." He clicked on another tab on the browser window. "These."

"Numbered. And those figures are ridiculous."

"Uh-huh. All the transfers go to other numbered accounts, but I'd bet in short order…."

"We'd find out where those go too. Yeah. Save that. We can follow the money more later."

Quincy picked up Dee's phone and turned back to see Miles had finished and bandaged Dee for the moment.

"Best way for him to heal the rest of the way will be to shift."

Quincy nodded. "Yeah. They'll have to wait a little while, though." He squatted in front of Dee. "In a few minutes, we're going to pack up and get out of here. You'll wait an hour. I don't give a fuck if you shift before that, but you'll wait an hour before you leave. And you will leave me, my father, my mate, and my friends alone. If I hear the *slightest* hint that you tried *anything*, I will find you. And I will kill you."

Dee nodded. "I'm done. We'll be gone."

Quincy tilted his head toward Dumber. "Get him to his family for a proper burial. He's an asshole, and he almost killed my mate, but he's already facing Osiris and the test of maat over that."

"We'll take care of it." Dee shook his head. "Good luck, dude. I wouldn't want to be you."

Quincy snorted. "Right now, *I* don't want to be me." He glanced at Miles. "Except for one thing."

Chapter 13

MILES WORRIED over Quincy's silence the whole way back to the hotel. When they'd gotten to the Challenger, Quincy had climbed into the back seat without speaking, then Jamie slid in the front on the same side, and Miles and Chad put the bags into the trunk. Before they closed it, Chad turned to him.

"Watch him. This is gonna fuck with him for a while." Chad frowned. "In the time I was on the force, I discharged my weapon four times in the line of duty. Twice, it didn't hit anything. Once it injured a guy in the leg. Once… once it killed. I spent a year in counseling. Some of that was for other stuff, but the idea that I took a life seriously fucked with me."

Miles nodded. "I… it's not the same when I lose a patient, but it's hard. I can imagine well enough, and Quincy… for all his aloof exterior, he isn't nearly as cold as he'd have people believe."

"Exactly. It'll fuck with him. Unless you're a sociopath or psychopath, anytime life ends fucks with you, especially if you cause it." Chad took a deep breath. "I might suggest getting him alone when we get back and giving him a chance to deal with it. This might seem… crass, but sex might help. He'll need to *stop* thinking."

"Thanks. Gods, how fucked up was that?" Miles asked, shaking his head.

"No shit. I've interrogated a lot of assholes—both innocent and not—over the years. None of it was anything like this. I think I'll have to help my own mate deal with some of this stuff. He's never been through any of it either."

"Yeah. I'm just glad we're here to do it. Let's get back to the hotel and go from there."

Chad nodded and shut the trunk. Miles went around and climbed in next to Quincy before Chad got in and started the car. Before they were out of the parking lot, Quincy was against him. Miles put his arm around Quincy's shoulders and kissed the top of his head.

They made the trip back in silence. Even Chad didn't cuss New York drivers when they got into the city. As a measure of just *how* fucked up it all was, Chad even let the valet park the car.

Miles guided Quincy straight into the bedroom when they got to the suite.

Quincy looked at him for a long moment, but couldn't seem to say anything.

"How about a shower?" Miles suggested.

Quincy nodded and turned to the bathroom. Miles helped him get undressed and under the hot water.

"Do you want company?"

Quincy shook his head. "No, uh, no, I'm just going to get clean."

Miles nodded and kissed Quincy's temple. "I'll leave the door open. Call me if you need me."

"Okay." Quincy bent his head under the water, and with nothing more he could do, Miles went back out to the bedroom.

He checked the lube to make sure they still had some, then unpacked and put the suitcase and his medical kit away. By the time he'd undressed himself, though, and Quincy hadn't come out, he decided to check. Quincy was usually quick at showering, and while Miles knew he needed to try to deal with the death, it still seemed to be taking too long.

Quincy's pale skin was almost red, and he was still scrubbing furiously, despite the fact that he looked quite clean. Miles frowned, not sure if he should interrupt or not. But when Quincy put *more* soap on the scrubby and went back to cleaning himself again, Miles stepped into the shower.

Without speaking he took the scrubby from Quincy and set it aside, then guided his mate under the spray. It was a testament to how messed up Quincy was that he didn't even speak, much less fight. Miles helped Quincy rinse, then picked up the shampoo.

"It's not maat," Quincy finally muttered. "Is it?" He looked up at Miles.

Miles paused in scrubbing Quincy's scalp. "Did you pray to Thoth? Talk to Bastet?"

Quincy swallowed. "Yes. Of course, they don't answer directly or right away. I just…." He shook his head, looking away for a moment, then back up to Miles. "Gods… what must *you* think of me?"

"Hey, hey." Miles quickly rinsed Quincy's hair, then pulled him back in. Miles wrapped both arms around him, kissing one temple. "I think you did an incredibly difficult thing that you had to do."

"He was going to kill you," Quincy whispered.

"I know. And he would have killed us if he'd gotten free. If you hadn't done what you did, things could have gone very differently. Jamie might well be dead right now."

Quincy shuddered. "But you don't... you're a *healer*, Miles."

"That doesn't mean I won't do what's necessary. If it came down to choosing between him and any of us, I'd have squeezed that trigger too, Quince." He brushed one of Quincy's cheeks with his thumb. "This is why it's maat. It *is* justice. How many people do you think he's killed in his life? I guarantee you his attempt on me wasn't the first time. Isn't it balance to stop him from killing again?"

Quincy swallowed and stared at Miles's chest. "I don't know. Maybe?"

"What does your heart tell you? What wisdom might Thoth give?"

With a sigh Quincy closed his eyes. "I... gods, Miles, I took a *life*." He shook his head, and to Miles's surprise, tears leaked from his eyes. "Bastet, help me," he whispered.

Miles tightened his arms and kissed Quincy's hair, giving his mate the opportunity to let it out. He didn't speak, didn't push, just held Quincy tightly, running a hand over his back. The sound of the falling water almost drowned out the soft sobs, but he could still hear them. Shakes accompanied the sobs, and Miles wished there was some magic thing he could say, some way he could make Quincy's pain lessen—and not just because he was feeling it across their bond either. The helplessness chafed, but he pushed it aside to focus on Quincy.

When the trembling stopped, Miles turned the water off and tugged the towel down. He dried Quincy off, then gave it a cursory run over himself before tossing it back on the rack. Taking Quincy's hand, Miles led him into the bedroom and guided him to the bed. As soon as Miles slid in on the other side of the bed, Quincy rolled into his arms.

"Please, I...." Quincy shook his head, and Miles stilled it, cupping a cheek. He leaned in and caught Quincy's lips with his own. He rolled them, settling on top of Quincy, and deepening the kiss, doing his damnedest to keep his mate's focus on him, on their bodies, on *feeling* rather than thinking. He rocked into Quincy's hardening cock, his own stiffening just as quickly.

Quincy slid his hands down Miles's back, nails scraping over his skin. His legs came up, and he wrapped them around Miles's waist. Miles pulled back long enough to grab the lube and was gratified to see heat and need in Quincy's eyes, rather than the pain that had been there before. It was still there, Miles was sure, but, for the moment, buried. With another deep kiss, he did his damnedest to make sure it stayed that way for just a little while longer.

THE NEXT morning Miles was glad Quincy seemed a bit less fragile, even if his skin was still paler than usual and he was still quiet. When they went out to the living room, Chad and Jamie sat at the table, talking quietly.

Quincy crossed over and stood next to Jamie. "How are you?"

Jamie swallowed but nodded. "Better. How are you?"

Miles joined them and took Quincy's hand.

Quincy glanced up and squeezed it, then looked back at Jamie. "Better. Have you... have you dealt with it?"

Jamie nodded again. "Mostly. What about you? I can't imagine what that must have been like."

"Some." Quincy swallowed. "It'll take a while for me to really deal with it completely."

"Yeah. That's what Chad said."

Quincy turned to Chad. "Have you?"

Chad nodded. "Yes. Once. I hope I never have to again. You're a hell of a man... cat.... Q."

Quincy cleared his throat, his lips tilting slightly, and turned back to Jamie. "I'm... sorry."

Jamie held up a hand and stood up. "I would very likely be dead right now if you hadn't done that."

"It's my fault you were there in the first place!"

Shaking his head, Jamie reached out and touched Quincy's shoulder. "No. It isn't. I was there because I wanted to be. I was there because my friend needed help. If it hadn't been last night, I'd still have a first of being in a situation like that someday. With what Chad and I do? It was bound to happen."

Quincy took a deep breath. "Thank you. I'm still sorry you had to go through it."

Jamie shrugged a shoulder. "I'm sorry I didn't do it for you. I saw him move, but… I froze."

Quincy shook his head. "Oh hell no. If it had to happen, between the two of us, I'd rather be the one to have to deal with it. I'm glad you don't have to go through this."

Jamie didn't speak for a moment, then, to Miles's surprise, hugged Quincy. To Miles's *further* surprise, Quincy hugged him back. "Thank you," Jamie whispered.

"You're welcome." He squeezed Jamie gently, then pulled back and turned to Chad. "So, chief, what do we do?"

Chad waved a hand at the other seats. "We order breakfast and decide what the next steps are."

Miles had to nudge Quincy to eat more than a few bites, but eventually got a decent amount of meat and eggs into him. When they'd cleared the dishes and had more coffee, Chad got up to pace.

"Okay, Jamie."

"What, me?" Jamie blinked.

Chad snorted. "You're the only Jamie here."

Jamie flipped him off.

Chad grinned. "That's my mate." He kissed Jamie's temple, and Jamie rolled his eyes but was smiling. "Now. What are the three biggest motives for most crimes?"

Jamie frowned. "Love, money, and revenge."

"Right. So, out of those three, what seems the most likely for what's going on?"

"Money," Quincy said.

"Not revenge?" Miles asked.

Quincy shook his head. "I don't think so. I mean, the wolves have almost wiped the cats out a few times over the millennia, but since they established peace a couple hundred years ago, the cats have focused mostly inward. There's no love lost, of course…."

"But that's a long way from revenge." Chad nodded.

"Right. And as far as I know, no one in the pride is old enough to have fought in the last war."

"Then money." Chad pointed at Quincy. "However, I'm not sure how the cats could benefit financially by starting a war, but my *guess* is one of two things. The first possibility is that they thought they'd get a hold of your money. I'm betting there's at least a trust for you from Dad."

Quincy nodded. "There is. If he died I'd inherit. Not that I *want* it—"

Chad held up a hand. "Yeah, I get that. But these guys don't. So if you survived and Dad died, you'd have all that money they could get to. And a puppet that let them run the pride however they wanted."

Miles coughed. "Idiots."

Quincy grinned. "Indeed."

"Right. Or the other possibility: they're being paid to help start a war."

Miles, Quincy, and Jamie all blinked. "But... why? Who?"

Chad shrugged. "I don't know. We have a lot of questions and very few answers. But we have a starting point. If it's about money?"

"Then we follow the money," Jamie said, nodding.

"Precisely." Chad looked at Quincy, then back at Jamie. "That's on you two. I can look at some of it, but it's not my forte." He turned to Miles. "It'll be up to you and me to brainstorm the rest of the questions and how to find the answers."

"I'm not sure how much help I'll be." Miles shrugged a little helplessly.

Chad waved a hand. "Sometimes I just need a live body to talk to."

"Does that mean you've talked to dead bodies?" Jamie asked, eyebrow raised.

"As a matter of fact, yes. When I was on the force. But those conversations were usually pretty one-sided."

"Usually?" Quincy smirked at him.

"Hey. Dead bodies can tell you a lot."

Miles nodded. "That's true. Can I just say, though, doctor or not, I'm glad we don't have to talk to any for this?"

Chad snickered. "Yet."

"Please, can we try not to end up with any more dead bodies?" Quincy asked.

Chad cleared his throat. "I don't want them either. Okay. Let's start with the money. We should print stuff out, though. There's too much chance it'll disappear."

Miles frowned. "I'm sure the hotel has a printer, but... do we trust sending stuff to it?"

Quincy shook his head. "No. There's an Apple store across the street. We could go there and get one."

"You use an Apple?" Chad asked, wrinkling his nose.

Quincy rolled his eyes. "Artist? Of *course* I use Apple."

"Dude, we're Windows guys, all the way."

Miles held up his phone. "I, uh, have a smartphone. Android for the win?"

All three of them burst out laughing.

"Right," Chad said, chuckling. "I think I saw a Staples up a few blocks. We can go get stuff there for the Win machines."

"Okay. Um… I might sound a little paranoid, but I'm not sure how far we should go right now. I'm sure it'll take the elders a couple of days to dig up someone new, but they probably will," Miles pointed out.

Quincy nodded. "Yeah, probably. I think we're okay today yet, but let's not go far. We'll stick to room service or delivery and these two short runs."

Chad rubbed his hands together. "Good. Let's get that taken care of. Then we can work on the rest."

MILES WAS impressed despite himself. Chad had brought back a whiteboard and markers, and set it up on the wet bar counter somehow. He'd also bought sticky notes in a bunch of colors and a big package of Scotch tape. Miles had no idea what he was doing. It didn't look like anything he'd ever seen before.

Across the very top of the board, he wrote, *Start a war?* then *Control the pride?* Below it, he'd written four words: *money, power, greed, revenge.* Down the left side of the board, he'd taped driver's license pictures of Abraham Thomas, Charles Ross, Quincy, Aubrey, Miles, and Payne Stewart a.k.a. Tweedle Dee.

"Investigations board?" Jamie asked. "My profs said those were just, like, stuff they made up on TV."

"Your profs were idiots, then," Chad said, stepping back. "Or, well, I don't know what other detectives did. I did my boards at home usually, not at the station, because I did my best thinking at home." He shrugged. "This works for me. I like to see it laid out visually. I can sometimes see stuff that way that I might miss otherwise." Chad picked up a pad of sticky notes and started writing. He took the top one off and stuck it up next to the pictures, then wrote *timeline* above it. The first one he'd put up said *hired to find Q.* He went back to the sticky notes and started writing again.

Miles left him to it, moved over to Quincy, and kissed the top of Quincy's head. "How's it coming?"

"Slow," Quincy said, sighing. "It takes a while to dig through and find the right things."

"Can I do anything to help?"

Quincy looked up. "Would it be horrible if I said, 'make sure to keep the coffee coming'?"

Miles chuckled and shook his head. "Not horrible at all. It's something I can do." He glanced at the clock. "How about I keep track of food and such too, hmm?"

"Thank you. I love you."

"I love you too." Miles chuckled and kissed Quincy quickly, then went over to the iPad to put in a fresh order for coffee and some food for everyone. Then he went back and stood next to Chad.

He'd added several more sticky notes in the same place as the first, all with events written on them. "Timeline?"

"It helps me if I keep track of exactly when stuff happens. I can sometimes see connections that I couldn't before."

"Makes sense." Miles frowned. One whole section of the board was still blank. "What goes there?"

"That'll be the 'how' part. We'll put some of the money stuff we find there. But there are still some great gaping holes in all of this, and until I figure out exactly *what* they're trying to do, I don't know that I'll be able to figure out all of the how."

Miles nodded, pursing his lips. "If the New York wolves know about the cats, is it possible one of them is involved?"

"Good point," Chad said, picking up a blue marker. He drew a box under the pictures and put *wolf?* inside it. "What would he have to gain by helping the cats, though? Or is he working against them? And for what?" Chad shook his head, rubbing his face. "Too many fuckin' questions."

"I ordered coffee," Miles said, chuckling.

"Maybe we need to simplify a little," Jamie suggested.

Chad turned and raised his eyebrows. "Oh?"

Jamie blushed a little but nodded. "I mean… okay, yeah, it may be about starting an interspecies war. But maybe if we just focus on the parts that involve Quincy, we'll *get* to the rest of it."

Chad nodded slowly. "That makes sense. So…." He picked up the red marker and drew a line between Abraham Thomas and Charles Ross, then an arrow to Dee, then from Dee to Quincy. "They hire Dee—and Dumb and Dumber—to rough Quincy up to convince him to come back.

That goes along with the puppet idea. But, of course, Quincy gives them the metaphorical finger."

"I'm pretty sure I gave them the literal finger, too, before they beat me up."

Miles chuckled. "I'd be surprised if you didn't."

"Me too," Chad said. "Okay, so they leave—message delivered. But obviously it doesn't work. Dee and Dumb follow Q, but Dumber stays behind and goes after you." Chad pointed at Miles, then drew a box for Dumber by the pictures and another red arrow from Dumber's box to Miles's picture. "Except that fails too."

"Everyone disappears for a while," Miles said, "then…. New York."

"Right." Chad set the marker down and paced for a few moments. "It comes back to the fact that whatever the elders want, it's bigger than Q. The amounts we've seen so far are just too big. So if they wanted his money, was it to help finance a war? What would they get out of one?"

Miles frowned. "Power?" He pointed to the word on the board. "Maybe they actually think the cats would win?" He turned to Quincy. "No offense, babe."

Quincy snorted. "None taken. We wouldn't. Just from sheer numbers."

"So, they're not that stupid. Something else is going on here, but I don't know what and it's driving me nuts."

Miles patted his shoulder when a knock came, and he went to the door to greet room service. He waited for the server to bring in the food and set it down. The guy sent a look at the board Chad stood in front of and his eyebrows went up.

Miles smiled, handed the guy his tip, and looked pointedly at the door. "Thank you."

He gave a polite smile in return and beat a hasty retreat.

Miles made sure everyone had food and Quincy was actually eating it, and then he took his plate and burgers back to the board. "Wolves."

Chad looked at him. "What?"

"I wonder if they weren't promised somehow that not only would they survive, but that they'd be put in charge of whatever cats were left. And if so… that means they'd be working with a wolf."

Jamie frowned. "How do you figure?"

"No, he's got a point," Chad said, nodding. "When you think about the fact that two or three *packs* have more wolves than a pride that covers several *states*, they can't be that idiotic to think they'd win. Which means they have a promise from *someone* that they'd be left alone. And who else would they be fighting?"

"Humans?" Jamie asked.

Chad shook his head. "No. Truthfully, if they wanted to start killing humans, as fragile as they are compared to shifters, if they were halfway sneaky about it, they wouldn't need assurances."

"We're not that much stronger," Miles said, frowning.

"Think about how many bullets you pulled out of Dee. If a human took that many?"

"Well, they might survive, but I see your point. They're certainly not going to recover in a few hours."

"Exactly," Chad said, turning back to the board. "Besides, I don't think the cats hate humans the same way they do wolves. I mean…." He turned to Quincy. "Hey, Q. Do you guys have a name you call humans?"

Quincy shook his head. "No. They're just humans."

"But you call wolves dogs, right?"

Quincy nodded. "Yeah. There's still a lot of hate among the cats for wolves, even if it's not, like, what would spawn revenge, if you know what I mean."

"Yeah. No, I don't think it's got anything to do with humans. I doubt they'd cry over human collateral damage, but I don't think the humans are the target."

"Are there other shifters?" Jamie asked.

That brought Chad up. "Or other creatures in general?"

Quincy turned around and raised his eyebrows. "Other shifters? Not that I know about. And creatures? You mean like vampires?" He smirked.

Chad shrugged. "Three months ago, I didn't know there were people who could take the shape of a wolf, much less a jaguar."

"Point," Quincy said, nodding. "But no, not that I am aware of. There might be, but… what? I don't think so, and if so, not someone the cats have any kind of issue with."

"Then that leaves a wolf," Miles said, sighing.

"But who?" Jamie asked.

Chad frowned. "Aye. That's the question, isn't it?"

Chapter 14

QUINCY SAT back in his chair and sighed. "As far as I can see, it all leads back to Abraham Thomas. There are transfers to and from Charles Ross, but the majority of the money goes to—and from—Thomas."

Chad stepped up behind him and peered over his shoulder. "So, he's likely the one we need to look at."

Quincy nodded. "Yeah. Now, that's all I've found so far. And that's all that's under that name. I'd be surprised, if they're dealing with anyone with half a brain, if they don't have other names."

Chad glanced over at Jamie. "Think you can find them?"

Jamie hesitated. "Maybe? I don't know. I mean… I'm not any better than he is." He tilted his head toward Quincy.

Quincy shrugged. "I don't know about that, but working together, we should be able to find it."

"Still, it's a step in the right direction. Let's see what else we can find. Cell phone records, e-mail, anything like that. We need more than just numbers transferring. And we still need to figure out where those are going *to*." Chad rubbed his face.

"There are at least three separate accounts the transfers are coming from, and a couple that they're going to. I just haven't found yet what those go to." Quincy shook his head. "That's going to take more time. Following numbered accounts takes a while."

Chad nodded. "Then it takes a while. We need that information before we do more."

Quincy went back to the computer and brought up the bank records again. He frowned. "Part of the problem is that the transfer goes to another bank, right? But once there, the amounts aren't the same. The money then gets held there before the transfers get split up, which makes it hard to track what the next step is."

"Makes sense, though, doesn't it?" Miles asked. "If all the amounts were exactly the same, it'd be too easy to follow."

"Yeah. So… we have some math to do. Ugh. That is not my favorite thing." Quincy picked up his coffee cup, only to find it was empty. "How many have I had?" he asked, scowling into it.

"Um, I think that makes ten," Miles said, smirking. "Good thing you've got such a high metabolism."

"Maybe," Quincy said, snorting. "Or maybe I wouldn't need eleven cups to get this shit done if I didn't."

Miles laughed and took the cup, kissing the top of his head. "You worry about the work. I'll worry about the coffee."

Quincy nodded. "Thanks," he said before turning his attention back to the data. "Any luck on e-mail accounts?" he asked Jamie.

Jamie shook his head. "Not yet. Going to take a while for that, I think. Same with cell phones. So far, I'm not finding any registered under either name. There was a number in Dee's phone, but it went to the house phone at Thomas's address, which we already knew. And I can't believe he'd do all his work out of his house like that. That's just *asking* to be caught."

"Maybe he doesn't care," Chad suggested.

"Hmm." Miles set Quincy's refilled cup on the table. "Dee said he was arrogant. Maybe he thinks he's untouchable?"

Quincy blinked. "Well, Abraham Thomas has attitude. He was one that always pissed both me and my father off. Charles Ross wasn't much better." He frowned. "It could be that we won't find anything."

"Uh… why not?" Jamie asked, tilting his head.

"They're both pushing two hundred years old. Telephones weren't even invented when they were born."

"Maybe they're Luddites?" Miles asked.

"That's definitely possible." Quincy made a face. "They always claimed technology was just going to cause problems." He sighed and took a sip of coffee. "That means, though… there's only so much we'll find this way. There *will* be a trail. It's impossible not to have one, but I'd bet we won't find e-mails or cell phones or the like."

"Ugh," Chad grumbled. "Well, let's get what we can, and we'll worry about the rest later."

Quincy sighed. "Yeah. There has to be a money trail back. So… math. Whee."

"OKAY, MY eyes are crossing, but… I think I've got it. You're not going to like it, though," Quincy said, sighing.

"Wolf?" Chad asked.

Quincy nodded. "Yeah. I know the name, and he's based here in New York. I, of course, don't know where he is on the hierarchy of the pack or anything like that. But…. The cats aren't the only ones he's getting money from."

Chad blinked. "No?"

"No." Quincy shook his head. "There are also transfers coming in from a bank… in Denver."

"What the fuck?" Jamie asked, scowling.

"Denver? What am I missing?" Chad asked. "Why does that sound familiar?"

"Denver is the American wolf headquarters," Miles said quietly. "Where the alpha prime lives."

"Oh fuck me," Chad whispered. "But… would he really be involved in this?"

Jamie shrugged. "I have no idea. I could believe the xenophobia, but… this goes *way* beyond that."

"That's even an understatement," Quincy said, frowning.

"Well, how the hell do we prove something like this? And what do we do with it?" Chad asked, looking from one to the next.

Quincy shook his head. "I don't know. Has Noah gotten back to you about the cats?"

"Oh yeah," Jamie said. "As far as he's been able to tell, no one but New York and Forbes knows—and, he's assuming, the prime."

"Oh yeah, the prime knows," Quincy said. "I'm sure of that."

"Well. That narrows down the involvement, at least. What does that wolf have to do with it? And what's his name?"

"Morgan Daniels," Quincy said. "I have no idea."

"A go-between?" Miles asked.

Chad frowned. "That's possible. If the prime *is* involved in this, then he wouldn't want a direct connection."

"But… why?" Jamie asked, shaking his head.

"That I don't know, and I suspect we won't unless we get the prime to tell us himself. Suffice it to say, he is for now. The transfers

are too coincidental. And I don't believe in that much coincidence."
Chad turned to his board and wrote a big dollar sign at the top of the
how column, then below it, Thomas's name, Morgan Daniel's name,
and alpha prime, then drew lines between them. "Okay. We have a trail.
Now… we have to prove it. A money exchange isn't enough to prove
they're planning a war."

Quincy shook his head. "No, it isn't. I don't know if your prime
disdains technology as much as the elders do, but I'd bet anything we do
find would be too vague to be useful."

"Yeah, I'm sure it would." Chad pointed to Jamie. "Look anyway.
We might get lucky. In the meantime we need to see if we can find out
where this guy is in pack structure. Miles, could you call Noah? Make
sure, at least, he's not the alpha here?"

Miles nodded. "Done." He pulled his cell phone out and started
dialing.

Quincy met Chad's gaze. "I can't believe what I've landed myself
in." He shook his head.

"Good thing Miles doesn't shy away from a bit of trouble." Chad
grinned.

Quincy laughed. "Really." He sobered. "Fuck, though. This has the
potential to seriously fuck with both our kinds."

Chad nodded. "Yeah, it does. If it's true. We could be off base."

"But you don't think so," Quincy said.

"No, I don't." Chad sighed. "We need proof. Then, I guess, we
figure out where to go. If we do have proof of what your elders are up to,
your father needs to know."

"He'll probably need to go to the tepey-iret." Quincy frowned.
"This is a fucking mess."

"You can say that again," Chad muttered, turning back to his board.
"More fucking questions." He shook his head. "Let's get answers we can
prove, then we'll figure out who to talk to."

"THIS CLUSTERFUCK just keeps getting better and better," Chad groaned
later that evening. He leaned back in his chair and rubbed his eyes. "Okay,
so, we have no e-mail, no phone records, *nothing* electronic except some
driver's license pictures and the bank records, is that right?"

"Yup," Jamie said, sighing. "It's just not there. Even the wolf—who I was glad to hear *wasn't* the alpha—doesn't have much we can track. We can connect the money, but that's all, and that's no proof of anything except… they gave each other money."

Quincy had to fight the urge to growl, knowing it'd come out just like his cat. He wasn't sure he wanted to try to explain that to the hotel staff. "We're going to have to find physical evidence." He dropped his face into his palms. "I so don't want to do that."

"I don't want to spend the rest of our lives in the Plaza either," Miles said, pouring fresh coffee into each of their mugs. "Not that I don't like it here. It is nice, but…."

Chad shook his head. "I want to shift and run. My wolf isn't happy being stuck this long."

"None of us are," Quincy said. "My cat is about to claw through my skin. The stress alone…."

"Yeah, well, unless we want to take a chance and go over to Central Park, we're stuck for now." Jamie sighed. "Okay, so… where do we start looking for physical evidence?"

"Thomas's place." Chad got up and stood in front of his board again. "I'm thinking that's the place to go." He shook his head. "Everything from this end—from Quincy's—leads back to him. I have no idea if he's stupid enough to keep records or anything, but I think we need to try."

"I should call my father," Quincy mused. "Or see him somehow."

"Get him down here," Miles suggested. "Even if they know he's meeting you, that doesn't tell them much. I mean…." He shrugged. "You're in New York and yet haven't admitted to being back. They'd have to be *completely* stupid to not realize you've figured *something* out by now."

"True. Okay." Quincy grabbed his cell phone and stared at it for a moment, then sighed and typed out. *Meet in Palm Court. An hour?*

It took less than two minutes for a reply. Quincy would have been more shocked if his father hadn't behaved the way he had at dinner the other night.

Will be there.

"Well, that was easy." Quincy sighed. "If everything could go the way that and Noah's report did…."

"Yeah, right," Chad said, snorting. "We wouldn't still be here."

"Okay. That's set up. What's next?"

"We need to figure out how and when to get into Thomas's house."
Chad grinned. "Luckily, that's something I have a bit of experience in."

QUINCY HAD found a corner table, away from most of the other
patrons. Miles, Chad, and Jamie all sat with him, and if Aubrey Archer
was surprised to see everyone, he didn't show it. He did look everyone
over as he approached the table, but that was all.

"Quincy. Miles. Good to see you again." He nodded at each of them.

"Chad Sutton—you should remember him," Quincy said, smirking.
"And his mate and partner, Jamie Ryan."

"Nice to meet both of you," Aubrey said, shaking their hands
before taking a seat.

Quincy refused to be shocked by his father's behavior. He'd always
been much more abrasive than this, much more standoffish, and Quincy
wasn't sure what to do with it. Still, he had bigger issues than his father's
change of attitude. "So... we've found some things out that you need to
be aware of, both because you are my father and because you are tepey."

Aubrey's eyebrows went up. "Oh?"

Quincy nodded. "Yes. You might want a good strong scotch—"

"Or two," Chad said.

"—or two," Quincy agreed. "Before you hear all of this."

Aubrey blinked but nodded. "Very well."

Quincy glanced around, and just as he did, their server materialized
next to the table. Aubrey put in his order, and the man disappeared almost
as swiftly.

"All right, then."

Quincy took a deep breath. "Okay. Here goes...."

It took three scotches, more than an hour, and a good deal of help
from the others, but they finally managed to get everything outlined.

Aubrey sat back, looking thoughtful for a long time. "That's... I
never really thought it went beyond our pride." He sighed. "We're going
to have to go to the tepey-iret. This is way beyond my jurisdiction."

Chad nodded. "I had a feeling you'd need to. Don't just yet, though."

Aubrey raised his eyebrows. "Why?"

"We need more evidence. What we have right now doesn't prove
a damned thing. Most of this is more or less conjecture until we have
something more linking these guys." Chad shrugged. "If we don't find

anything in Thomas's place, we'll have to look elsewhere. But it's a place to start."

"What if you don't find any more evidence of this at all?" Aubrey asked.

Quincy frowned. "Then we're back at the beginning, more or less, because either we're wrong or we need to find another way to prove it. Let's hope we find what we need."

"I'm not sure I want to prove my pride is involved in something like this," Aubrey said, shaking his head. "But—" He held up a hand when Quincy opened his mouth. "But, if they are, then I simply don't want them in my pride. But this… you're talking *treason*. This is beyond any punishment I can give."

"Proof first," Chad said. "We'll worry about the rest when we have it."

Aubrey nodded. "How can I help?"

Chad cleared his throat. "We need all we can get on Thomas's habits. Employees, schedule, anything like that you can give us. Do you know if he's got a security system—he seems to not like technology in other ways, but does that extend to his house? That sort of thing."

"I can get that, sure. Are you planning on breaking and entering?" Aubrey asked with a raised eyebrow.

Chad flashed a grin. "I don't have to break to enter."

Quincy snorted. "He got into my place without leaving a trace."

Aubrey inclined his head in acknowledgment of that. "Very well. We just don't need to bail anyone out of jail."

"No way I could go to jail right now," Chad said, shaking his head.

"Is there a particular reason?"

"He's a newly made wolf," Miles said. "He's only had his wolf for a couple of months."

"And you're controlling him this well already?" Aubrey asked.

Chad shrugged a shoulder. "We seem to understand each other, for the most part."

"Except for skunks." Jamie snickered.

Chad elbowed his mate. "But in extreme stress, I can't keep him contained yet. If I were locked up, he'd likely break free."

"Well, then, don't get caught," Aubrey said.

Quincy blinked at his father. "Did you just make a joke?"

"I've been known to, now and again." Aubrey tilted his head. "When this is all over, I think you and I need to have a long talk."

"I guess so," Quincy muttered.

"Well. I'm going to go. I'll get that information to you as soon as I can. Look for a cat messenger directly to your door."

"Are there cats you can trust?" Quincy asked, frowning.

"Yes. There are a few I'm sure are not involved." Aubrey looked at Quincy. "Let me know when you make your attempt. If nothing else, I'll be ready to bail you out right away."

Chad chuckled. "Thanks."

"Yes, thank you, Father," Quincy said, standing.

"You can thank me later. Good luck."

Quincy stared at his father's back, shaking his head. "He's changed," he muttered.

Miles wrapped his arms around Quincy from behind. "Good or bad?"

"Good." Quincy swallowed, not sure how to put it in words. "I… back when I was growing up, he'd never have cracked a joke like that. He'd never have greeted Chad and Jamie so… nicely. I don't…." He shook his head again, then sighed. "Well, we still have work to do."

"Yeah. We can't depend on Aubrey for all our information. Thomas pays bills like everyone else. Let's see if his electric usage tells us anything," Jamie mused.

Quincy blinked at him. "It's no wonder I didn't stand a chance against you two. Really glad you're on my side now."

Chapter 15

"ARE YOU fucking kidding me?" Chad asked, taking the coffee cup Miles handed him and peering at the printouts he'd spread across the table.

"Nope. Eleven acres. The house itself has nineteen thousand square feet. Thirty rooms, including twelve bathrooms." Quincy shook his head.

"Fuck me," Miles whispered.

"Later," Quincy replied, smirking.

Miles grinned and waggled his eyebrows.

"Much later. This is going to take work." Chad rubbed his face. "I guess there are rooms we can immediately ignore—the kitchen, the bathrooms, but…." He shook his head. "Jesus. That leaves seventeen possible rooms."

"Well, we could probably ignore the steam room too," Jamie pointed out.

"Yay. Sixteen." Chad rolled his eyes. "Okay, we're going to have to do more than a little surveillance on that one. There's no way we can just sneak in, even *if* there's no security system, and look around. We'd need hours."

"I think some of this wing," Quincy said, pointing, "is actually servants' quarters. I *have* been here, but it's been a long time, and he's likely changed at least a few things. Not a lot, he's very much a traditionalist, but…."

"But we can't count on your memory, no offense."

Quincy shook his head. "None taken. I'm not an elephant shifter. I'm a cat."

Chad blinked. "Do those exist? How the fuck would that work?" All three burst out laughing, and Chad grinned. "Good. I'm not *that* crazy."

"The problem I'm seeing," Jamie said, frowning, "is that there's no way to get close in a car." He opened his laptop wider and turned it to show the Google map. Forest surrounded the estate for quite a distance.

Chad wrinkled his nose. "No, there isn't."

"We could shift," Miles suggested.

"That means we watch naked." Chad frowned. "And with no equipment. I'm not sure I like that either. We'll need to give it some thought and hope your father comes through soon," Chad said, glancing at Quincy.

"What if we park near the access road and watch it first? Maybe here?" Jamie tapped the screen. "I bet the Challenger would fade in pretty well, especially at night."

Chad pursed his lips. "That's a possibility."

"I mean, we're not going to see everything, but we could start with a feel for how much traffic goes in and out."

"That would be good to know." Chad nodded. "We could do that while we wait for more from your father, Q."

"And maybe while we're there, we'll come up with another idea for how to get closer." Miles leaned in and peered. "Is that… a putting green?"

"And a swimming pool with pool house, and tennis courts. Two English gardens, a three-car garage, and a carriage house." Quincy shook his head. "And he's *alone* there."

"Where's the partridge in a pear tree?" Chad asked, shaking his head. "And what the fuck does one guy need with a place like that?"

"He doesn't." Miles couldn't keep the disgust out of his voice entirely. "I mean… I make good money. I could own a house, probably one of those huge ones in Squirrel Hill, but…."

"Yeah, I don't see you doing that either." Chad shook his head.

"Okay. Well, I think we can rule out the pool house too." Jamie sighed. "When do we want to watch the road?"

Chad looked up at the clock. "Q, how long would it take to get there? Without the cemetery traffic this time?"

"Less than an hour."

"All right. We can do this one tonight. We'll see how far we can get in the car, then go from there."

"WOW, THIS *is* worse than waiting for the cats to show up," Jamie said before taking a sip of coffee.

"Told you it would be. This is *the* most boring part of investigation ever." Chad chuckled. "Hey, Q, any donuts left?"

Quincy sniffed. "I'm not that much of a pig. Of course."

Miles grinned and kissed Quincy's temple. "Of course you're not." He handed the box up to Chad.

Chad opened it. "Okay, pick a donut," he said, holding it out to Jamie, who did. Chad set the box down, then took one for himself. "Okay, now. You have to break these in half, 'cause they're too big."

"Okay," Jamie said, raising an eyebrow.

Miles buried the snicker, sure he knew where this was going.

"Now, you gotta hold the cup close to your mouth so you don't drip, and you can't dunk for more than a couple of seconds, or you'll soak the donut too much and it'll end up a lump in the bottom of the cup."

Quincy snorted. "Are you seriously showing him the proper way to dunk a donut in coffee?"

"Hey! It's a delicate operation. Takes a steady hand and good timing!" Chad managed to sound truly offended.

Miles lost the battle and started laughing.

Meanwhile, Jamie had dunked his donut and was already eating it.

"Bastet, give me strength," Quincy muttered, but Miles noted he seemed to be fighting a smile too.

Miles was about to say something when a car pulled out of the access road.

Chad sat up slowly, watching it carefully. "Get that plate number?" he asked.

"Yup," Quincy said. "Already working on it." He'd set his coffee down and was furiously typing into his computer. A few moments later, he chuckled. "That was his, all right. One of…." He tapped a few more keys, then nodded. "Eight different vehicles. All registered under his name."

"Ugh. Too damned rich," Chad muttered. "What does he do with eight cars?"

"My father probably has as much money, maybe more than Thomas does, but even he doesn't have eight vehicles. As far as I know, he owns three, including the one he's driven in."

"He has a driver?" Chad asked, looking into the rearview.

Quincy nodded. "Yeah, for events and the like and when he's in the city. Cabs stink too much, but driving is just…."

"Yeah, no," Chad said, shaking his head. "Not something I'd want to do all the time."

"Was Thomas being driven just now?" Miles asked.

"Yeah, why?" Quincy said.

Chad stared at him in the mirror for a moment. "Nothing. Or, well, it could be. Something to consider, though, if we do manage to get in, is how many servants he has."

"So, how are we going to get to the house?" Jamie asked.

Chad sighed. "I've been trying to figure that out."

"What kind of equipment do we need?" Miles asked.

"Binoculars. I'd like a good camera with a decent telephoto lens. Listening equipment would be nice, but I doubt we can get that close." Chad shook his head. "We can walk, I guess. It doesn't look *that* far."

"Four men walking through these woods would throw up so many alarms, it isn't funny," Quincy said, shaking his head. "While Thomas may not have a security system, everyone else around here will, and most of those woods actually belong to other properties. I have no idea what *kind* of security, but there are enough animals in the area that I'm sure it's calibrated to ignore them."

"What if…," Jamie said, then shook his head.

"What?" Chad asked.

"What if we tied it on somehow?"

Quincy raised an eyebrow. "Tied it on?"

"Uh, when Tanner had to go get Finley, he took a cell phone he'd tied up in a bandana and put around his neck. What if we found a way to put a bag or something with the equipment in it and put it on one of us."

Miles blinked. "That's not a bad idea."

"Those cameras aren't tiny like a cell phone," Chad pointed out.

Quincy nodded. "Yeah, but… it doesn't have to fit in a bandana. I have an idea. When do you want to do this?"

"How much time do you need to put together your idea?"

Quincy shrugged. "A few hours and a bit of shopping."

"Let's go tomorrow, then."

"I'M GOING to look ridiculous," Chad muttered, shaking his head.

"Who's going to see you?" Miles asked.

Jamie sighed. "You don't have to carry it."

Chad waved that away. "I'm joking. Mostly."

"Well, go ahead and shift." Quincy took the backpack he'd bought earlier in the day, now filled with the equipment Chad wanted, and, once Chad had shifted, squatted next to him. "You're such a cute little puppy!"

Chad growled.

Miles grinned. "Go ahead and bite him. He'll heal."

Quincy glared up at Miles, who winked.

Chad chuffed and lifted his head.

Quincy got the bag onto Chad's back, and then they worked the straps around him the way they'd figured out earlier. Each of the big straps crisscrossed over his ribs. One smaller strap went around each of his forelegs at his shoulders, and two larger straps anchored it to his back legs by his hips. Chad had tested it a bit in the hotel room, and though his movement had been limited, the bag hadn't come off his back.

A few moments later, the other three had locked the car and shifted. It didn't take too long to get through the trees, and none of them tripped any alarms, thankfully. Finally they got to the edge of the huge lawn surrounding the estate. Jamie was shifted before the rest of them, pulling the bag off Chad's back. In mostly silence, Chad handed the binoculars to Quincy and took out the camera and lens. Then he glanced at Miles, pointed to the left, and nodded.

Miles nodded, then shifted back to wolf form. He was grateful for the way Chad was focused, and the jealousy of having his naked mate near two other gay shifters wasn't nearly as bad as it might otherwise be. Pushing the thought away, he turned to do as Chad asked, picking his way around the edge of the lawn to the other side of the house. There were very few lights on, but Miles counted no less than five doors on that end, two on one wing and three on the main part. Windows galore too. He glanced around and saw another stretch of trees that got closer to the house on one side, so he crept through them as silently as he could.

Sure enough, when he got there, one of the windows on that end of the house had the drapes wide open. Miles could just make out a high-backed leather chair, bookshelves along one wall and what looked like a desk of some sort in front of the chair. He made note of any other obvious rooms—including the location of the kitchen—then hurried away.

When he got back, Chad glanced at him, then back to the house before speaking. "This place is a security nightmare." He shook his head. "How old is this place?"

Quincy lowered the binoculars. "I believe the main house was built not long before Thomas was born, somewhere around 1800."

"Fuck me, that's old," Chad said, turning back.

"We've got some that old in Pittsburgh," Miles said.

"True. Okay, so what did you find?"

"I think the office is on the other end of the main part of the building. First floor, there's a section that sticks out a bit, and I saw bookshelves and what was probably a desk. I'd guess that would be a good one to check, anyway."

Chad nodded. "Excellent. I'd say we'll go there first. Q, how many rooms did you say this had?"

"Thirty, according to the tax assessment."

"How many servants does it take to keep up with a thirty-room estate?" He glanced over at Jamie.

Jamie frowned. "My former alpha's place was smaller than this, but he had at least four or five. Cook, butler, maids…." Jamie tilted his head in thought. "And a gardener."

"Yeah, and how many maids would it take to keep that place clean?" Chad pointed at the house.

"At least three or four," Miles said.

"Uh-huh. Q… how many cats did you say were in the pride?"

Quincy frowned. "Last count, we had about a hundred and fifty."

"For how many states?"

"Thirteen."

"One hundred and fifty cats in thirteen states. And how many live here in the New York area?"

"Maybe… ten? Fifteen? Three of the elders live here. My father, of course. There are two families—husband, wife, and a kid. *Maybe* four or five others. Maybe."

"So… who's cleaning, cooking, opening doors for him? Driving him around?" Chad asked.

Quincy blinked. "Humans."

"And how much do human servants know?"

"A lot," Miles said.

"Yeah. Are they *supposed* to be allowed to know he's not human?"

"No one's supposed to know what we are," Quincy said. "Especially humans."

"Is there any way at all that these people could live with him and *not* figure it out?" Miles asked.

Quincy snorted. "Oh hell no."

"I'm guessing your father knows this, then?" Chad asked.

Quincy frowned. "Actually, I don't think so, come to think of it. But… none of the other cats have homes like this either."

"Your father knows how big this house is, though, right?"

"Yeah."

"So, who does he think cleans and cooks?"

"I don't know, but I think we need to find out," Quincy said, frowning.

"Yeah. I'd be interested in that answer too," Chad said, turning back to the house.

"OKAY. I count four different maids in these pictures," Chad said, pointing to the prints spread out on the table.

"The cook was still in the kitchen," Jamie said, pulling another one out.

"And the gardener was in his room in the carriage house next to the driver."

"So, there's no way they *don't* live there," Miles said.

"Yup." Chad nodded. "Now, if we rule out the gardener and driver, since they more or less live in the carriage house, that still leaves how many for the servants' wing?"

"Six. With the cook and butler," Quincy said, sighing.

There was a knock on the door before anyone could say anything more. Quincy glanced at Miles. "Did you order food?"

Miles shook his head and got up, but Chad held a hand up. "I'll answer it. Q, get the SIG."

Quincy hurried into the bedroom and returned a moment later with his weapon. Jamie had his Glock out, and Miles said a prayer to Diana that they were overreacting.

Chad opened the door and stepped back in surprise. "Mr. Archer."

"Chad, good evening," Aubrey said. He glanced behind him quickly. "Uh, may I—" He waved a hand into the suite.

"Oh, duh, yeah." He stepped aside, shaking his head. "Mind isn't really where it should be. Sorry."

"That's fine," Aubrey said, turning to the rest of them.

Quincy and Jamie relaxed. Aubrey glanced around with his eyebrows up. "I suppose I'm glad you're prepared. I didn't know you could use one of those." Aubrey nodded at Quincy.

"I taught myself some time ago." Quincy tucked the gun into the holster in his jeans. "Is everything okay?"

Aubrey held a hand up. "Yes. I actually decided it'd be safest to bring you the information I have myself." He held up an envelope Miles hadn't noticed.

"Oh, thank you," Quincy said, taking it.

"Please, Mr. Archer, have a seat. Coffee?" Miles asked, waving a hand toward the couch.

"Sorry," Quincy muttered, blushing.

Aubrey took a seat on one of the couches but shook his head. "No, thank you. I don't think I should stay long. I'm pretty sure I'm being watched."

Miles joined Quincy on one of the other couches. He leaned over to see what Quincy held. The top page held a daily schedule, including departure and arrival times and office hours and even some evening activities.

Quincy's head whipped up. "I knew you were being tapped, but watched?"

Aubrey nodded. "Yeah. They don't dare do anything to me yet. They don't want Frank Lewis in my place, so until they have you taking over, they're not going to do anything. But they're keeping tabs on me."

Chad wrinkled his nose. "Somehow I'm not surprised. Um… it might be best if you keep someone with you most of the time. Like… I'm sure you can bathe yourself."

Aubrey smirked. "Yeah?"

Chad chuckled. "Yeah. But you're bound to have security you trust in your company, right?"

"Sure."

"I *highly* suggest you pick one. Tell him whatever you have to, but have him stick to you like glue for now."

Aubrey considered Chad for a long time, then nodded slowly. "I can do that."

Quincy let out a breath, and Miles put an arm around him and hugged him.

"Good." Chad frowned. "Also… I have a question. Is it common for jaguar shifters to have live-in human servants?"

Aubrey blinked at Chad. "No. In fact, we're not supposed to. Too much chance they'll figure us out."

"Yeah, that's what I thought too. Do you know if Thomas has servants living at his estate?"

Aubrey shook his head. "No. He told me he hires a cleaning crew to come in a couple times a week and temporary ones for events and the like."

Miles met Chad's gaze, and Chad shook his head briefly. It took him a moment, but then Miles realized he didn't want to give away their thoughts about the servants just yet. He wasn't quite sure why, but he trusted Chad to know what he was doing.

"Why?"

Chad smiled. "Just curious, that's all. It's just such a huge house. I was sure he wasn't taking care of it himself."

Aubrey laughed at that. "No way. I can't see Abe in rubber gloves and an apron." He shook his head. "The estate didn't used to be that big. But it's been in his family since before the Civil War, so they've had it a long time and added on quite a bit."

"Father, what's this?" Quincy asked, pulling a card from the envelope he held.

Aubrey grinned. "Apparently Abe is having a party. Some big merger with his firm and another finance firm. I thought it might be a way for you to get in. There'll be a few cats there, but also quite a few humans."

"Ooh, very Bond," Chad said, grinning.

Quincy rolled his eyes. "You are such a puppy," he said, shaking his head.

Chad laughed. "Well, you know...."

"I figured you could walk right in," Aubrey said, turning to Quincy. "There's no way he could turn away the tepey-sa—whether you want it or not, that's what you are—and his *partner*, even if the party isn't exclusively cats."

Quincy nodded slowly. "That's true. So, the invite...?"

"Is for them," Aubrey said, pointing to Chad and Jamie. "Once inside, you distract Thomas, and Chad, Jamie, and Miles go looking for what you need."

Quincy grinned. "Looks like we're going shopping."

Miles groaned. "I have to wear another tie, don't I?"

He didn't like the twinkle in Quincy's eye. "Not just any tie. A *bow* tie. It's a black tie affair."

Miles sighed.

"Hey, I wonder if we can buy exploding pens at Staples...," Chad mused.

MILES REFUSED to be nervous. He refused, but it was damned difficult. He tugged at his collar again, unused to wearing a tuxedo, much less a bow tie, and tried not to think about walking into the lion's—or jaguar's—den. In fact, Miles would have preferred to face off a wild jaguar in their natural habitat to the ones he was about to meet.

The four of them currently sat in the back of Aubrey's limo. It wasn't a stretch or anything, nothing that would have made him roll his eyes, and he was glad for that. It still had nice leather seating, a television on the divider between the driver and the back, and an ice bucket—complete with champagne, which Quincy opened and the four of them downed in short order. Apparently Miles wasn't the only one nervous.

He took a moment to let his gaze trail over his mate's body. Quincy seemed to be one of those men that could make any clothes look good. But a tux… well, Miles decided then and there he could be talked into one again if it meant he'd see Quincy in one. The slim fit jacket showed his lean musculature well. Miles was going to enjoy taking it off him later.

The limo rolled to a stop in the courtyard in front of the house, pulling Miles's attention back to their task. He had to remember to wait for the driver, but only a few moments later, they were approaching the front door of the mansion. Quincy held his hand firmly, making it *quite* clear what they were to each other. Miles wasn't sure if that was the best idea, though he *did* appreciate it. He was still dealing with a bit of jealousy from earlier.

As they'd been getting ready to go, Quincy had decided the best way to help camouflage Chad and Jamie was to put his scent all over them. Chad had wrinkled his nose but recognized the importance of not smelling like a wolf around the other cats. So he'd agreed to let Quincy scent-mark him.

Miles hadn't expected the surge of jealousy that had hit when he watched Quincy marking them. He was used to the smaller spikes of jealousy now and again, though Quincy seemed to go out of his way to make sure he didn't put himself in a situation to cause it. Even so, this one hit him hard, and Miles knew he was being ridiculous. They were *dressed*, for Diana's sake, but it didn't seem to help to tell himself that. What did help, though, was having Quincy come mark *him* right after.

Now all three of them smelled enough of cat to confuse the senses. Chad had made a comment about stinking, which Quincy had flipped him off for, making everyone laugh. Now Chad and Jamie hung back so the four of them didn't appear together, getting a little lost in the others coming into the party.

As Miles and Quincy went through the door, it was to be stopped by a man taking invitations. Quincy smiled—and Miles hoped he was never on the receiving end of it. It was downright *creepy*. "Please inform Mr. Thomas that Quincy Archer is here."

The human looked down his nose at them, but turned to another man with him in the same suit-and-tie uniform and whispered something in his ear. The second man left while Mr. Haughty stood over them, smirking.

The smirk turned to a scowl when Abraham Thomas himself approached. He didn't look much like his driver's license picture. His hair was quite a bit whiter, he had more than a few more lines in his face, and the picture didn't have the creepy, fake smile on his face that was there now. Miles had also expected him to be taller somehow.

"Quincy! Welcome! That's quite all right, Simmons, thank you." He turned to Quincy again, holding out his hand.

Quincy shook it. "Good to see you, Mr. Thomas," he said, smiling.

Miles had to admire the hell out of his mate in that moment. He had the brief thought that Quincy ought to be on Broadway with a performance like that. That smile looked downright genuine.

Thomas's wasn't nearly as good, but he still held a hand toward the open doors on the left. A huge crystal chandelier lit a long, narrow ballroom, sparkling off champagne glasses, satin dresses, and an absurd number of diamonds adorning necks and ears. Highly polished marble tile led up to the small dais in the corner, holding a string quartet.

Miles pulled his attention back to Quincy and Thomas. "Mr. Thomas, allow me to introduce my partner, Dr. Miles Grant."

It took all Miles had to smile politely and shake the man's hand. He wanted to bite it, but resisted the urge to let his canines drop. "Nice to meet you," he managed to say instead.

"And you, Doctor." Thomas turned to Quincy with a barely concealed sneer. "Quincy, I wasn't aware you were… interested in men."

Quincy smiled—again frighteningly well-acted. "Well, of course, one in my position is encouraged to put our own interests aside for the good of the… group. So, I haven't exactly made it well-known."

Thomas inclined his head. "Indeed."

Miles caught a glimpse of Chad and Jamie in the entryway. He turned back to Quincy and Thomas. "If you'll excuse me, I need to take a few moments."

"Of course. It's nice to meet you, Dr. Grant." Thomas smiled that same grating smile again.

"And you. I'll be back shortly," Miles said to Quincy.

"See you soon." Quincy turned to Thomas. "So, Mr. Thomas, please tell me how you've been. I'm afraid I've been out of the loop."

Miles had to force himself to walk slowly as he left the ballroom and caught up with Chad and Jamie. "Any trouble?"

Chad shook his head. "Barely looked at the invite."

Miles rolled his eyes. "Mr. Haughty tried not to let us in. Quincy ought to win an Oscar. Anyway, let's see what we can do. If I have to stay here too long, I'll get hives."

Jamie snorted. "Not my cuppa either. You go with Chad to the study. I'll see what I can find on the rest of this floor, since there doesn't look like a lot of rooms not occupied."

It turned out to be easier than either expected to get to the office. Guests filled the hall, spilling into the ornate dining room, the billiard room, and one that appeared to be a music room with a grand piano in one corner, currently silent. The last door along that hallway before it turned toward the kitchen was their target. Miles was relieved when the knob turned easily. They slipped into the room, Chad watching the hallway, but no one seemed to notice them.

Miles had been right about the room's purpose. Bookshelves lined three of the walls. The fourth held an enormous marble fireplace, currently dark. Thick burgundy carpet covered the floor and leather, high-back armchairs sat in front of the fireplace. They hurried over to the desk first. The bookshelves behind it had cabinets from waist height down, so Miles went to those.

Unfortunately all it had was common office supplies, more books, and a few other mundane things. Disappointed, he moved to the next, but again, nothing but bottles of liquor and boxes of cigars. Miles wrinkled his nose and stood.

"Hey," Chad whispered.

Miles went over to the desk to see what Chad had. "This look familiar?" he asked, holding up a copy of the picture Quincy had received in Maryland.

"Well, hell. That at least proves he was involved in the attack on me. There'd be no other reason or way for him to have that," Miles said as Chad flipped it over to see a message at the bottom. *A.T.—Witt will take care of it tonight.—P.S.*

"Bingo," Chad said, handing the picture over. He closed that drawer and moved to another.

Miles went around to the other side, but all this had was pens, a notepad, and in the bottom drawer, a decanter of scotch and a glass. "Nothing," he reported.

"Yeah, same here." He stood and looked around. "I don't see him hiding shit in the books, not if he left this in his drawer."

"I don't think so either."

"And there's nowhere else here. Let's see if Jamie found anything, then we'll figure out how to get upstairs."

JAMIE HAD come up empty-handed, though. All the other rooms on that floor were being used for the party, including another parlor and a receiving room. They found a set of servant's stairs in one corner of the main house and made their way through the bedrooms on the second floor. Unfortunately, yet again, they found nothing. Each of the guest bedrooms had a desk and side table, all of which were empty. And Thomas's bedroom had a disgustingly rich and huge closet, too many watches and other pieces of jewelry, but nothing of interest, even in his bedside tables.

"We need to get out of here. I'm pretty sure our luck is going to run out soon," Chad whispered.

Jamie slapped a hand over Chad's mouth. "Don't jinx us!" He shook his head.

Chad snorted and led the way back to the servant's stairs. They made it to the first floor without incident, and Chad and Jamie went out into the garden to call for the driver. Miles went in search of Quincy.

He found his mate still talking to Thomas, and a man Miles recognized as Charles Ross from the driver's license picture. "Miles! I'm glad you're back. What took so long?"

Miles chuckled. "I'm afraid I got a bit lost. Ended up outside, then took a wrong turn when I came back in."

"Easy enough to do here," Ross said. "Still think Abe ought to find something a bit smaller."

Thomas ignored him, and Miles had the feeling it was an old discussion. "Miles Grant, this is Charles Ross, another member of Quincy's group," he said, waving toward Ross.

Ross looked quite a bit younger than Thomas did, and Miles wondered about that. If he looked closer, though, threads of silver ran through the dark hair and the lightest of lines surrounded the deep blue eyes. Miles forced himself to smile and shake the man's hand. "Nice to meet you." He turned to Quincy. "I'm sure we should probably not steal all of Mr. Thomas's time. He does have other guests."

Quincy smiled at him. "Of course. Wonderful to catch up with you." He turned and nodded to both Thomas and Ross.

"Do enjoy the rest of the party," Thomas said, and he and Ross left.

"Let's get the fuck out of here," Quincy muttered.

"Chad and Jamie are in the garden, calling for the car."

"Good. Did you find anything?"

"Not as much as we hoped, but I think it's something. Let's get to the car," Miles suggested.

Chapter 16

SEEING THE picture again, knowing it was in Thomas's hands, and reading the message that confirmed Thomas had ordered the hit made Quincy want to go right back into the house, pull his SIG out, and just shoot Thomas then and there. He was glad they were well on their way back to New York when Chad handed him the photo.

Quincy took a deep breath. "This is all you found?"

"Unfortunately. Whatever messages are being passed between them are either not there or have been destroyed. There was a fireplace in the study, and I suspect that's where they went." Chad sighed.

"Well, it was a long shot. This, at least, proves his part in Miles's attack. That's still not something to ignore."

Chad nodded. "No, that's true. And we *do* have bank records that tie him—even loosely—to the wolves in Denver and the one in New York."

"So, what now?" Miles asked.

"Now, we talk to my father. I think it's time to go to the tepey-iret."

"Is this enough for that?" Chad asked, frowning.

"I don't know, but I don't see us getting anything more, not without taking risks I don't think we should take." Quincy shook his head.

"Well, let's see what your father says. You know… if nothing else, maybe we could get him on the secrecy thing," Chad suggested.

"I thought about that. It doesn't take care of Ross, but at least it'll get Thomas out of the picture."

"Maybe the bank records will be enough to convince your tepey-iret that Ross was involved," Jamie said.

Quincy frowned. "Maybe. He's a fair man, though. I don't think he'd want to punish someone without being sure."

"We'll just have to wait and see on that," Miles said. "First, your father."

QUINCY JUST wanted it all over. He was tired of investigating and research and hunting and all of it. He wanted to go back to selling information and drawing pictures. Especially since he hadn't picked up a pencil in almost four months. He wanted to spend quiet nights with his mate, curled up under the stars in their animal forms. He wanted the freedom to *claim* Miles and be able to let go of all of this.

They decided to wait until the next day to contact Quincy's father. It was already late, and they wanted a chance to talk it out a little more first, anyway. So they tucked the picture away, and they focused on getting to the hotel.

But when they got back to the room, they realized they were all a little too tired to try to hash it out that night. Quincy didn't think he was tired enough to sleep, though, and thought about spending the rest of the evening in the bedroom with Miles. He'd just turned to say as much when his phone went off. He frowned at the unknown number, but opened the text message.

Tried to hire me again. Said no. Hired someone else. Doc's the target. Watch your back.—P

Quincy blinked at the message, momentarily at a loss as to who it was from. And why were they sticking their tongue out at him? It took him a full minute to figure out that wasn't a smiley, but was the person's initial. *Payne*. Tweedle Dee. Warning them.

Thomas and Ross had apparently not appreciated his appearance at the party. Did they know the picture was missing?

Quincy wasn't sure, but there was *no* way they were leaving the room now. He'd requested the one they had for one major reason: there was *one* way in and *one* way out. The windows didn't open and were triple-paned and thick. No one was getting through them without warning.

He stared at the message for several moments, until Miles came up and touched his shoulder. "Baby? You okay?"

Quincy sighed. "Not really. I don't think I'm going to be okay until it's all over." He shook his head, paused long enough to send a reply of *TY*, and handed the phone to Miles.

Miles read the text message, his eyebrows going up. "P?"

"Payne. A.k.a. Tweedle Dee."

"Tweedle Dee?" Chad asked, coming up to them.

Miles handed the phone over. "Payne."

"Aw, fuck. I was hoping we'd have more time." Chad sighed. "Well, I think the best bet is to stay put for now. This place is about as secure as it gets."

"That's what I was thinking." Quincy wrinkled his nose. "On the other hand, it's *one* door. No one's going to stop someone coming up to this floor. If they get through it…. Fuck." He frowned, looking around.

"Why not keep watch?" Jamie asked.

Quincy blinked. "Watch?"

Chad nodded. "Not a bad idea. We'll take shifts for now. Jamie and I can go first. We'll stay out here, one sleep for a couple of hours, then switch off. That way we'll at least hear anyone trying to get in."

Miles nodded. "That will work." He glanced at his watch. "It's midnight now. Come get us at four?"

"That works." Jamie sighed and went straight for the iPad. "I'm thinking… espresso…."

Quincy chuckled. "Thanks, that makes me feel better."

"This is going to end soon," Chad said. "Just hang in a little longer."

"Yeah." With a sigh, Quincy turned to Miles. "Come on. I have something to talk to you about."

"Uh-oh. Did I leave my socks on the floor?" Miles asked.

Chad laughed and Jamie snickered.

Quincy chuckled and took Miles's hand. "Not exactly."

When they were in the bedroom, Quincy turned around. "I want us to claim each other."

Miles blinked. "Uh… I do too, but didn't we say we were going to wait until this was over?"

Quincy nodded. "We did. But this—" He held up his phone. "—this makes me want to reconsider that. I…." He took a deep breath. "If anything happens to you… it's not going to take a bond for me to not want to be without you."

Miles stared at him for a long moment. "You remember what I told you?"

"Yes." Quincy stepped a little closer. "I'm well aware of what could happen to me if you died."

Miles cupped one of Quincy's cheeks. "Maybe we should just strengthen what's there for now."

Quincy frowned. "Do you *want* to wait? Are you worried about *me* dying?"

"Oh hell no." Miles shook his head fast. "No, no. I mean, yes, there's still that fear. But… if something happens to you, well, I feel the same way as you do." He blew out a breath. "I'm just worried about you, baby. I'm hoping you could handle being alone better than I could."

"Before you? Yes. Now?" Quincy shook his head. "I don't think so. The bond we do have is too strong, I think. It's not like we haven't gone out of our way to strengthen it." He smiled.

Miles grinned. "True. Very true. If you're sure…." He took a deep breath. "Then I'd like that. I'd like it very much." He paused. "Hey, uh, where do you bite when you claim a mate?"

Quincy frowned. "I'm not sure? When I topped the first time, my cat was pushing me to bite the back of your neck. I don't know if it has to be there, though."

"I think I can work with that," Miles murmured, pulling Quincy in. "I know it can be anywhere for us. Usually the shoulder, here," he said, running his finger teasingly under Quincy's collar. "But it could be… here too." He lifted Quincy's hand and brushed his lips over Quincy's inner wrist. "While your cock is buried inside me."

Quincy refused to put a name to the sound he made over that. His dick hardened, his vision turned gray, and his teeth dropped almost at once.

"You're so hot like that," Miles whispered, leaning in. Skipping Quincy's lips, he kissed his way along Quincy's jaw. He pushed his hands up, threading his fingers into Quincy's hair, nibbling softly at the soft skin just above his collar. "I love you, Quincy Archer."

This time Quincy would openly admit he whimpered. His heart skipped a beat and he swallowed. "I love you, Miles Grant. So much." Quincy closed his eyes, sliding his hands up over Miles's chest.

Miles kissed his way back along Quincy's jaw, then caught his lips in a long, thorough kiss. When he pulled back, Quincy saw Miles's eyes had bled black and his teeth had dropped. It never failed to get him going when he saw his mate like that. Miles reached up and gently removed Quincy's glasses. "Don't want to mess these up." He set them on the bedside table, then turned back.

Slowly, he slid his fingers along the edges of Quincy's jacket and eased it down over his shoulders and off. He laid it over a nearby chair, then lifted one of Quincy's hands. Kissing the inner wrist, he took the cuff link out, then did the same with the other arm.

Quincy was stunned by the slow seduction. He and Miles had taken it slow before, but nothing quite like this. But it fit, was what they both needed, especially for this.

Miles turned his attention next to Quincy's shirt, and the incredibly slow button-kiss pace had Quincy almost insane by the time Miles pushed it off Quincy's shoulders. He went for the pants next, but Quincy stopped him, putting a hand over the one at his waist.

"My turn," he whispered when Miles raised his eyebrows.

Miles smiled and dropped his hands as Quincy slid his jacket off now. Just as Miles had done, as each cuff link came off, he brushed his lips over Miles's wrist. And he chased each button on the shirt with a kiss to Miles's chest. He paused to take in Miles's lean, defined chest, running his hands over it, then kissing his way over one pectoral to the other. Eventually Quincy worked back up to Miles's neck and caught his lips again. He poured everything he couldn't possibly articulate in that moment into the kiss—every promise, every emotion, everything.

Miles returned it, then pulled back and guided Quincy to the bed. Quincy sat on the edge, smiling when Miles knelt, taking off each shoe and sock before running his hands along Quincy's thighs. Quincy lay back, eyes glued to his mate as Miles opened his pants.

The moan Quincy let out could not have been contained for anything because Miles decided to kiss Quincy's cock over the *very* brief black briefs he'd put on under the tux. Miles eased Quincy's pants off him, grinning when he saw the rest of the briefs.

"I approve," he murmured, making Quincy grin.

"Glad you like them—*Miles*." Quincy was interrupted when Miles turned his attention to Quincy's inner thighs, brushing his lips over the sensitive skin there, slowly making his way from groin to knee. The sounds only got louder when Miles turned and gave the same attention to the other thigh. By the time he got back to hover over Quincy's cock, Quincy was damned near incoherent.

With a grin Miles eased Quincy's briefs off next and tossed them aside. He licked a long line from the base of Quincy's cock to the tip, then back down again, but before he could do more, Quincy tugged on his hand. Miles looked up, raising his eyebrows.

"You're wearing too many clothes," Quincy managed, making Miles smile.

"Perhaps you should fix that oversight."

Quincy grinned, sitting up and sliding to the floor as Miles stood. He kissed a line slowly across Miles's stomach, just above the waistband, his hand cupping and rubbing the lump under the zipper. Miles moaned and Quincy's cock jumped in reaction. He loved hearing the evidence of Miles's pleasure. Finally he let himself open Miles's pants. He couldn't quite take it slow on the shoes and socks like Miles had, and instead let Miles dispense with them quickly. As soon as Miles finished, Quincy was back, leaving more kisses over his stomach, then outside the briefs before slowly pulling those down as well.

Quincy would never get enough of his mate's cock. Thick and slightly longer than his, it was *perfect* in his not-so-humble opinion. He copied Miles again, dragging his tongue along the length to the tip, then back, but he didn't stop there. Instead, he closed his eyes, forced his teeth to retract, then used his tongue to tease each ball. He pulled one in, sucking it lightly, then moved to the other to do the same.

"Gods, Quince, your mouth is too talented," Miles groaned. If Quincy's mouth hadn't been full of a ball, he might have grinned. As it was, he sucked lightly, teased a bit more, then let go and turned back to Miles's dick. One more trail, this time of light nips with his lips along the length, and then, eyes locked to Miles's, he opened his mouth and swallowed as much at once as he could.

Miles gritted his teeth, but a moan still escaped. His hand went to Quincy's head, and Quincy loved seeing the involuntary touch. He ignored his own need, focusing on Miles's cock, bobbing his head shallowly, then taking it all in again and sucking before doing it all again.

In only a few moments, though, Miles tugged on him, groaning again. "Gonna have to stop that or we'll have to put off the claiming," he muttered.

Since it was the ultimate goal of the evening, Quincy—reluctantly—let go and stood. Miles kissed him again as he guided Quincy back. When he felt the bed against his legs, he broke the kiss and scrambled to settle in the middle.

Miles followed him down, kissing his way up one leg, then, with a grin, turning his attention to Quincy's balls. Quincy groaned at the feel of the tongue running over them. Miles didn't stop there and sucked on each lightly just like Quincy had done to him, then before Quincy could so much as blink, Miles took Quincy's cock into his mouth in one move.

"*Ohgodsyes*," Quincy moaned. He gripped the comforter in one hand and his other landed in Miles's hair, unable to *not* touch. It took all he had to keep from thrusting in need, but he managed. Miles took no mercy on him, moving his mouth in long bobs.

Quincy was so aroused, though, after tasting and touching so much of his mate, he had to stop Miles after a short time, just like Miles had with him. "Cat's pushing me. Need to claim you…."

Miles pulled off and sat up, reaching for the bedside table. He dug into the drawer and pulled out the lube, then handed it to Quincy.

Quincy tilted his head and they switched places, Quincy kneeling between Miles's legs. He paused briefly, staring at the vision before him. "Even in grays, you're the hottest guy I've ever seen."

Miles beamed at that. "I'd argue, but I'll save it for later."

Ignoring that, Quincy focused on opening the lube and coating a finger. He was grateful to find Miles already somewhat relaxed. The first finger quickly became two, and then he was coating a third.

"Really, don't need all that. You were just inside me last night." Miles grunted, pulling his legs back. "Need you inside me, baby."

Quincy couldn't really argue and gave up, coating his cock liberally, then crawling into place. Gaze locked to Miles's, he pushed slowly against the muscle. Thankfully it was stretched enough, and with just a little effort, the tip popped in.

Even as he started thrusting, he knew in short order he wasn't going to last long. There was too much build up, too much emotion, too much *everything*. He pulled out again and tilted his head.

Miles didn't say anything, simply rolled over. Quincy worked his way back into Miles's tight heat, pausing when he was fully buried, his balls against Miles's ass. He closed his eyes, dropping random kisses over Miles's back as the import, the enormity of what they were about to do, filled him. There would be no going back. Once he'd claimed Miles and Miles had claimed him, they'd forever be linked.

He eased out slowly, then thrust back in at the same pace, wanting to build the pleasure up. Miles turned his head, and Quincy leaned in for a sloppy but oh so good kiss. Then he moved a little faster, thrusting a little harder. This earned him a moan, and Miles reaching back to touch, hand resting on one of Quincy's hips.

Quincy rested his head on Miles's back, groaning himself. "So good. So tight, baby…."

Miles rolled his hips, rocking to meet each of Quincy's thrusts. The pleasure built quickly, and Quincy did everything he could to fight to hold back, but it wasn't working.

"Stroke yourself. Can't hold back much longer," Quincy murmured, kissing Miles's back again.

Miles did, moaning Quincy's name. "Not… can't, oh *gods*, I'm close, baby."

"Me too." Quincy leaned forward, brushing the long red hair away from Miles's neck. Quincy's cat pushed harder, but Quincy paused one more time. "You sure, Miles? You want me as your mate?"

"*Fuck yes*," Miles said without the slightest hesitation. He shifted, taking one of Quincy's arms.

"Oh gods…. Then, *now*, Miles," Quincy managed, then sank his teeth into the back of Miles's neck.

A second behind that, Miles shouted, then bit into Quincy's wrist. The climax slammed into Quincy, forcing him to let go of Miles's neck. As he did, something drew his gaze up, and he gasped at what he saw.

A spirit form of his cat and a spirit form of Miles's wolf rose above them, swirling around each other. So beautiful, it stole Quincy's breath. They danced briefly, then merged before fading.

The invisible something that pulled them together when they'd strengthened their bond drew them in once more. At the same time, the link between them snapped into place, thicker and more secure than anything before. His pleasure amplified, and he realized he was feeling the echo of Miles's orgasm too. It sent another shockwave through him, and he gasped again.

Quince!

Miles?

Miles laughed. *Yes!*

I didn't know we could talk telepathically! Quincy grinned into Miles's back, not wanting to lose the physical connection just yet.

Claimed mates, baby. That's it. You're stuck with me now.

Just don't chew on my slippers. Quincy chuckled as Miles laughed. *I will make no promises of the sort.*

Quincy chuckled again and wrapped his arms tight around Miles, kissing his back one more time before slowly pulling out. They lay together, facing each other, huge grins on both their faces. *This might take some getting used to. Did you know about the spirit animals?*

Miles shook his head. *No. I once observed a claiming, but all we saw was sort of sparks of light. I guess only we get to see our wolves— or cat.*

Do I want to know why you were watching someone fuck? Quincy raised an eyebrow.

Tanner, as future alpha of the pack, had to claim his mate publicly. The wolves are very sexual and open about it, and watching gives the observers proof that they're really mated. Shows the pack the leadership will be held by a strong, bound couple.

Quincy blinked. *Can I just say I'm glad we didn't have to do that publicly?*

Miles grinned. *Yeah, no way I'm sharing you. Though, it's so amazing when it happens, I'm not sure I'd even notice.*

It was *beautiful.* Quincy swallowed, his throat suddenly tight. He ran his fingers over Miles's face, brushing at a bit of hair. "I can't believe we did it. My cat is insanely happy right now."

"So is my wolf. I'm… gods, Quince, I don't know what to even say. Thank you? For not pushing me away. For not rejecting me when you came to see me."

Quincy shook his head. "I… I don't know if I really could have." He gave a wry smile. "You fascinated me. And cats and fascination are a *bad* combination."

Miles laughed. "Duly noted."

"So, no…. Thank *you* for waiting. I know you didn't expect a cat, but I'm infinitely grateful you didn't push me away either." He chuckled. "Even if I didn't want a mate at all to begin with."

Well, we're mated now, for good or ill.

Good thing I'm mated to a doctor, then, eh?

Miles laughed. "Indeed." He sobered, swallowing. "Let's hope this is over soon, yeah?"

Quincy nodded. "Yeah. I can't wait to start our life together."

That put a huge grin on Miles's face. "Me either, baby."

He kissed Quincy's forehead, and Quincy burrowed into his arms. They lay in silence for a long time, and Quincy simply savored the feel of their new, stronger bond, the arms around him, the love he felt from his mate. Despite the rest of the hell going on around them, he'd never been happier in his life. He just hoped it didn't come crashing down on him.

Chapter 17

CHAD WOKE them at four, and Miles and Quincy went out to the living room to give them time to sleep. Miles didn't get a lot of sleep himself, but he wouldn't trade what had happened for anything. Despite the solid feeling of their completed bond, he still had trouble believing they'd done it.

Quincy was working on coffee, and Miles just took a moment to enjoy the freedom to watch. The first two months had just about done him in, always worried—despite the messages from Quincy—about where he was or if he was safe. He really hoped he wouldn't have to worry about that anymore, but there were still a hundred different ways this all could go wrong.

Miles crossed the room, stepped up behind Quincy, and put his arms around his mate.

You okay?

Miles nodded. *Yeah. Just… absorbing everything.*

Quincy hit the start button on the coffeemaker and turned around. "It's a lot to accept, isn't it? That we're really mated now?"

Brushing some of Quincy's hair back, Miles sighed. "Yeah. And…."

"Still worried." Quincy smiled. "But I just don't see the iret letting this go completely. Especially with the picture evidence of the human servants in the house. We'll get out from under this, *somehow*, soon."

"I know. I guess I'm just a little impatient." He smiled sheepishly.

Quincy laughed. "I'd hardly call this impatient. I've been running for too long. You've been hiding for too fucking long." He shook his head, then frowned. "What did you tell the hospital?"

"Just that I needed to take a leave of absence. They always need ER docs, so if I want to go back, I can."

"If?" Quincy tilted his head.

Miles took a deep breath and let it out. "I've been thinking about starting a small private practice. Out near pack lands."

The smile spread slowly, but was no less wide for that. "Yeah? Like… where we could maybe have a house?"

The relief made him almost giddy. "Yeah. I was thinking maybe we could find a spot, kind of like Tanner and Finley's, and build something… Japanese in style."

Miles loved that he could still feel their emotions. The happiness he got across their bond thrilled him. "Oh, that would be gorgeous. I never thought about that, but then again, I never expected to really own my own house."

Miles grinned. "We can certainly afford one."

Quincy laughed. "Well, yeah. Just… by myself, you know?"

"Yeah, I know. Same reason I didn't. But that's not the case anymore."

Quincy shook his head. "No. And… as weird as it sounds, I'm glad for that."

"Yeah, silly solitary cats," Miles teased.

This got him more laughter. "Goofy puppy. Go lay down. I'll take the first watch and wake you in a couple of hours. I'm sure you're used to sleeping in snatches."

Miles chuckled. "Oh yeah." He kissed Quincy softly. "No heroics," he warned, then took one of the couches.

"I promise," Quincy said, then, to Miles's surprise, threw a blanket over him. "Sleep, baby."

Miles didn't remember so much as closing his eyes.

QUINCY LET him sleep too long—more than three hours—but when Miles woke, it was to daylight, and he sent Quincy back to bed instead of him sleeping on the couch. He ordered fresh coffee from room service, then picked up the living area a bit. They'd been keeping housekeeping out because they didn't want to give *anyone* the chance to get to them. He was sure they'd been in when they weren't there, but at least while they were in the room, they'd kept up the Do Not Disturb sign.

Three wolves and a jaguar could sure make a mess. Shoes, socks, electronics of every variety, printouts, and more were scattered across the coffee table, dining table, the wet bar counter, and even stacked on the side tables. He even found one of Chad's shoes on the console table under the TV. He had no idea what had caused that and decided he didn't want to know.

By the time the coffee and breakfast was delivered, the room was more or less presentable. Just as he was sitting down, he noticed something poking out from under one of the couches. He dug it out to discover it was Quincy's sketchbook.

And on the top page, a drawing of him asleep. Miles stared at it for several long moments, stunned. His long hair had fallen down over his chest, and Quincy had made him look… seriously sexy. He blinked and his cheeks got hot. Clearing his throat, he closed the sketchpad and set it aside for later.

One by one the others got up for the day. Chad was first, sheepishly collecting his shoe, then hitting the coffee. He carried a second mug into the bedroom, then came back out. Clearly not quite awake yet, he sat at the table to sip from his own cup.

Miles pushed a covered plate over to him. "Get some protein into you."

"Thanks," Chad said with a smile. "Always taking care of us."

Miles flashed a grin. "That's what I do."

"I thought you were supposed to put Band-Aids on us, then tell us to shift."

With a laugh, Miles shook his head. "Naw… I'll actually clean the wound first."

Chad laughed and picked up another piece of bacon. Jamie stumbled out then, plopping down next to Chad and stealing a slice of bacon. "Hey! Get your own. You're not allowed to steal it in this form."

Miles raised his eyebrows. "There's something there?"

Chad grinned. "When he was stuck in wolf form—before I knew what he was—he was having a bit of a freak out about being mates. But he couldn't tell me what was wrong. I sensed it, but, of course, had no idea what it was. So, I just did my best to calm 'Murray' down. Well, to try to cover it up, he stole a piece of bacon."

Miles chuckled. "That sounds like him."

Jamie rolled his eyes. "Fine, I'll go order my own," he grumbled, but Miles was a step ahead of him and got another plate from the cart.

"I already ordered for everyone. Figured we'd want to have time to talk."

You all up already? Quincy asked.

Yup. And have breakfast and coffee out here, if the lazy cat wants to join us.

Ha. Ha. A moment later, though, Quincy emerged and collected a coffee cup, then sat next to him.

Chad and Jamie stared at them for a moment, noses twitching, then they both grinned. "You claimed each other?" Chad asked.

Miles blushed but nodded. "Yeah. Decided not to wait any longer."

Quincy leaned over and rubbed his face across Miles's shoulder. "Yup. I don't think my cat's ever been this happy. I'd swear if I was in cat form, he'd be purring… even though he can't physically."

"You purr," Miles said, looking over at Quincy. "And… why are you marking me?"

Quincy smirked. "Mated doesn't mean I'm not going to make sure everyone knows you're mine."

Miles laughed and shook his head. He leaned in and kissed Quincy's temple, then turned back to his plate.

"And I do *not* purr. I… growl." Quincy sniffed and picked up his cup.

The other three laughed. "Growl. Right," Miles said, getting up and retrieving a plate. He set it in front of Quincy, then sat again. "So…."

Chad sighed. "Yeah, so. I'm still pissed we couldn't find more. I was so hoping for… a letter or… *something*."

"Yeah, well, he's an asshole and overconfident, but not *completely* stupid," Quincy said.

"So, what do we do? Do we have enough to go to anyone, or do we want to try to look further?" Miles asked.

"I honestly don't know where else we'd look. I doubt sincerely Ross has left anything to be found." Chad frowned.

"I don't think he would either," Quincy said, frowning. "Especially after seeing me last night. I think we should call my father. Maybe get him to meet us here again and see what he thinks."

Chad nodded. "Yeah. I think that'll work. I swept the room last night to make sure nothing new was added and didn't find anything, so this is as good as any place."

"All right, then. I'll call him."

TWO HOURS later, Aubrey sat in one of the armchairs, muscles jumping in his jaw as he looked at the picture. "I'd still kind of been hoping one of our own pride wouldn't be involved," he said quietly.

"Is it enough to do anything with?" Chad asked.

Aubrey sat back with a sigh. "I don't think the iret is going to let it go. I don't know how much he can do with this, though."

Miles glanced over at Chad and raised his eyebrow. Chad nodded, and Miles retrieved the folder they'd been holding in reserve. "Maybe these will give the iret something to work with."

Aubrey raised his eyebrows but took the folder. The line on his forehead got deeper as he paged through the pictures of Thomas's servants.

"We counted six in the main house, plus the gardener and driver in the carriage house," Quincy said. "All human. We confirmed that last night. Chad and Jamie made a point of looking for them during the party."

"Nothing but human smells. In fact, the only cats I smelled were Thomas and Ross."

Aubrey frowned. "But the cats suppress their scents."

"To a point," Chad said. He tapped his nose. "I still haven't managed to learn to filter things completely. Which *totally* sucks down on the street, let me tell you." He shuddered, making Aubrey chuckle. "But I smelled Dumber in Miles's apartment, and he was suppressing his scent then."

Aubrey nodded. "Fair enough. It would be easy enough to check, anyway. All cats are registered. I don't recognize them as part of my pride, and I know every single cat under me. If they *are* cats living here without me knowing, that's its own problem."

"They're not, Father," Quincy murmured. "The problem is, even if that gets Thomas out of the way, what do we do with Ross?"

"Well, we *do* have this," Chad said, handing over the stack of printouts.

Aubrey took them and paged through them like he had the pictures, frowning more and more as he went. "Let me get this straight," he said, going back a few pages, then looking at Quincy. "Thomas—and Ross—send money to this wolf. Morgan Daniels?"

Quincy nodded. "Yes."

"I'm guessing you're the one who pulled this information?"

"Jamie and I, yes," Quincy confirmed.

Shock echoed over their bond at the unmistakably proud smile on Aubrey's face. "That doesn't surprise me. Okay, so, Thomas to Daniels, who then sends money to an account in Denver, attached to a fake business that's registered under the alpha prime's name."

You okay, Quince?

Yeah. Is he ever going to stop surprising me?

Probably not. Miles kissed Quincy's temple, then sighed. "Yes. There are money transfers to Payne Stewart, the enforcer hired to come after us, as well."

"Okay. It doesn't prove a conspiracy to start an interspecies war, but there's *no* reason they'll be able to come up with to explain the money transfers. Why would they send money like that to a wolf?"

Chad shook his head. "There's no reason. Morgan Daniels is otherwise clean. He works a basic nine-to-five office job. He has a mate—legal wife—and kid and a mother in hospice."

Aubrey raised his eyebrows. "Hospice? Isn't she a shifter?"

"No, actually," Miles said. "She's human. Her shifter mate actually claimed her, which is why the pup came out wolf."

"Huh. So, human with frailties."

Chad nodded. "Yes. I'm thinking that's probably what the money was for." He shrugged. "That's pure conjecture, though. Anyway, he's otherwise clean."

"But we have ties between the cats trying to hurt you—and you have the picture to prove it—and two separate wolves, including alpha prime." Aubrey pinched the bridge of his nose. "I don't know if this is enough to get both of them, but I think we need to try. I want to talk to your alpha, though, first," he said, nodding toward Miles.

"We thought you might. Perhaps a conference call from here?" Miles asked.

"FOR THE love of Diana, that's a mess and a half," Noah said after they outlined everything to him. "And a problem and a half. I suspected the prime was xenophobic. I'd been hearing the rumors. A few other folks said he'd been seeming... not unstable necessarily, but worrisome. But this goes beyond that. He knows the alpha council wouldn't go along with a war."

Miles felt a little better hearing that, but with the suspicions they had about *how* the prime was going to try to start the war, it didn't help much.

"Does he *need* the council's approval for that?" Aubrey asked.

"No, but if we don't cooperate—if we don't fight or send our wolves to fight—he can't force it either."

"True. So... he finds another way to start a war. Something that'll make you *want* to fight."

"That's about the size of it." Noah sighed. "I don't think I should go to the prime yet. I don't want to give him the chance to cover things up. I'm thinking it might be best to approach your iret first."

"I agree, Alpha," Aubrey said. "I have a few thoughts to share with the iret. If he agrees, I'll call you back."

"All right. I'll be waiting."

Aubrey disconnected the call and sat back, glancing at Chad. "Let me ask your opinion on this before I take it to the iret. I know you're used to dealing with human justice, but jaguar justice isn't hugely different."

"All right. I'll help if I can."

Aubrey nodded. "So, we have to make sure that the prime can't find out what's happening until he's faced with it. That means we need to make sure that anyone who might tip him off can't contact him. Your best suggestion?"

"Get them all into custody at the same time somehow. I don't know what the rules are for arresting them, but I'm sure you've got something that'll allow you to hold them, right?"

"Yeah. We don't even have to tell them *why* right off the bat—unlike in the human courts."

Chad grinned. "Even better. Don't tell them anything. It might prompt them to spill."

"Oh, I like that," Miles said, nodding. "Maybe they'll confess? Or turn someone else over?"

"Possible," Aubrey agreed. "And that kind of evidence would go a long way toward getting them for the treason, not just the secrecy accord—though that's serious as it is." He looked at Quincy. "I'm assuming you know where to find Morgan Daniels?"

Quincy smiled. "Oh yes. I do."

"Good. Let me call the iret and go from there."

THE CALL ended up being a bit shorter than Miles expected. Aubrey had kept it to the minimum facts, explaining they had evidence to back their theories up. Though not hugely damning, it was pretty bad.

Tepey-iret Cesar Martinez apparently respected Aubrey quite a bit. He listened to Aubrey outline a few of the things they offered and agreed taking Thomas, Ross, and Daniels into custody was the best chance.

"Call your alpha contact and make sure arresting the wolf isn't going to cause a bigger issue, but if not, then we will take it from there."

"Thank you, Iret," Aubrey said. "I'll be in touch." He disconnected and immediately called Noah back.

"Noah Pearce."

"Alpha, this is Tepey Aubrey again."

"Ah, Tepey. Please, just call me Noah at this point."

Aubrey chuckled. "All right. If you'll call me Aubrey."

"Sure."

"Good. My iret is concerned with one thing and asked me to discuss it with you first."

Noah listened in silence about Daniels. He took a deep breath. "I think, as long as you have *some* proof of his involvement—which you do, right?"

"We have the bank records."

"Right. Make sure he isn't harmed during the arrest and transport, and I don't think it'll be a problem. We can explain it fairly well, anyway."

"Good. I was hoping you'd say that."

"Thank you for checking with me."

"Of course, Noah. I'll call you when we have things finalized."

SEVERAL PHONE calls, some not-so-minor hair-pulling, a slight panic when Thomas couldn't be immediately located, and at least three pots of coffee later, they had everything set up. It would take some careful timing, but by that same time the next day, all three should be in custody and they could move on to the next part of their plan.

Miles was exhausted. He hadn't been able to do much except keep the coffee going and try to soothe Quincy as much as possible. He'd gotten them to eat, but beyond that—and answering a few questions—he'd felt pretty useless. It turned out, being useless was as tiring as everything else.

Aubrey loaned them a security officer for the night. He was human and had no idea who or what was going on, just that he wasn't to let anyone through the door. With that, Aubrey had gone home to his city condo with his own security guard to hopefully get a bit of rest.

Quincy, apparently, still didn't trust the guard completely. He slept with the SIG right next to him.

Miles didn't blame him. As up in the air as everything still was, he was more than a little freaked out. So, even with the security in the living room, even with the exhaustion, it took forever for him to fall asleep.

IT TURNED out the tepey-iret had enough of his own enforcers that he could collect all three men at once. Daniels disappeared on his way back to the office from lunch. Thomas and Ross had been on the golf course together. They were all tight-lipped for now, but Miles would bet Chad was right and they'd started talking when they realized where they were going.

Noah's call to the alpha prime to report the attack on Miles had gotten them the reaction they'd expected. He'd immediately called the iret—while Noah was still on the line—demanding he answer for the attack. It took some fast talking, according to Noah, by both Noah *and* the iret, but Alpha Prime Ezekiel Adams had finally agreed to *deign* to meet with the iret.

And now they were on their way to the airport. Miles had insisted he be given time to make the tea the wolves needed. The cats had a similar herbal combination, but he wasn't sure it would work on the wolves and he didn't want to take chances. Private jet or not, too much could happen.

The limo actually felt a bit crowded with three wolves and two cats in the back. They all stayed silent, sipping the first cup of tea, and Miles guessed the combination of the unknown ahead, the stress of the last several days—weeks?—and the lack of sleep was getting to all of them. He was hoping they might pass out on the flight.

He wasn't sure what he'd expected of the jet. The interior of the small plane sat ten people in thick leather chairs. Two walls held TVs, a small sofa toward the back provided a place to lie down, and several folding conference tables filled the space between the rows of facing seats. Miles took a seat next to Quincy, across from Chad and Jamie, while Aubrey took a seat across the aisle from them. Aubrey's security guard—who had apparently been riding with the driver in the limo—took a seat in the back by himself.

Chad fidgeted, and Miles raised an eyebrow.

"Are you okay?"

Chad nodded. "First flight since I was made a wolf."

"Ohhh. You drank the tea, right?"

"Yes. But… I'm still not sure how well I could hold him back if the stress gets to be too much."

"We can have the attendant make more of your tea," Aubrey said. "But don't worry. The pilots won't come back and the attendant is a cat."

Chad blew out a breath. "That helps, though… I still don't want to shift. My clothes are all in the luggage hold."

Everyone chuckled.

"Don't want to greet the tepey-iret naked?" Quincy asked.

Chad stuck his tongue out.

Jamie rolled his eyes. "I don't remember mating a puppy, I swear I don't."

Chad kissed his temple. "I was a 'pup' *before* we mated, remember?"

That made Jamie laugh. "True, true."

The pilot's voice came over the speaker. "Good afternoon. Our flight plan is set for McCarren International Airport. If the winds hold, we should be arriving in Las Vegas just shy of 6:00 p.m. Attendant, please prepare for departure."

Everyone scrambled to fasten their seat belts and settle in. Miles held Quincy as close as he could, closing his eyes and resting his head on Quincy's. He didn't even feel them take off.

Chapter 18

LAS VEGAS was not one of Quincy's favorite places. He'd only been there a few times, but it never really appealed. It was just too bright, too glittery, too *much* for him.

He was glad to get to their suite at the Bellagio. There were definite advantages to being able to stay in a penthouse suite, and not waiting for the normal registration desk was one of them. They took a minute when they got into the suite itself to sort out the three bedrooms, but when Chad saw one of them had an exterior hall door, he and Jamie volunteered to take that one.

The security guard would take the sofa, though Quincy tried to offer him their bedroom since Jamie and Chad's had two beds. He refused, insisting the sofa was fine, and Quincy didn't argue further. He didn't really *want* Miles that close to an outside door, anyway.

Now that they were there, he wanted to get everything over with. They were *so* close, and yet it could still all fizzle out and end up being nothing. If that happened, at *best* they would delay things. At worst he and Miles—and likely Chad and Jamie—would have a big fat target painted on their backs for a long time to come.

Quincy didn't want to get settled and eat dinner and all that crap. He wanted to get to the meeting and see what would happen. Thomas and Ross could still be let go. The alpha prime could still squeak out, and then they'd end up with *him* coming after them because Quincy didn't think for one minute he'd let that go.

Were it not for Miles's determination to help keep him sane, Quincy was pretty sure he'd be climbing the walls. And in cat form, that was quite doable, though seriously inadvisable. He had no idea how he'd explain claw marks on the walls to hotel staff.

Quincy and Miles, like Chad and Jamie, spent most of the evening alone in their room. He introduced Miles to another of his favorite animes—this one the loud ninja kid in orange. Then they spent *quality* time focused on each other.

He slept much better after that than he'd expected to.

QUINCY HAD only met the tepey-iret a couple of times over the years. The tepeys met every few years, and with so few of them, there wasn't anything to discuss more often than that. The last time Quincy had gone with his father had been some twelve years before.

Tepey-iret Cesar Martinez didn't look much different. At his age, though, cats didn't change much. He still had pitch-black hair, deep brown eyes still smooth at the corners, and a lean, defined, if not muscular, frame. Quincy couldn't remember exactly how old the iret was, but he guessed, based on looks, he was at least fifty, though probably closer to a hundred.

He greeted Quincy and Aubrey warmly. Miles, Noah—who'd flown in commercially the night before—Chad, and Jamie were currently on their way to meet with the alpha prime. Quincy had only been comfortable letting Miles go because of their ability to talk telepathically. They hadn't been sure they could still talk when Miles was those few miles away, but apparently, it did, in fact, reach.

"Tepey Aubrey, Tepey-sa Quincy, it's good to see you," Cesar said as they shook hands. "I'm sorry it's under circumstances such as this."

Aubrey nodded. "Indeed. I would much prefer the tepey meeting to this, but it's necessary. May I ask where Thomas and Ross are currently?"

"They are in separate rooms down the hall, under guard. The wolf has his own room, also under guard. If things work out, I intend to release him to the alpha you have been talking with."

"Good. Noah will appreciate that. It seems he's friends with the wolf's alpha in New York. I'm sure they'll work something out with him."

Cesar nodded. "Indeed. But first we must get through the questioning with Thomas and Ross and then the meeting with Alpha Prime Adams."

"I am very sorry my pride has caused such problems."

Cesar waved that away. "We are responsible for the pride in general, but we cannot take blame when an individual—or two—cause problems. Thomas and Ross made their own choices. Now they must live with them."

Q?

Miles? Everything okay?

Yeah. Prime's pacing and kind of nuts. Nothing too bad and no hint that he's onto us or that he thinks we suspect anything.

Good. Let's hope it stays that way. Be safe, yeah?

Oh yeah. You too. I don't like you so close to Thomas and Ross, now that they know we've figured it out.

I'll be fine, baby. I have the SIG. And my father.

Okay. Chad's armed, as is Jamie. Love you.

Love you. See you soon.

Quincy refocused on the conversation in the room with him.

"He'll be here shortly," Cesar said, hitting a button on his cell phone. "I figure Thomas first."

On the coffee table in front of him sat the folder—open—they'd brought with the evidence. The picture on top was the one of Miles that had sent Quincy racing back to PA. His blood still boiled when he saw it. He took a few deep breaths and forced himself to calm down.

He tuned out the small talk between his father and Cesar. Too nervous to be able to participate, he instead mentally drew the house he and Miles would have. Before he could get beyond the front porch, however, the doors to the suite opened and Thomas came in, escorted by two of the biggest cats in human form Quincy had ever seen. They stood just about as tall as Thomas, but both were pure muscle—not just toned, but muscular in a way few cats could manage.

Thomas's normally immaculate suit was covered in wrinkles and his usually perfect hair stuck out in disarray. He was in handcuffs, though everyone was aware they were a formality. Any cat could break simple handcuffs if they needed to. Quincy suspected it was the behemoths next to Thomas that kept Thomas in line more than any little metal bracelets.

Abraham Thomas stopped short at the edge of the living area of the suite, gaze bouncing from Quincy to Aubrey to Cesar to the open file folder and back again. Time seemed to stand still as they waited for him to react. He swallowed once, lips compressing into a thin line.

"I told Ross we should have had that brat killed instead of his mate," Thomas muttered, face turning red. "But no—" He seemed to realize he was speaking out loud, and his mouth snapped shut audibly. He looked from Quincy to the iret again. "Uh, I mean—"

Cesar held up a hand. "I've heard enough. And I thank you for your cooperation." He smiled, and Quincy hoped to hell he never had to go up against the tepey-iret for anything. That smile was downright terrifying.

Thomas's eyes widened and he paled. "Wait! Uh... there's a dog! Daniels! And the prime—the dog leader! They started it. They wanted the war! It wasn't my idea! Ross wanted it more! He financed the whole thing!" He shook his head hard.

"I'm well aware of who all is involved. Thank you for confirming it. However, if I were you, I'd be more concerned about your test of maat."

If possible, Thomas's skin turned even whiter. "I—"

"You were brought here initially to answer for your breaking of the secrecy accords with your human servants." Cesar shook his head. "With that and, now, your confession of involvement in the attack on the wolf, you have enough to answer for. You might consider trying to figure out how to face Osiris. You'll be taken back to your room and we'll discuss sentencing when we return to LA."

The enforcers bodily picked Thomas up by his arms, turned around, and carried him back out of the room.

Quincy did not pity the man even a little. He turned his attention to the iret and his father. "That went better than I'd hoped," Quincy muttered.

Cesar nodded. "Indeed. Though I've seen many guilty parties behave that way." He shrugged a shoulder.

"Thank you," Aubrey said.

Cesar shook his head. "No, thank you. If they'd have succeeded, we would have been in a hell of a mess. I wasn't iret when the peace treaty was signed—I wasn't even born yet—but we're all too well aware of what could happen if it's broken. I can't imagine there'd be any cats left if they'd gotten their way." He sighed. "For the record his confession only ties him officially to the attack on the wolf. However, his breaking of the secrecy accords could bring a death sentence. Officially he'll be convicted of that, since it has the strongest punishment potential."

Aubrey nodded. "I'd expected as much. The evidence is...."

"Not quite solid enough to get them on treason. However, there's enough here for both of them to, if not get a death sentence, be locked up for a *really* long time."

Quincy let out a breath. "They hired another enforcer to go after Miles. I can try to find out who, but I don't know—"

Cesar held up a hand again. "We can take care of that too. I can find out who it is."

"Thank you," Quincy said, swallowing hard. *Miles?*

Yes, baby?

Thomas and Ross were officially arrested. They'll be taken to LA for sentencing.

Oh thank the gods. Did they ask about Payne?

No, and I'm not going to tell them. He tipped us off to the enforcer that's out after you, and we did enough to him, I think.

I agree. See? Maat. Anyway, now to deal with the prime.

Indeed.

"The meeting is scheduled for about an hour from now at the Aria. My driver can take us over. Let's hope this goes the way we hope, yes?"

Aubrey and Quincy both nodded. "If he knows we know and he gets away with it...." Quincy shuddered.

"Then you and your mate will go into protected custody for a while until we figure something out," Cesar said.

Quincy raised his eyebrows. "You'd do that?"

Cesar smiled—in a nonterrifying way. "Of course. You are my cat, he is your mate; that makes him my responsibility by extension. I care about all my cats. But hopefully it won't be necessary."

THEY WERE the first to arrive at the neutral hotel. They'd agreed on the Aria, with its Sky Villa suite, because it would comfortably accommodate any number of cats and wolves. The living area had seating for seven, plus a desk, as well as additional seating around the outside of the room. Two walls were made entirely of glass, showing miles of Las Vegas buildings and landscape.

Cesar, two of his guards, an aide Quincy didn't know, and Cesar's second-in-command—a smaller version of Cesar ironically named Jesus—chose one side of the living area. The aide took the seat at the desk behind a computer and immediately started working. Quincy guessed he was going to record the proceedings somehow.

Jesus—who turned out to be Cesar's younger brother—immediately went to the bar and poured drinks. He handed out tumblers of scotch before taking a seat next to his brother. Quincy happily chose a seat at the bar, by the windows, near the guards. He sipped his scotch and tried not to let the wait unnerve him.

Miles? Are you guys on your way?

Yes, but he's making the driver circle a few times. Wants to make the iret wait on him.

Quincy may not have been able to see his mate, but he could almost *hear* the eye roll in Miles's words. *Power play. Ugh. This is why I don't want to deal with politics.*

I don't blame you. I'm sure it'll only be another minute or two until we finally get into the hotel.

Okay. Thanks, baby.

Quincy sighed. "The prime's making his driver circle to make you wait," he said, shaking his head.

Cesar laughed. "Somehow that doesn't surprise me."

"Power games," Aubrey said, nodding.

"That's all right. I am a patient cat." Cesar smiled again before taking another sip of his drink.

They sat in silence as they waited, which, thankfully, wasn't *much* longer. The door opened and the alpha prime and his entourage came in. It took Quincy a moment to count all of them. Not counting Miles, their friends, and Alpha Noah, there were no less than ten other wolves with the prime.

Is he fucking kidding?

Miles looked over at him. *I wish.*

Who are all these people?

Prime is the one with silver in his hair. Four of them are guards, two aides of some sort, and I think three are random wolves who don't seem to have a clue why they're here. Can you believe this ridiculousness?

Somehow… I can.

Noah's wired, by the way. Just like you were for the dinner with your father, only this time he has most of the alpha council on conference.

Oh… really?

Miles gave a small smile and a minute nod.

Cesar stood but didn't move from his spot otherwise. "Alpha Prime Adams. It's nice to see you, though I do wish it was under other circumstances."

"Save it. This isn't even close to nice," Adams said, scowling.

The only reaction Cesar gave was the slightest raising of his eyebrows. "Very well. Will you take a seat and we can get started discussing things?"

Wow, can he be more of an asshole?

He wasn't always like this. I met him once, back when I was doing my residency in Denver and studying wolf physiology. He didn't seem like such an asshole then.

I wonder what happened.

Adams hesitated very briefly, then slowly walked around the chairs and took a seat. None of the wolves joined him. Noah, however, did step forward, standing closer but not *with* the prime. The guards took up spots behind him, and the aides and other wolves retreated to the seats by the windows. Chad and Jamie casually took two of the last three seats next to Quincy at the bar.

I'm staying near Noah for show.

I figured. Love you.

Love you.

Cesar finally sat, his face still in friendly lines. "It is unfortunate, what has happened."

"Unfortunate? You call an attack on my wolf *unfortunate?*"

"Is this the wolf in question?" Cesar asked, waving at Noah.

The prime shook his head, pointing at Miles. "This was the one attacked. Luckily he survived, but my understanding is that wasn't the intent."

Did you guys tell him that?

Nope. Just that I was attacked.

Yet again Cesar didn't show an outward reaction. "It wasn't? Are you implying the intent was to kill?"

"I'm not implying anything. I'm quite sure of it."

"May I ask how?" Cesar glanced at Noah. "Are you the wolf's alpha?"

"You'll talk to me," Adams growled.

"My apologies," Cesar said, bowing his head briefly. "Is this the wolf in question's alpha?"

Adams hesitated, then nodded. "Noah Pearce."

Cesar nodded at Noah, then turned back to Adams. "Was there evidence, first, that it was a cat? And second, that the intent was to kill?"

Yet again the alpha prime hesitated. He pointed at Chad and Jamie. "Those two were at the scene and smelled your cat."

Cesar raised his eyebrows. "We are very adept at hiding our scent. I find that hard to believe."

Adams looked at Chad and raised his eyebrows.

Chad stood and cleared his throat. "I'm a relatively newly made wolf. My senses—especially smell—are still more sensitive than most wolves. I don't filter things as well as they do yet."

"Ah," Cesar said, nodding. "Very well. I will accept that it was a cat."

Quincy admired the way Cesar was handling all of this. He didn't think he could be so calm in the face of such hostility.

"Do you have evidence of the intent to kill?" Cesar asked again.

Adams lips compressed into a thin line, and his eyebrows came together even more harshly. Finally he more growled than said, "No." He shook his head. "But the cat was in the process of trying to strangle him. What else could he be trying to do?" Adams raised an eyebrow as if he had a trump card.

Cesar shook his head. "He could have been attempting to make your wolf pass out. Not that I excuse the attack, mind you," he added when Adams opened his mouth. "But that alone does not guarantee an intent to kill."

Quincy had the brief disconnected thought, wondering if the scowl would permanently embed itself in Adams's face, it was so deep.

"The fact is, there was an attack. What are you going to do about it? I believe it is my right to demand recompense for the attack. Since you were the ones so insistent on the peace treaty, then you should be willing to give more to maintain that after being the ones to break it."

Once more Cesar didn't react except to incline his head. "What are you looking for?"

The smile on Adams's face sent a chill down Quincy's spine. "I *insist* you execute those involved. The cats who ordered it, the one who carried it out, as well as their tepey."

Um… did he just give away that he knew there were people who ordered it?

Yes, yes he did. Miles looked over at Quincy with wide eyes.

"I don't recall admitting the attack was a paid hit. Is there something else you're implying?" Cesar asked, still as calm as could be.

It seemed the calmer Cesar was, the more riled Adams got. "Of course it was a paid hit! This is why these damned animals need to be put in their place!" Adams turned to Noah. "Do you see? This is why they should be wiped out! Two hundred years of watching them act as if they did nothing wrong! They should have been gone then, but *no*! They had to form peace! We could have wiped them out then! Instead they put a treaty in place because the scaredy-cats couldn't handle the fight with the wolves. Well, it's about time we fix that, and I'm not going to let this… this… cat get in the way. This may not have worked, but the next plan will!"

Noah calmly pulled the cell phone out of his pocket and held it up, his eyes fixed on the alpha prime. He touched the screen, then spoke. "Alpha council, did you hear that?"

A chorus of *yes*es came through the phone.

Noah turned to Cesar. "Could you give us a moment, please?"

"Of course," Cesar said, and he and the other cats made a quick exit.

Quincy stayed, unable to not watch. Adams seemed to have forgotten he was even there.

"I move to remove Alpha Prime Adams from office on the grounds that he no longer has the capacity to carry out his duties."

"Seconded!" someone said on the phone.

"Does anyone oppose?" someone else asked.

Adams's nostrils flared, and he was panting hard as he stared at Noah when no one answered the question. "How *dare* you? You can't do this!"

"I can." He spoke to the phone this time. "All those in favor?"

Another chorus came through this time, all *aye*s.

One of the aides stood and crossed over to them. "I, Calator Riley, hereby excuse Ezekiel Adams from the duties of the Alpha Prime of the United States. You are also hereby placed under arrest, pending investigation in conspiracy to commit murder."

Two of the guards stepped forward. One reached out and put a hand on his shoulder. "You need to come with us."

Adams angrily shrugged the hand off. "I don't have to do anything. I'm alpha prime! This is ridiculous."

"No, you're not," Noah said. "The council has spoken, and you're well aware we have the right to do this if we feel the alpha prime is not working in the best interests of the wolf population."

"It is legal and so decreed," Riley said.

Each of the guards took an arm, and Adams went with them. He muttered angrily the whole way out the door.

Quincy couldn't stop himself from staring after the man. *Wow, just… wow.*

You can say that again. Miles crossed the room and wrapped both arms around him. *Are you okay? It's over.*

I… yeah, yeah I am.

"Alpha Noah," someone said through the phone. "I nominate you as ambassador to the jaguar leader to finish the summit."

"Seconded!" a few other voices chimed in.

"Uh—" Noah said, looking a little confused.

"All those in favor?" Riley asked.

Another chorus of *aye*s sounded.

"Anyone opposed?" This question was greeted with silence. "And so it is." He turned to another man sitting on the bench. "Scribe Owen, will you please stay and take notes for the rest of the meeting?"

The aide, an obviously young wolf, jumped to his feet and practically bowed.

Riley rolled his eyes and shook his head. "Alpha Noah, this is Owen, apprentice scribe. He can contact me if you need anything. I have a former prime to deal with. And a new one to find." He turned to the phone. "Alpha council, we will be calling an emergency meeting in Denver in a few days' time. Please make arrangements as such. Thank you."

Noah touched the phone screen and tucked it back into his pocket. "I'll report to Denver as soon as I'm done here."

"Of course. Thank you very much for all you've done, Alpha Noah."

"I'm happy to do it. I'm sorry he really was involved in this. It's never good when a leader falls like that." He cleared his throat. "I'm just glad I was able to help."

"Well, thank you again. I'll see you in a few days." He shook Noah's hand, and then he and the three random wolves left. Two guards stood back.

Noah waved a hand. "I'm not worried, guys. Go ahead."

They raised their eyebrows, glanced at each other, then shrugged. "We'll be nearby if you need us."

"Thanks. Could you let the cats know?"

One of the guards nodded, and Noah turned to the rest of the room. "Holy… wow."

Everyone laughed, the sound full of relief and almost giddiness.

"I do not envy you, Noah," Aubrey said, crossing the room. "And it's nice to officially meet you."

"Indeed, Aubrey. I do hope it won't only be for this."

"I'm sure, if my son is going to be involved in your pack, we'll cross paths somewhere. For now I believe we are redundant and I'm sure they want a chance to rest."

Noah nodded. "I'm sure. Thank you for all your help."

"You're welcome. Good luck."

Quincy, Miles, Chad, and Jamie wasted no time getting out of there and back to the limo. It was time to go home.

Chapter 19

QUINCY FLOPPED into the seat and sighed. He still couldn't seem to wrap his brain around the idea that it was over. He was—they were—free. He and Miles could pick their apartment, decide where to live, go places, and do things without worry.

After so many months on the run, it almost felt weird.

"You know," he murmured, turning to his mate. "I'd be happy if I didn't see another hotel room for quite a while."

Miles chuckled. "I know what you mean. I wonder, though…."

Quincy raised his eyebrows. "Oh?"

Miles nodded. "I wonder if that would count a honeymoon?"

Quincy stopped breathing for a moment. "Honeymoon?"

"Yeah. I thought maybe we might consider doing the legal human thing. Then maybe go to, I don't know…. Japan for our honeymoon." Miles wouldn't look at him and both cheeks were turning red.

"You want to marry me?" Quincy managed to say.

Miles smiled and nodded. "If you're okay with that."

Quincy nodded. "Yes! Yes, I'll… holy shit, I never thought of it."

"I'm gathering that." Miles finally met his gaze. "So… Japan?"

"Um… duh?"

Miles laughed. "We'll talk about that after we get settled at home, yeah?"

"Yes," Quincy said, settling in. "What made you think of it?"

"Well… Tanner and Finley were the first. Chad and Jamie committed to each other in Rome, but want to have a legal human wedding too. I really liked the idea. Especially since legalities can get sticky with just partners."

"That makes sense, if we want it all legal… until we're too old."

Miles nodded. "Right. But we've got some time before that's an issue."

"Yeah, we do." Quincy pulled Miles down to him and kissed him softly. *I love you.*

I love you, Quince.

Quincy closed his eyes and settled in against Miles. He didn't even hear the pilot announce takeoff.

THEY LANDED in Denver long enough to drop off Noah, who would be meeting Carol at the airport a few hours later, and to refuel. Once they were in the air, Aubrey turned to Quincy. "Could we talk?"

Quincy glanced at Miles and dropped a kiss on Miles's lips, then moved over to sit across from his father. He took a deep breath and let it out. "Hi."

Aubrey laughed. "Hi. So… do you know where you are going to live?"

Quincy didn't sigh, though he wanted to. "We're going to live in the Pittsburgh area. Forbes pack lands."

Aubrey nodded, looking down. "I have to admit I'd hoped you'd changed your mind."

"Father, if this whole thing has taught me anything—aside from being more resourceful in hiding—it's all the places I'd fall short for a tepey. I was pretty sure before this, but…." He shook his head. "I couldn't have handled any of this nearly as well as you did."

"You could be taught," Aubrey said.

Quincy took a breath. "Probably. But… Father, Miles needs his pack. He's been uprooted enough, and Forbes pack is his home. I can't take him away from that."

Aubrey nodded. "I had to try," he said, smiling wryly. "Who's going to take over?"

"Maybe you can convince my uncle or cousin to come back. I know they don't *want* it, but I'm pretty sure Danny would be much better adept at dealing with the politics than I would be."

Aubrey looked thoughtful for a long moment. "Maybe. I don't plan to go anywhere for a good long while, so there's plenty of time to teach Danny what he needs to know." He chuckled. "My brother's going to kill me for that."

Quincy snorted. "No, he's not. If it's what Danny wants, then Uncle Alan won't get in his way."

"True." He sighed and looked up. "Does this mean no grandcubs?"

"Um… I'm not built for giving birth," Quincy said, deadpan. He waited a heartbeat. "But that doesn't mean we won't consider surrogacy sometime in the future. Neither of us is ready for cubs or pups yet."

Aubrey gave a nod to this. "That's fair. So…." The attendant interrupted them for drinks, and after putting in their requests, Aubrey took a deep breath. "I thought, maybe, I might… I don't know, make a trip now and again to Pittsburgh. If I'd be welcome."

Quincy blinked at him without speaking for a long moment.

Baby? You okay?

Uh, yeah. Tell you in a minute.

"You want to visit us?"

Aubrey shrugged a shoulder. "Unless you don't—"

"I'd like that," Quincy said quietly. "Maybe… maybe Miles and I could visit New York a few times a year… when we don't have to hide it. I still want to attend festivals."

Aubrey smiled. "Good. I'd like that. So, tell me about your art," he said, sitting back.

Quincy hesitated for another moment. "You're different," he said instead.

"I'm going to tell you something I'd never say in front of another cat." Aubrey dropped his gaze to his hands, then met Quincy's again. "When I couldn't find you, I was terrified. Not scared, not a little afraid. I was *terrified*."

Quincy swallowed, blinking at his father. "Terrified?"

Aubrey nodded. "I know I will never be a candidate for Father of the Year—even among the cats. But I always loved you. I always cared about you—not just because you were tepey-sa, but because you are my son. And the thought that you might be gone…." He closed his eyes and took a deep breath, then shook his head. "It woke me up," he said, looking back up at Quincy. "As tepey, I *am* supposed to put the pride before everything else. But there is still a balance between the pride and family. Yes, we're solitary, but maybe we shouldn't be as solitary as we are. We still have a human half, a part of us that needs people. And the most important of those should be your family."

Quincy glanced over at the wolves, then back to his father. "That's something I've recently understood better too."

"So, I realized I needed to pay more attention to those closer to me. Relax a little more. Remember what's important."

"I… that's…." Quincy shook his head, at a loss for what to say to that. He stared at his father for another moment, then smiled. "Miles asked me to marry him."

Aubrey's smile lit up the entire cabin of the plane.

THAT HAD to have been *the* most surreal flight Quincy had ever taken. He was still trying to deal with talking to his father about Miles and his art for the better part of two hours. There'd been too many revelations, too much for him to absorb. By the time the plane touched down in Latrobe, Quincy wanted time to not think. It seemed the other three were already thinking something similar.

Tanner picked them up from the airport and drove them back to his place. The four of them were barely out of the Outlander before they started stripping. Finley managed to get them in the house to leave their clothes inside before he too stripped.

"It's been *way* too long since I've been in my fur," Chad declared as he waited for the rest to finish undressing.

"I imagine it's worse for you than the rest of us," Miles said, nodding.

"I don't know, but he's been pushing me for a while. Come on, babe. Race you to the stream," he said, then immediately started shifting. Jamie was only a couple of seconds behind him, and they took off for the trees.

Quincy let his cat take control, growling in pleasure when he landed on four paws. *Definitely too long.*

Same here. Let's see what we can scare, yeah?

Quincy would have laughed if he'd been in human form. As it was, he immediately took off. *If you catch me, you can top!*

I am so *catching you!*

"YEAH, WE found a rental place on the edge of Latrobe," Miles said to Carol. "Just until construction is done. It'll take a while, of course, but we're not far from pack lands, so it's good. And it's close enough to the office we're looking at for my practice."

Carol nodded. "I wonder, though. Didn't Tanner and Finley offer you one of their rooms?"

Miles grinned. "Yeah, but, uh...."

"We prefer a bit of privacy," Quincy said, deciding to save him.

Carol smirked. "I suppose I can see that." She sighed. "Well, I'm going to miss this place. I mean, Denver is beautiful, but this is home."

"Is Noah still in shock?" Miles asked.

Carol laughed. "And stressed."

"How can you tell he's stressed?" Quincy asked. "He's so...."

"Stoic?" Carol asked.

Quincy nodded.

"He used the word *hell* the other day."

"Wow," Miles said, eyes widening.

Quincy blinked. "What am I missing?"

"My dad is, like, allergic to cuss words," Tanner said, joining them, Finley, Chad, and Jamie right behind him.

"Ohhh... and he used *hell*?"

"Yes. You could have knocked me over with a feather," Carol said, chuckling. "Well, I'll leave you kids to talk. I see Laura's here." Carol waved and took off.

"Well, that's... something," Quincy said, shaking his head.

"I think my dad is still expecting to wake up. He keeps saying he must be dreaming... or in a nightmare. No one was more surprised than he was when they voted him alpha prime." Tanner chuckled. "Of course, that means I now have to be alpha." He wrinkled his nose.

Miles laughed. "You'll do fine. So will your dad. He's a good leader."

"Yeah, he is." Tanner nodded. "He's going to officially pass the pack to me tonight." He took a deep breath and turned to Jamie. "I'd like you to be my beta."

Jamie's mouth fell open, his eyes nearly bugged, and he stared at Tanner so long, Chad reached over and closed his mouth for him. "You want *me* to be your beta? But... wouldn't someone else be better?"

Tanner raised his eyebrows. "I can't think of anyone I'd want watching my back more than you. Besides, part of the beta's duties is as our religious guidance. No one's more devout than you are."

Jamie swallowed, looked over at Chad, then to each of the others before turning back to Tanner. He took a deep breath and finally said, "I'd... be honored."

Tanner grinned. "Good." He glanced up at the sky. "We should get started since we have so much to do tonight."

They moved over through the pack clearing and stood next to the fire ring. Noah joined them, along with Noah's beta, Bob, and his wife, Laura. Carol took her place on the other side of Noah between her husband and Bob.

"Okay, everyone," Noah called. "We've got quite a bit of business tonight to discuss, so we should get started. Gather around!"

Quincy tried to take a quick count of the number of pack members in the clearing, but couldn't manage it. He hit fifty and gave up. It was *full*. He'd never seen so many shifters in one place, except their big festivals. *Do all these people gather every month?*

Not always. Tonight's a big deal, but sometimes they handle the moon at home or, like Jamie was, are stuck somewhere else.

Ah.

"Thank you for making a point of being here tonight," Noah said when everyone was settled. "I'm sure some of you have heard, but I'll say it anyway." He shook his head. "I have been made alpha prime by the alpha council."

A huge cheer went up throughout the clearing, and Quincy added his applause to the mix.

Noah waved but still had to wait a moment for it to calm down. Finally the crowd quieted enough. "Thank you. I'm still figuring things out. I will be able to spend some time here, but a big chunk of my time will be in Denver. More than that, though, my duties as prime mean it's time for me to step away as alpha of the Forbes pack." He turned to Tanner. "Tanner Pearce, do you promise to put the pack first, doing everything in your power to lead fairly?"

"I do," Tanner said solemnly.

"And do you promise to do all in your power to help the pack grow?"

"I do," Tanner said again.

"I hereby pass leadership of the Forbes pack to you. May you lead with wisdom, strength, and love."

Yet again a cheer went up through the clearing. Tanner had the biggest grin on his face. He held Finley's hand tightly, then leaned down and kissed Finley quickly, earning himself—and Finley—another round of applause.

"All right, all right! We're not done yet!" Noah called. He turned to Tanner. "And now it's up to you to take over." He grinned.

Tanner rolled his eyes. "Thanks, Dad." Laughter followed, then Tanner held his hand up. Quincy was a little impressed how quickly they quieted for him. "First, Bob has an announcement." He turned and waved Bob forward.

"I will be resigning my position as beta. It's been a good run, but I wanna focus on Steeler football and serving beer." This got some more laugher, and Laura elbowing him. "'Sides, a young pup like Tanner needs another pup watching his back." He waved and he, Laura, Noah, and Carol all moved over and took seats in the grass.

Tanner nodded at them. "Most of you know the man who is my choice for beta, though he's been spending time down in Pittsburgh at college. More recently, he found a mate." This brought a new cheer. "Yes. First, I'd like to announce my choice for beta." He turned to Jamie. "Jamie Ryan, do you accept the position of beta to the Forbes pack? Do you promise to do all in your power to help protect the pack, treat its members fairly, and guide us in our faith?"

Jamie took a deep breath and swallowed several times. "I do."

Tanner put a hand on Jamie's shoulder. "Couldn't have a better man for the job."

Jamie took a few hard breaths, and Quincy smiled. *He's trying not to cry, isn't he?*

Yeah. Jamie can be a little emotional, but Tanner did *kind of blindside him with this.*

"Now, next order of business, I want to formally introduce Jamie's mate, Chad Sutton." Chad stepped forward and waved. The pack cheered and clapped. "Chad is a new wolf," Tanner said and silence fell. "Yes. He was human when Jamie found him. There is much to go over, but there's a lot that's been withheld from us. For one thing, there are human mates out there. Human *destined* mates. There is also at least one other shifter species."

Quincy took a deep breath and stepped forward.

"I'd like to introduce Miles Grant's mate, Quincy Archer. A jaguar shifter."

A ripple of talk went through the pack. Tanner let it go for a moment, then turned to Quincy and nodded. Quincy tugged off the sweatshirt he wore and handed it to Miles, then turned around, more than a little shy. He still wasn't used to stripping in front of people, much less a clearing full of wolves. With a deep breath, he shucked his sweatpants, closed his eyes, and let his cat out. When he landed on four paws, he turned around.

The entire pack had gone silent, all staring in obvious shock.

"Quincy is now a member of our pack, despite preferring catnip to ham bones."

Quincy growled softly and twitched his tail, and the pack laughed, breaking the tension.

"I don't have to tell you they are to be kept as secret as the rest of us. In fact, we should be *more* careful with them, at least for now. The jaguars have many, many less in their population than the wolves do. Quincy is, in fact, the only jaguar in the southwestern Pennsylvania area, possibly the western half of the state." He waited a beat for that to sink in. "And... that's it. Thank you for accepting me as your alpha. I promise to do my best for everyone, though I still plan to call the old man quite a bit."

Noah rolled his eyes and the pack laughed.

"Now! Let's enjoy the moon!"

Quincy was surprised by the number of people who came up and welcomed him to the pack. He found himself shifting back and tugging his pants on quickly to greet them. He lost count of the number of hands he shook and of well wishes for him and Miles. In fact, it was quite a while later that they finally stopped and he and Miles could get ready to run with them for the full moon.

When they were both shifted and sitting together for the moment, Quincy turned and worked his head under Miles's. *I can't believe how welcoming they are.*

I told you they would be.

I'm sure some of it is because I'm mated to the pack doctor.

Ha. Hardly. They're a good group of people.

That.... I can see that. Thank you, Miles.

For what, baby?

Thank you for accepting me. For giving me a home.

Thank you for wanting it. Now... let's go have some fun, yeah?

Yeah, with our pack.

Miles gave him a wolfy grin. *Yes. With our pack.*

Epilogue

Eight years later….

MILES KEPT one eye on the bundles of fur streaking around the outside of the clearing as he talked to Chad and Jamie.

Chad shook his head and called, "Hey! You really *don't* have to chase the cat just because you're wolves!"

None of the four blurs even acknowledged his shout.

Miles had a nagging suspicion about what was going to happen, but he ignored it and turned back to Chad and Jamie. "So… he seriously called you?"

Chad nodded. "Yeah. Imagine my surprise. I mean, it's been, what, eight years?"

"Something like that."

"And he's *still* calling me for consulting. I mean, I can't believe the leader of the cats doesn't have someone else that can do that work for him, you know?"

Miles shrugged. "He trusts you—you and Jamie."

Jamie grinned. "Him more than me."

Chad shook his head. "He knows how good you are."

Jamie blushed and cleared his throat. He glanced behind Miles and his eyes widened just a second too late. Claws dug into Miles's legs, ass, and back before a thirty-pound weight settled on his shoulder.

He shouted, unable to hold it in. "Gods dammit!"

Three more fur bundles scrambled to a stop at his feet, all looking up at the cub on Miles's shoulder. One black paw swatted toward them, and all three wolf pups—one with black fur, one with auburn fur, and one with red fur—all started barking.

Miles glared down at the pups. "All three of you quiet down! Noah and Eric, I *will* get your dads."

The black and auburn pups dropped their heads and whined. The red pup simply rolled over and showed his belly. "Uh-uh, Chad. That's not going to get you out of trouble," Miles said, shaking his head. "I've told you before to stop chasing your brother, haven't I?"

Chad rolled over and sat up.

"Shift," Miles said, staring at him.

Noah and Eric tried to slink away.

"Uh-uh. You two stay put."

They both froze in place, then turned around slowly.

"Now. Let's try this again. All three of you. Shift."

A moment later, three preschool boys squatted in the grass, looking like Miles had just taken their favorite toy away.

Noah, the black-haired boy, looked up first. "I'm sorry, Uncle Miles."

"Me too," Eric, the auburn-haired boy, said.

"Sorry, Daddy," Chad said, looking about ready to cry.

"You two," Miles said, pointing at Noah and Eric, "Need to go sit in time out for a few minutes." Miles looked up at Jamie. "Could you take them over?"

Jamie nodded. "Happy to."

"And I'll take my namesake. Come on, squirt," Chad said, lifting Chad-the-pup.

Miles looked up at his shoulder and carefully peeled the black jaguar cub out of his skin. He held his son up by the scruff of the neck. "And how many times have I told you not to climb people, Aubrey?"

Aubrey drooped, his tail and head hanging down.

"Trees, Aubrey. You climb trees, not people. Your claws are too sharp!" Miles took a deep breath. "You need to shift too," he said, changing the hold he had on his son.

A few seconds later, the black-haired little boy looked up at him, ready to cry. "I sowwy, Daddy!"

"Not sorry enough if you keep doing it. You've got sharp little claws, bud. You don't like to hurt people, do you?"

Aubrey shook his head. "No."

"What's this?" Quincy asked, walking up to them.

Miles turned. "Oh good, you're here. *Your* cub climbed me. Again."

Quincy took Aubrey from Miles's arms and held him up. "Aubrey, I will forbid you from shifting if you keep this up."

Aubrey's blue eyes widened. "But… Papa!"

"Uh-uh. Don't 'but, Papa' me. We've told you before, haven't we?"

Aubrey drooped again. "Yes, Papa."

"Time out, bud. And you'll sit quietly the whole time. If you ask me even *once* if time is up, I'll take you home. Do you understand?"

Aubrey nodded several times. "Yes, Papa."

"Good." Quincy took out his phone, set Aubrey in the grass at his feet, then set the timer on the phone and put it between Aubrey's feet. "Not until that goes off."

"Yes, Papa."

Miles didn't think Aubrey could sound any more bummed and had to turn around briefly to keep from grinning. Finally clearing his throat, Miles turned back to Quincy. "How was the meeting?"

Quincy wrinkled his nose. "It went. I'm not a big fan of meeting people like that in person. These two were clients from the deepest parts of the underworld, I swear."

Miles winced. "Sorry, baby."

Quincy shrugged. "That job is done, though. And I think I'm going to cut down on the number of those types of jobs I do. Stick to the graphic design projects that really interest me."

"I've been saying that for a while now."

Quincy rolled his eyes. "Yeah, yeah."

Miles chuckled. *Well, I'm glad to hear it. You've been too stressed. You started chasing yarn last night.*

Quincy sniffed. *I did not.*

Miles simply stared at him.

Quincy's nose twitched. *Okay, fine. I did. I get it. But I'm done. But you were eyeing my slippers the other night.*

Guilty. Miles grinned. *But I hired the new nurse today, so no worries there.*

Good. Now, when Aub gets up, let's run as a family. I could use some time doing simple things.

Me too.

"You guys ready for the run?" Tanner asked, coming up with Eric in his arms.

Finley approached right behind him, holding Noah. "I know I am. If I hear one more 'but, Papa,' I think I'm going to explode. It'll be nice to hear nothing but a few barks and a whine or two."

All the adults laughed.

Chad brought back the third pup and handed him over to Miles. "You know, every time I wonder if we should consider pups of our own, we get to deal with yours and remember that… we're happy being uncles."

Finley grinned. "They're not that bad, are they?"

Chad laughed. "Naw. But we are. We get to spoil five pups and a cub, and send them home to their dads."

"Seriously, what's not to like there?" Jamie asked joining them.

"I mean, we got to feed babies," Chad said, grinning.

"And change diapers," Jamie added.

"*And* we get to be the cool hero uncles. I'm thinking that's a pretty sweet gig."

"Did I mention Eric has started singing 80s songs?" Tanner asked, raising an eyebrow.

"I've been teaching him all the classics," Chad said, nodding.

"If he asks me one more time to drive fifty-five, I'm going to duct tape his mouth shut."

Chad tried to look innocent and failed. "I don't know what you're talking about."

Jamie glanced around. "Hey, where are Ben and Eric?"

"Ben called a little bit ago," Tanner answered. "Apparently Diana spilled an entire cup of juice on her dress, so they're running a little late."

The alarm on the phone beeped, and Aubrey picked it up and stood. "I did it, Papa!"

Quincy squatted in front of his son. "Yes, you did. You were a good boy. Now, you can shift, but don't climb anyone or we go home."

"I won't, Papa!" He threw his arms around Quincy's neck. "Lub you!"

"Love you, bud," Quincy said, rubbing his nose against Aubrey's.

A few seconds later, the little black jaguar cub took off. Not ten seconds after that, three wolf pups gave chase. However, when Aubrey got around the clearing, he made for the tree nearby.

Miles couldn't stop himself from laughing when all three pups sat at the base looking up with their heads tilted. He elbowed Chad. "Look familiar?"

Chad snorted. "Not in the least."

Jamie laughed. "Uh-huh."

A pine cone fell from the tree and landed on Chad-the-pup's head. He growled up at his brother.

Miles looked over at his mate. "And where did he learn *that* little bit from, hmm?"

"I don't know *what* you're talking about," Quincy replied, smirking.

Miles shook his head, badly suppressing the snicker when another pine cone fell, landing on Eric next. But the third pine cone didn't hit Noah. It landed on Chad-the-adult instead, making everyone laugh. Chad turned around, looked up, and tilted his head.

"Uh-huh. Not in the least familiar," Miles said, grinning.

Chad kept it mature. He stuck his tongue out.

Miles's grin widened, and he let himself simply enjoy watching his family—all of it. Uncles Chad and Jamie, making faces at the cub in the tree. His closest friends and "nephews," his own mate and kids. He couldn't wait to spend the rest of his life with them.

Chapter One

TANNER STEPPED into the club and moved to the side to let his eyes adjust. Even with his heightened eyesight, going from the bright lights of a city block to the dim room took a little while. When he could see well enough, he shifted his gaze from one group to the next, working slowly around the dance floor and bar. The interior looked to him like every other gay club on the planet.

He resisted the urge to inhale deeply and look for the scent he knew so well. His oversensitive nose was already being bombarded with too much sweat, deodorant, cologne, alcohol, and arousal. No matter how well he knew his recalcitrant mate's scent, he'd never be able to find it masked by all of that.

He skipped the bar and moved out toward the dance floor. Thankfully, this particular club only had one level. The last two Finley had disappeared to had been the multilevel clubs full of side rooms and lounges.

If I have to do this one more time, I swear I will spank his ass until he can't sit for a week! Tanner pushed the annoyance away, saving it for when he found Finley. When a hand ran over his ass, he fought the urge to growl, carefully peeled it away, and decided it might take until he got his mate home—to Finley's parents' house—before he could reasonably control his temper.

Besides, he couldn't spank Finley yet. Not for another four years. If he survived another four years, at this rate.

The owner of the hand gave him a beguiling smile, but the wafer-thin, spritelike twink looking up at him held zero appeal. Even if he'd been built like Finley, he wouldn't be appealing to Tanner. Finley was his mate, the one given to him by Diana, their patron goddess, and the only one he wanted.

"Sorry, not interested," Tanner grunted and almost felt bad when the smile melted. "I'm sorry, really. Uh, here with my partner." He didn't think he could be heard clearly, but the boy gave him a slight smile and nodded before moving on, obviously at least getting the gist.

Tanner turned his attention back to the dance floor. It shouldn't be this difficult to find Finley, and Tanner's blood pressure and anger were rising quickly the longer he looked.

Then he spotted black hair and blew out a breath in an effort to cool his ire a little. He gritted his teeth to keep the newfound calm in place as he stalked across the floor, dodging hands and asses, and other body parts. He couldn't exactly rip the man currently rubbing against his mate limb from limb, no matter how much he wanted to.

His wolf—the other half of his soul—disagreed.

He reminded his wolf he had a human half, and tearing a full human to shreds was a bad thing. His wolf grumbled but curled up, though he still watched from a distance. Mine, he growled in Tanner's head, and Tanner agreed.

Finley was his. Finley knew it. And these stunts he was pulling were getting old.

He stood in front of the man and crossed his arms. Finley spun around and his green eyes widened in surprise; then he stepped away from his dance partner. The dance partner, Tanner noted, was built much like he was, though with blond hair instead of dark auburn. And was human. Even without drawing a deep breath, he could smell it from there.

Said man reached out toward Finley, but Tanner's hand shot out and gripped the wrist. "He's with me," he growled. It couldn't have been heard over the music, not by human ears, but the guy obviously got the drift.

One blond eyebrow rose. "Didn't see you here a moment ago."

"I'm here now," Tanner replied, letting go of the man's wrist and grabbing Finley's hand. Finley took advantage of it and slid up against him, grinding to the music. Tanner tried—he really did—to hold himself in check. But his wolf was already frustrated with the other guy for touching Finley, and calming him further was nearly impossible. He needed to put his scent back on his mate.

And, well, he was a normal, healthy twenty-four-year-old guy. He could only take so much of Finley rubbing against him before he took advantage of it. He gave in, wrapping his arms around Finley, wedging one leg between Finley's, and picking up the beat.

Even with his superior hearing, he felt more than heard Finley's groan of appreciation. Tanner slid his hands down to Finley's hips, gripping them as they moved. Finley held Tanner's shoulders to steady himself, but Tanner kept him off balance deliberately, forcing him to lean into Tanner's body.

He slid one arm back around Finley's waist and held him close, moaning when Finley's hard cock rubbed against his through their jeans. With the other hand, he couldn't resist cupping Finley's amazing ass. God, Finley felt so fucking good in his arms, against him. He tilted his head, burying his face in Finley's neck and inhaling the scent deeply. His wolf growled in appreciation, and Finley—and, undoubtedly, Finley's wolf—echoed it back to him.

One of Finley's hands found its way into Tanner's hair, the other cupping Tanner's face. He leaned in, pulling at Tanner, who couldn't find it in himself to resist. Their lips met, mouths hot and wet, and Tanner groaned at the taste. Finley slid his tongue into Tanner's mouth and they fought for domination of the kiss.

Tanner broke the kiss and glanced around. He spotted a quiet corner nearby and danced them to it, then pushed Finley against the wall when they got there. He pinned Finley with his own body, grinding their hard cocks together. He caught Fin's lips with his again, the kiss hot, wet, and full of so much need he could barely breathe.

Finley's hands flew over Tanner's body, cupping his ass and gripping his hair. He rocked into Tanner, meeting his movements. Tanner pulled back from the kiss, his gaze taking in the look of his mate: hair messy, lips wet and kiss-swollen, eyes bled black in arousal, teeth lowered. Tanner's own vision had gone gray, eyes shifting because of his own need.

Tanner growled again, dove for Finley's neck, and nipped his way along the skin. It took everything he had to keep his canines out of Finley's neck. Instead, he sucked the skin in, biting with his human teeth, unable to resist leaving at least a minor mark.

His wolf didn't like it, was pushing for Tanner to flip their mate over, yank the jeans out of the way, fuck him hard, and bite when he filled Finley's ass with cum. When he realized he'd stepped back to do just that, he shook his head hard, grabbed Finley's hand, and pulled. "Let's get out of here," he said, not bothering to raise his voice. He knew Finley could hear it quite clearly.

Finley raised his eyebrows in shock. "You're taking me home?"

"To your parents' house."

The shock morphed to anger. "No," Finley said, pulling his hand out of Tanner's.

Tanner sighed. "Look. I've got a lot of work to do tomorrow. I don't have time for this tonight."

Fin shrugged a shoulder. "So go home. I don't need you here." He turned on his heel and started back onto the dance floor.

Tanner took a deep breath and immediately regretted it. He wrinkled his nose at the assault and grabbed for Finley again. "I'm not leaving you here. You're coming with me."

"Fuck you," Finley replied too cheerfully and melted back into the crowd.

Tanner silently counted to ten before following. He didn't even give Finley a chance to argue this time. He yanked Finley back against him, then lifted the man up and over one shoulder. It was a good thing he had the strength he did, because Finley wasn't a small man. In fact, he only had about two inches and fifty pounds on Finley. He didn't want to think about how they'd match when Finley finished filling out.

"Tanner!" Finley pounded on his back with both fists, but Tanner ignored it. "Put me down!"

"No." The dancers parted for him, and his long legs ate up the distance to the door.

"Problem?" one of the bouncers asked, stepping in his way. The guy looked like he came by the muscles honestly—rather than at a gym—but he'd still be no match for preternatural strength.

"Just taking him home. Someone put something in his drink," Tanner lied smoothly.

The bouncer raised an eyebrow and leaned around Tanner. "He telling the truth?"

Finley didn't reply at first. "I don't know. Maybe."

That was apparently good enough. He stepped back and waved them through. Tanner was relieved Finley at least didn't make a scene with the bouncer. He knew better than to bring any kind of authority down on them. They'd get out of it, but it'd be a mess and a half in the meantime.

Tanner set Finley down on the sidewalk and immediately swung him around to glare at him. "What the fuck?"

"What?" Finley bit off, crossing his arms.

Tanner realized Finley was furious. He blinked. "What do you mean, what?"

"What do you mean by 'what the fuck'? It's not like I can't come down here if I want."

"You're not of age."

Finley rolled his eyes. "I'm old enough for here. I turned eighteen two months ago, as you are well aware. You were at my fucking party."

Tanner didn't growl this time, but he wanted to. "Twenty-one, genius."

Finley sighed and pointed with his thumb at a sign by the door: Under 21 Night. 18 to 21 Only.

Fuck. Tanner rubbed his face. He didn't know how he got in, but he let it go and sighed. "Why?"

"Why not?"

Tanner scowled. "You know what? No. We're not doing this. Let's go." He grabbed Finley's wrist, but Finley twisted it out of his grip.

"No. I'm not going home. I'll get a cab and go somewhere else, since you've ruined this place for me tonight."

"No you are not!" Tanner roared.

Finley simply blinked at him, jaw working as he held in his own fury. Tanner knew the signs. Though Fin was usually a cheerful, easygoing person, he'd been known to get pissed now and again, and Tanner had seen it. "Are you quite through?" he asked, too calmly.

Tanner chose to ignore the fire spitting from Finley's green eyes. "No. Can we not do this on the street?" He glanced around to see a few other club-goers staring at them.

"Sure. You go home and I'll get a cab."

"Do I need to pick you up again?"

This time Finley was the one who growled. He jabbed a finger hard into Tanner's chest. "No. You're not going to pick me up. You're not going to take me home. I can do whatever the fuck I want. I'm an adult. I have permission from my legal shifter guardians. And until you claim me, you can't do a fucking thing about it." He stepped around Tanner and stalked away.

Despite his anger, despite his frustration, he couldn't resist eyeing the smooth grace of Finley's movements. Just like he couldn't resist the dance. Every time he was in his mate's company, his wolf surged forward, the mating instincts kicked in, and he had to wrestle them back into place. His cock, in fact, was still painfully hard.

He sighed and dropped his head. The most frustrating part of it was… Finley was right.

According to shifter law, once he'd claimed Finley—even underage, which shifter law said was twenty-one—Finley became his responsibility. But unless and until he did, Finley still answered to his parents, who Tanner thought were batshit insane.

Because they didn't see a problem with him claiming their son. They seemed almost as upset by it as Finley was, though not because they wanted to get rid of him or anything. Because they loved him and saw how much Finley was frustrated. Or, at least, that's what they claimed.

Tanner didn't understand it. Finley was young—too young. He needed to finish growing, for fuck's sake, much less finish school, go to college, experience things—nonsexual, thank you very much—before he mated. Never mind that, as the future alpha, there were certain semipublic events that happened when he claimed his mate. Finley was too fucking young for that. So Tanner was doing his damnedest to make sure they waited.

And Finley was doing his damnedest to fight him every step of the way.

He'd never forget the night they met as long as he lived. They'd taken one look at each other and reacted almost violently, both of them partially shifting on the spot. There'd been no question in that moment: Finley was his destined mate. And the first part of their bond had already formed. He was so screwed—or not, in this case, as Finley was much too young for that.

Finding his or her destined mate wasn't common, much less at that age. Destined mates weren't exactly rare, but some shifters never managed it. Tanner had assumed, since he was gay, he didn't have a destined mate. He was, as far as he knew, the first gay shifter in their pack. He was the first out gay shifter, anyway.

He'd listened to the lessons the pack teachers had given them about mates. It was one of the biggest parts of a shifter's life, finding their mate. There were two types of mates in their world: destined and chosen. A shifter was supposed to be able to recognize a destined mate immediately—their wolves would recognize each other and their scents drove each other crazy. Simply meeting started the bonding process, which was finished through sexual intercourse and biting.

Chosen mates formed a similar bond, but only after the sex and bite. They didn't have the same recognition as destined mates did, but they were usually still quite happy, their wolves happy, and their bond almost as strong.

His teacher, one of the pack elders, had described the bond like a thick vine made up of many twisted strands. Meeting Finley had connected them by those first strands, and their bond had begun to form already. If either experienced very strong emotion, the other could sense it. Protective and possessive instincts kicked in, and the urge to mate and claim usually happened fast.

Tanner had been fighting it for the last two years. Two years of being around his mate—two years of smelling him, two years of sharing strong emotions—and he still couldn't claim the man, because he was just barely a man. His wolf thought he was being ridiculous, not that he would think quite that coherently, but Tanner got the message all the same. His wolf wanted their mate, period. He didn't understand why Tanner was hesitating.

But Tanner thought he had a damned good reason. Tanner had seen the disastrous results first hand of what could happen if two people mated too young, and he wasn't going to let that happen to them. He sighed, turned on his heel, and followed Finley's scent around the corner to the small set of stairs he sat on, took the spot next to him, and looked over.

Finley's anger had obviously died. Tanner couldn't read the expression on the handsome face, and the emotions weren't strong enough to sense, but he was certainly not happy. "Why?" Finley asked, for probably the millionth time in two years. And the thousandth in just the last month.

Tanner sighed again, feeling really fucking old, even though he only had six years on Finley. "We've been over this, Fin."

"Yeah, well, maybe if you explain it again, I'll get something that I didn't before."

'Tanner shook his head. "Nothing's changed, Fin. You need to finish growing up. You need to—"

"Go to college, experience things, blah, blah, blah." Finley shook his head. "First, I am grown up. Second… shouldn't that be my decision to make?"

While Tanner knew Finley had a point—the same point he'd had for two years—Tanner could all too readily see Finley resenting him for tying them together so soon. To make matters worse, Finley would blame himself because he'd pushed for it. Then he'd feel even worse about the whole thing, and they'd end up in a big mess, if Finley didn't downright hate Tanner or himself.

"Look, I agreed to wait until eighteen. I got it. As much as we can weasel out of, we can't get out of everything associated with human law. So, I agreed to wait so no one got arrested for statutory rape. But for fuck's sake, Tan, I'm over eighteen now."

And still too young for some of it. He hadn't been able to bring himself to tell Finley that last part. While it wasn't the biggest hang-up he had over this, it was still something he didn't think Finley was ready to go through. He rubbed his face. "Look, I—"

"Never mind. Just take me home," Finley said, standing up.

Tanner frowned but wasn't going to argue. He reached out to take Fin's hand, but Finley stuffed both into his jeans pockets, making it clear the touch wasn't welcome. Tanner swallowed at the snub and focused on walking. When they got to the car and were settling in, he had to try again. He hated when they fought, which they'd been doing a lot since Finley had turned eighteen. "Baby, I—"

"Don't 'baby' me. Just drive," Finley said through a clenched jaw.

Tanner suppressed yet another sigh and started the car.

GRACE R. DUNCAN grew up with a wild imagination. She told stories from an early age—many of which got her into trouble. Eventually, she learned to channel that imagination into less troublesome areas, including fanfiction, which is what has led her to writing male/male erotica.

A gypsy in her own right, Grace has lived all over the United States. She has currently set up camp in East Texas with her husband and children—both the human and furry kind.

As one of those rare creatures who loves research, Grace can get lost for hours on the Internet, reading up on any number of strange and different topics. She can also be found writing fanfiction, reading fantasy, crime, suspense, romance, and other erotica, or even dabbling in art.

Website: www.grace-duncan.com
Facebook: www.facebook.com/GraceRDuncan2
Twitter: @gracerduncan
E-mail: duncan.grace.r@gmail.com

FORBES MATES

BOOK TWO

Patience

GRACE R. DUNCAN

Forbes Mates: Book 2

Jamie Ryan was almost ready to accept he'd never find his destined mate. They're uncommon to begin with, and same-sex versions are downright rare. Since his gay best friend found a destined mate, Jamie figured he was out of luck. Until end-of-semester stress forces him to go through the full-moon shift early. Stuck in wolf form, he runs into none other than his destined mate. Who's human.

Chad Sutton has always had good instincts. They served him well as a detective and continued on when he went private. Those instincts tell him there's something about the dog that comes up to him while running away from animal control that isn't quite right. He works to put the pieces together, but is unsuccessful until his dog turns into a human before his eyes.

Jamie has no idea what the mate bite of a shifter will do to a human. He's terrified to try—and possibly kill his mate. They hunt for answers while working together on one of Chad's cases. It's easy to see they belong together, but Jamie fears the gods gave him someone he can't keep.

www.dreamspinnerpress.com

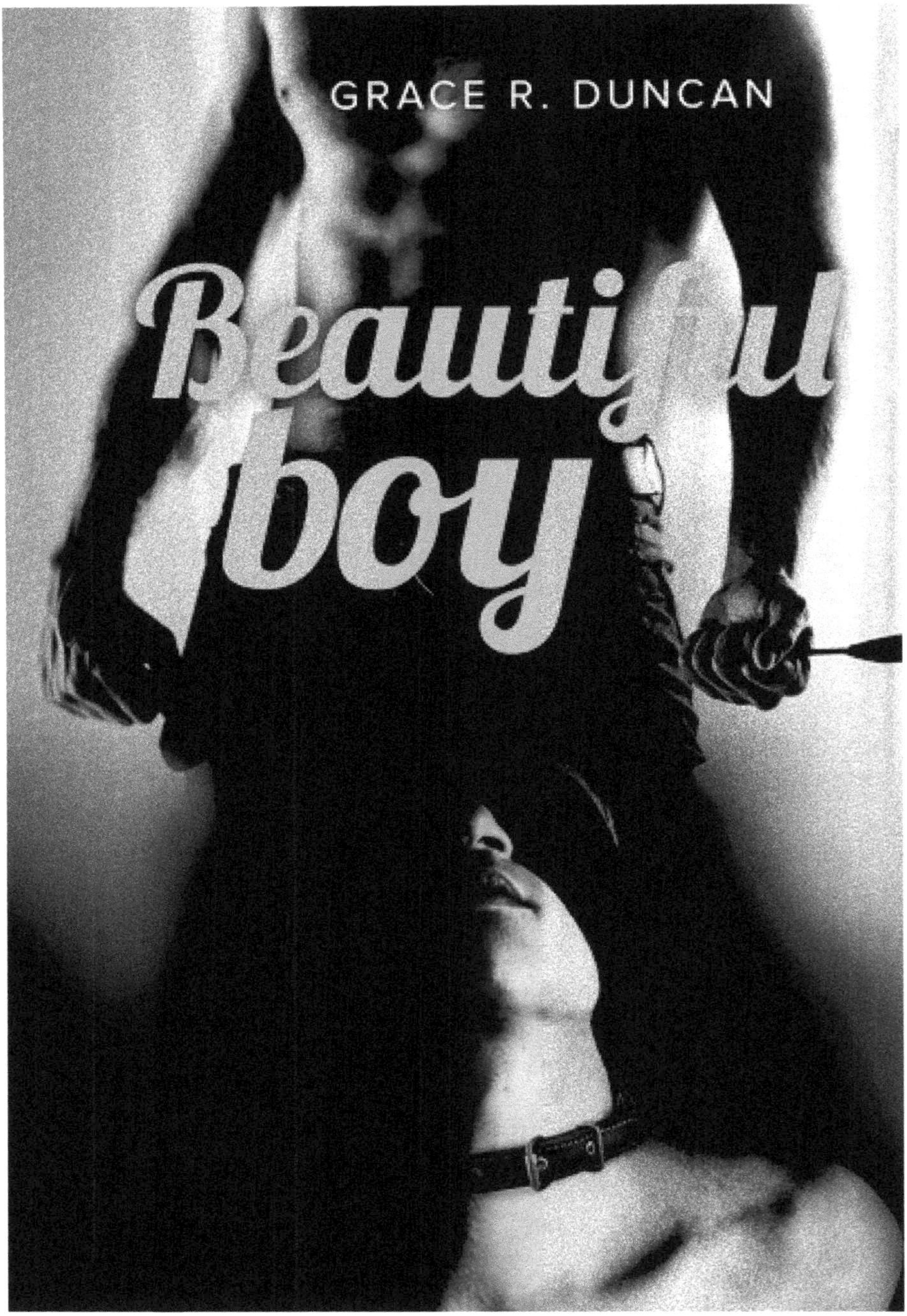
GRACE R. DUNCAN
Beautiful
boy

Malcolm Tate hung up his flogger when his submissive sought out another Dom and landed in the hands of a serial killer. Convinced his lack of dominance sent his sub away, Mal has spent two years blaming himself for what happened. But when his best friend finally convinces him to go back to the local dungeon, Mal's grateful. Especially when he wins beautiful, submissive, firmly closeted Kyle Bingham in a charity slave auction.

College grad Kyle hasn't earned enough to move out of the loft his conservative, homophobic parents bought, much less to buy any of the other things still in their name. When he's won at auction by the hot, amazing Mal, he's shocked that anyone would want him. No one else seemed to—not his parents, his former Doms, or any of his disastrous dates.

But Mal does want him and Kyle lets his guard down, only to be outed to his parents. With his world crashing down, he must find a way to trust Mal—and their developing relationship—or risk losing everything.

www.dreamspinnerpress.com

TURNING HIS LIFE AROUND

GRACE R. DUNCAN

When Kane Harris's world turns upside down, his lifelong best friend is the only one to catch him.

Years ago, Ian Kelly accepted Kane would never return his love, since he knows Kane believes he's incapable of it. Ian is willing to settle for what he can get—a best friend, sometimes casual lover, and occasional submissive. He's learned he can't live without Kane, but he can't let Kane know. Because when, not if, Kane confirms that Ian's love will never be returned, Ian won't be able to take it. But when Kane loses his job and asks Ian to step up their play to help him deal, Ian's ability to hide his feelings falters. Then Kane starts his own computer security firm and asks Ian to join him, and Ian struggles further.

It's not until they visit the exclusive BDSM club the Iron Door that things come to a head. Kane screws up big time, and he's afraid he can't fix it. He's sure he'll lose his best friend, his Dom, his everything… forever.

www.dreamspinnerpress.com

WHAT ABOUT NOW

Grace R. Duncan

Five years ago, everything went wrong. Braden Kirk and Rafe Jessen's long-term relationship started unraveling. They stopped talking, fears mounted, then Braden walked in on Rafe and another man, completely misreading the situation. Without giving Rafe a chance to explain, Braden walks out. Out of their home, their relationship, and the game development company they started together in college.

After months of therapy to deal with the attempted rape Braden walked in on, Rafe begins to understand that his dominant tendencies in the bedroom aren't a bad thing and that Braden's submission is likely what scared his partner into silence. But Rafe isn't ready to let go of the man he loves more than life itself. He arranges for himself and Braden to end up on the same charity cruise, knowing Braden won't let his phobia—terror of vast, deep waters—rule him.

With a plan and twenty-eight days, Rafe is determined to get Braden back, make him see there's nothing wrong with being submissive, and find a way to get Braden to stay with him when they get home to LA.

www.dreamspinnerpress.com